THE
BERLIN
WIFE'S
VOW

BOOKS BY MARION KUMMEROW

MARGARETE'S JOURNEY

A Light in the Window

From the Dark We Rise

The Girl in the Shadows

Daughter of the Dawn

GERMAN WIVES

The Berlin Wife

The Berlin Wife's Choice

The Berlin Wife's Resistance

Not Without My Sister

The Orphan's Mother

LOVE AND RESISTANCE TRILOGY

Unrelenting

Unyielding

Unwavering

WAR GIRLS SERIES

War Girl Ursula

War Girl Lotte

War Girl Anna

Reluctant Informer

Trouble Brewing

Fatal Encounter

Uncommon Sacrifice

Bitter Tears

Secrets Revealed

Together at Last

Endless Ordeal

WAR GIRLS ROMANCE SERIES

Second Chance at First Love

BERLIN FRACTURED SERIES

From the Ashes

On the Brink

In the Skies

Into the Unknown

Against the Odds

THE
BERLIN
WIFE'S
VOW

MARION KUMMEROW

bookouture

Published by Bookouture in 2024

An imprint of Storyfire Ltd.
Carmelite House
50 Victoria Embankment
London EC4Y 0DZ

www.bookouture.com

ISBN: 978-1-83790-277-4
eBook ISBN: 978-1-83790-280-4

1

BERLIN, MARCH 1943

David stood bent over a machine, sweat running down his back as he pulled the handlebar for what felt like the ten thousandth time. The noise inside the huge factory hall was deafening. A hundred different machines rattled, clattered and hammered into an ear-piercing orchestra.

That wasn't even the worst of it. As soon as the sun shone onto the metal roof, the temperature inside gradually rose to unbearable levels. Gritting his teeth, David yearned for his old job at the locomotive workshop. Under his mentor Baumann's tutelage he'd been—unofficially—promoted to head mechanic and had been given the freedom to roam the company's vast premises as he saw fit.

In contrast, here he was chained, not literally of course, to this damned machine, repeating the same action ten or twelve hours a day. David scoffed. Perhaps he should count himself lucky, because he was still alive and in Berlin. Perhaps he should be grateful for not having been deported to the East.

He was grateful for that indeed, although that didn't keep him from grinding his jaw and cursing the Nazis with every repetition of the same straining arm movement he performed, thousands of times a day.

What weighed even harder on his conscience was that the Nazis exploited his manpower to produce weapons that would later be used by SS or Wehrmacht against the very Jews, or half-Jews in David's case, who had been forced to manufacture them.

Ever since he'd been assigned to this godawful munitions factory two weeks ago after his release from the Rosenstrasse camp, he'd been racking his brain as to how he could get out of this job, and with every passing day his mood had become drearier.

None of the Rosenstrasse inmates had been allowed to return to their former workplace, presumably so their colleagues couldn't ask curious questions or come to undue conclusions. The government fully intended to sweep their defeat—by a bunch of housewives no less—under the carpet, lest it encouraged imitators. The Nazis feared public opinion even more than the Allied soldiers, because an uprising of the people would inevitably lead to their downfall.

None of the official media outlets had mentioned the protest of German women in favor of their Jewish family members, and definitely not their subsequent release a week later. Nothing had changed in public life and sometimes David believed he'd dreamed the six days he spent in the holding center, except when he was with his sister Amelie, or his father Heinrich, who'd both been imprisoned as well.

In their haunted eyes he read the truth of their narrow escape.

During the Gestapo's latest sweep, innocently called the *Fabrikaktion*, any and all remaining Jews in Berlin had been rounded up and taken into custody to be shipped off to places in the East, from where not a single soul had ever returned, but awful rumors were rife.

When the sound of the siren ended his shift, he stretched out his aching back and walked in line with the rest of the forced workers toward the exit. Having deported all but a few Jews, the Nazis had replaced their manpower with prisoners of war; scrawny, dirty and miserable men pressed into hard labor without proper food, clothing and presumably shelter.

The one good thing that had come with David's new job was the permit to use public transport for getting to and from work. But even this benefit was a double-edged sword, subjecting him to the worst kind of harassment by the other passengers on the subway.

He couldn't wear his reversible jacket with the starless side out, because many of the civilian workers and even some of the SS guards used the same train to travel to work, and the bosses were dyed in the wool Nazis, who would never turn a blind eye to David not wearing the yellow star.

It was unpleasant indeed.

Standing in a corner of the train cart, David molded himself against the wall, becoming as inconspicuous as possible, while lost in thought. After being liberated from the Rosentrasse camp he'd yearned to see Roxi again. Much to his disappointment though, she hadn't returned to her hiding place in the attic of the building where he lived with his family and the Falkensteins.

He gave a deep sigh. Roxi hadn't left an answer to his note either, therefore he feared for the worst. As a gypsy, *Romani*, he corrected himself, she was a member of yet another undesired minority and subjected to the same persecution.

Roxi is far too street smart to be caught, he reassured himself. Living as an illegal without papers, she wasn't forced into work and thus her risk of having been caught during the raid was minimal.

The train reached David's stop. In the hurried crowd of Berliners wanting to reach home before nightfall, he snuck into a corner, took off his jacket, reversing it to the unblemished side in one swift, often-practiced move, before putting it back on again.

In one instant everything changed. Passersby ignored him instead of hurling evil glances, insults and even spittle toward him. A young woman gave him a smile. A vendor offered a newspaper to buy. If it weren't so sad, he'd laugh at the gullibility of the people, falling for a yellow patch of cloth. As if that changed him into a better or worse person.

As soon as he arrived home, he raced upstairs, removed the extendable ladder into the attic and climbed up.

Nothing.

Dust gathered on the floor, not a trace of anyone having been up here in weeks. His hidden note remained untouched, as was the wire in the window to alert him if someone climbed through.

Roxi seemed to have vanished from the face of the earth. Having grown up in a traveling community, she was used to coming and going as she pleased and had perfected the talent of showing up out of nowhere, as well as leaving without a trace. Still, he sensed something was off.

They weren't officially a couple, but he knew deep in his heart that she would contact him if she had a chance. His stomach twisted into a tight knot as vivid images occupied his mind: the lithe, black-haired woman with the piercing blue eyes, who usually went barefoot, writhing in agony at the hands of Gestapo brutes.

He shook his head to dispel the images. Surely, there would be a perfectly reasonable explanation for her absence. Regrettably, the only other explanation he could come up with hurt almost as much as the notion of her being tortured. *No, she hasn't abandoned me.* Unlike Thea, she was loyal to the bone. If she grew tired of him, she'd have no qualms about telling him to his face.

Slumping his shoulders, he entered the apartment, where his mother Helga was preparing dinner.

"Evening, Mutti," he announced on his arrival.

"David," she greeted him, her face falling when she turned and saw his expression. "What happened?"

"Nothing."

One of her eyebrow's shot up. "Are you sure?"

"Don't worry, Mutti, nothing out of the ordinary." He shrugged. "I hate my new job, our situation and my life in general, but that's nothing new, is it?"

She wiped her hands on her apron and pulled him into an embrace. "Oh, sweetheart, I wish I could do something."

David rested his chin on his mother's shoulder, letting the comfort of her love fill him with new energy. "You've done enough already. After all, none of us would be here if it weren't for you."

"Ach..." She patted his back. "That's what mothers are for, isn't it?"

He gave a silent nod, well aware that not all mothers were like her. He knew of acquaintances where the Aryan partner had left the spouse and sometimes the children to save his or her own skin. Helga, though, fought fiercer than a lioness to protect her cubs and her husband, Heinrich.

"I love you, Mutti." He extricated himself from her embrace. "What's for dinner tonight?"

"Potato soup."

"Again." He wrinkled his nose in disgust. Just his mother and Frau Falkenstein received full ration cards, whereas the other four in the shared household were given the lesser rations for Jews.

"I know. Let's hope this war will soon be over, now that the Wehrmacht has been defeated at Stalingrad."

David didn't believe in a fast end to the war and Hitler's reign with it, but he still nodded.

2

Thea wrinkled her nose as she entered the public toilet and made her way to the sink. After splashing cold water on her face, she grimaced into the mottled mirror. Her characteristic blonde curls hung like cooked spaghetti from her head. It was a miserable sight. Even living as a submarine, as Berliners called the illegal Jews scratching an existence in the vast underbelly of the capital, she normally took great care of her looks. Her charming appearance was her most valuable asset—her flashing smile almost guaranteed to wrap any SS man or police officer around her little finger.

In the three weeks since she'd gone underground after the *Fabrikaktion*, she'd managed to always look well-kempt and neat, despite often sleeping rough after exhausting her few remaining Aryan friends. Each one was afraid to let her hunker down with them for more than a night or two. Even her estranged husband, Ralf, whom she'd married in the mistaken belief he could protect her from persecution, had disappeared without a trace weeks ago, presumed dead or transported to the East, which basically amounted to the same thing.

The night after the raid, she'd returned to her home to find

her parents had been taken with no trace left behind. She'd
the opportunity to grab a suitcase full of clothes, her
and her ration booklets, plus the little cash her mother
n beneath her mattress.

it, as important as it had been to give her a fighting
ing illegally, had almost been her doom. Not a
e'd left the building, SS men rushed inside to
ment. She gave a bitter cough. The seal was
uders away, so the Reich could later sell her
the highest bidder. These auctions were
many Aryans, presenting an opportunity
buying the "abandoned" property at
out her tongue at her own reflection

enstein, who'd risked his own life
id, she'd have been taken too. A
ng underground was hard. It
with deprivations. Hunger,
ompanions. But what she
who hadn't slept rough
properly wash himself
had to give. She was
lerground.

ted, middle-class
se for a woman
mind.

enstein
parents
had been
cables. A
so wealthy

pen without
state of the
assing several
dalized by the
e every piece of
rs.
her to turn on her
ilding, she had no
ting other Jews. She
led herself together.
ouldn't help, she'd be
e been preferable. At

ives' protest
rriage to
. She'd
er the
Thea
en
, and
more.

Today though, she'd finally visit and beg him for help.

He couldn't refuse, either. She'd saved his life months ago when he'd stumbled disembarking the tram, falling directly in the path of a van. Renewed hope coursed through her veins, erasing the frown on her forehead. A man with his connections simply must be able to find a way to end her life as a vagrant.

She considered washing her hair in the sink, which was a risk if someone came inside and found it suspicious, but oh s worth it if it helped her to look pretty enough not to be asked f papers in the street. Just as she fumbled for a scrap of soap her handbag, she stopped halfway.

For her plan, it would be more beneficial to look unke Not too horribly, because she didn't want Herr Falkenst be disgusted by her presence, but enough to stress the p her ghastly living conditions.

Thea left the stinking room and walked to the Fall residence in the same Jewish quarter where she and he used to live. The panel with bells for each apartment ripped out and left oscillating at the end of several testament to the social decline of the formerly Falkensteins.

She prodded the entrance door, which swung a sound—a peculiar experience given the sorr building. Nonetheless, she ventured inside, apartment doors hanging off their hinges, var same good Germans who *bought* or rather sto furniture left behind by their deported neighb

A shudder raced down her spine, urging heels and run away. If the SS entered the b excuse to be here, except for being a Jew vis almost gave in to the temptation, then *pu Herr Falkenstein was her last hope. If he resigned to a homeless life.

Even being rounded up would ha

least in prison one had a roof over one's head and received regular meals—something Thea certainly did not.

When she reached the highest floor, she almost wept with relief at the sight of an intact door. There was no name next to it, yet she was certain this must be the Falkensteins' place. At her knock it didn't take long for steps to approach the door. A female voice asked, "Who's there?"

Swallowing down her nerves, Thea answered, "Thea Dalke, I'm here to see Herr Falkenstein, we used to work together."

Seconds later, the door opened and Thea looked into the friendly face of a lady in her mid-forties with gray strands in her hair. The well-worn dress must have cost a fortune many years ago. Despite hanging slightly loose on her body, it still gave her the appearance of a queen.

"Please come in, I'm Edith Falkenstein. My husband will be home any minute, if you'd like to wait."

"If it doesn't cause too much trouble." Thea was tempted to curtsy at the elegant lady.

"Not at all. May I offer you a glass of water?"

"Yes, please."

"Have a seat." Frau Falkenstein pointed at the dilapidated sofa in the middle of the room. "I'll be back in a minute."

Thea used the time to observe the apartment. The furniture was a motley collection of styles and colors, every piece showing years of usage. It didn't look remotely like what she'd imagined the residence of the former owner of the Falkenstein Bank. But then, he had suffered under the Nazi reign the same way as every other Jew. Her gaze continued to take in the shabby but clean carpet and several doors leading to other rooms.

Inwardly she took heart. The apartment definitely was big enough to host more than two people.

"Here you go." Frau Falkenstein returned, offering Thea a glass of water. "My husband has been wondering about your whereabouts."

"Mine?" Thea gave her host a well-measured smile. This was shaping up better than expected.

"Yes, he told me about you hiding in the basement during that awful raid."

"It was horrible." Thea pouted. "But I'm immensely grateful to have gotten away with my life."

"Aren't we all?"

A key turning in the lock indicated the arrival of the man of the house and Thea jumped up as soon as he shuffled inside. "Herr Falkenstein."

Recognition hit his eyes, followed by a huge smile. "Fräulein Dalke, what a pleasant surprise."

He looked much older than just three weeks ago, dragging one leg behind as he walked over to a chair, while eyeing the comfortable sofa with yearning. "If I sit down there, I'll never get up again. The week in that miserable, damp building has worsened my arthritis."

"I'm so glad they released you." Thea smiled at him. "Thanks to your wife and all the other courageous women."

"Indeed, I owe my life to Frau Falkenstein."

While his wife blushed at the compliment, he scrutinized Thea's appearance, evidently taking in her less than stellar condition. "I must say I'm relieved to find out you escaped. It doesn't bear contemplating what they would have done to you if they had found you hiding in the basement." A barely visible shiver passed through him.

"Because you covered up for me, nobody missed me," Thea offered. "I couldn't see anything in that dark room down there. I just heard the shouting, trucks coming and going and then nothing. Still, I was too afraid to leave, for fear one of the civilian workers would see and betray me. So I stayed in that cramped and cold place until the change of shifts. When I heard the others walking down the stairs, I found the perfect moment to sneak out and fall in step behind them."

"That must have been awful," Frau Falkenstein said, sympathy etched into her face.

Thea pressed a hand over her heart, as if reliving the anguish she'd felt back then. "It was. I almost died of fear. All those hours alone in the darkness, frightened I'd be discovered." She gave a little shrug. "Anyhow, I was lucky. When I walked out behind everyone else, the guard only glanced furtively at our employee cards. Once I was outside the factory premises I took to my heels and dashed off. My first, admittedly stupid, action was to go home and check on my parents."

Herr Falkenstein had known Thea's mother who had worked at the same factory. He pursed his lips, seemingly bracing himself for what he was going to hear.

"They were gone. Vanished without a trace." She had to compose herself for a few seconds before she continued to speak. "I wanted to stay in the apartment, but was afraid the Gestapo might return."

"You were probably right about that," Herr Falkenstein said in an earnest voice.

"Very much so. I hurriedly filled a suitcase with a few clothes and my dearest things, including our ration books and a bit of cash. Then I left." Thea gazed at him with big eyes, tears gathering. "I hadn't fully rounded the corner when SS entered the building. Imagine if they'd arrived a few seconds earlier."

"You shouldn't have gone to the apartment," Frau Falkenstein injected.

"I know that now." Dread crept into Thea's bones. "Back then, it didn't occur to me. My only concern was my parents' safety."

"Do you have any news of them?" Herr Falkenstein asked.

"No. Just that they've been taken. Presumably to the Jewish Hospital, because my mother was sick. But I haven't been able to visit..." Thea launched into her attack. "I've been forced to go underground and live off the charity of strangers, sleeping every night in another place. Meanwhile I've used up all my ration cards and my cash." She gave a heartfelt, deep sigh. "Life as an illegal is so awful, sometimes I wish they had arrested me. It can't be that bad, can it?"

"Never think like that." Herr Falkenstein shook his head. "You haven't experienced what I did. The conditions in the Hermann Göring barracks, where they took me first, were appalling. Nonetheless, what shocked me most was the Nazis' cavalier behavior with us, as if they didn't even consider us humans. They truly do not care about the well-being of their Jewish prisoners. We're scum to them, worse than scum, we're cockroaches that must be squashed."

Thea felt herself blanching with every word he said. She knew the situation in the camps and holding centers were bad, but never in her wildest dreams had she expected it to be that terrible. "I... I don't know what to say."

"Say that you're grateful to be at liberty, however bad you may feel it is."

Herr Falkenstein's well-meant advice caused the bile to rise in her throat. Who was he to demand her to be grateful for her appalling conditions, while he himself lived like the King of France?

Swallowing down her anger, she feigned agreement. "You're right, I should... and I am, honestly. But it's so hard. If I at least had a roof over my head, a place to sleep every night, it would make life so much better."

Frau Falkenstein shot her husband a look, which Thea couldn't interpret.

"I'd offer to hide you in our attic—"

"Oh no," she interrupted him, since she would much rather stay in one of the many extra rooms in their apartment. He couldn't really expect her to be up in a drafty attic, exposed to the ever-increasing Allied bombings?

Just at that moment, the door swung open and David

stormed inside. When he recognized Thea, he stopped cold in his tracks. "Thea? What are you doing here?"

"David. I didn't know you knew the Falkensteins," she said sourly, racking her brain for why on earth he was here. Unfortunately, they hadn't parted on the best terms—to tell the truth, she'd cheated on him for months with another guy. She still remembered the bottomless hurt in his eyes when he'd confronted her.

"I live here." His voice betrayed no emotion he might still harbor for her. The indifference was worse than him still being angry at her, because scorn could be transformed into desire. A lack of feelings was much harder to overcome.

"I had no idea. What happened to your old apartment?" Thea kept her voice sweet and cast him the dashing smile that had always mesmerized him.

David rolled his eyes. "We were evicted, because it wasn't in a Jewish owned house."

"Oh yes, I remember," she said lamely. The *big move* of all Jews into Jewish quarters and buildings, affecting her family too, had happened while David worked at the Zionist training farm in Luckenwalde. "Does that mean your entire family lives here?" Her chance to move in with the Falkensteins was dwindling.

"In fact, we do. I thought you'd know. Weren't you a friend of Amelie's as well?"

"We used to be, but lost contact after finishing school." Thea didn't mention that she'd only befriended Amelie because the other girl was a gifted student in the boring subjects of book-keeping and mathematics and had generously allowed Thea to copy her homework. "It would be nice to rekindle our friendship."

David's eyes became big. It wasn't what she'd hoped for, but at least her response had teased some reaction from him.

"I don't think that's a good idea," Herr Falkenstein joined

their conversation. "Fräulein Dalke had to go underground after the *Fabrikaktion*. For her to liaise with us would only endanger her, as well as us. Therefore, it's best that none of us keep in contact with her, not even Amelie."

Inwardly Thea seethed. How dare this man brush her off in such an uncaring way? It took her some effort to put on a mask of pleasantness. Clutching at straws she said, "Actually, I'd love to take you up on your offer to hide in your attic."

The sheer look of horror on the faces of all three people told her immediately that she'd pursued the wrong path.

"I'm so sorry if I wrongfully got your hopes up." Herr Falkenstein fumbled awkwardly with his fingers. "Before we were interrupted by David, I was going to say that I'd offer you to stay in our attic, if that weren't much too dangerous for everyone involved, including yourself. A Jew hiding in a house full of Jews is not a wise move."

"I thought, perhaps, if I..." Desperation propelled her to come forward with such a bold suggestion and she blurted out, "I could legally live here and be safe from prosecution, if David married me."

"Me? You're joking," David drawled. "You seem to have forgotten that you're already married to someone else."

"You're married?" Herr Falkenstein seemed astonished.

"I was." Thea opted for a white lie. "My husband was captured and died in prison." He probably *was* dead by now, given what everyone knew about the living conditions in the camps.

Frau Falkenstein, looking worried about an unsavory discussion to unfold, raised her voice. "My condolences, that must have been a terrible blow."

It hadn't been. Regardless, Thea dabbed at her eyes. "I'm still reeling with grief."

"I can absolutely relate." Frau Falkenstein put a gentle hand on Thea's shoulder. "Now I'm even more sorry that we're not able to help you out. I'm sure you understand we would do you a disservice if we invited you to stay with us. This house is under observation and the Gestapo will be only too happy to find a reason to send us all to a holding camp. What we can do, though..." She looked at her husband, who apparently understood her without words, because he completed her sentence.

"... most of our money is gone, but we still have a few possessions left."

Frau Falkenstein disappeared into one of the bedrooms and returned several minutes later with a staple of fine linen in her hands. "These bedsheets are made from the finest damask, you should get a good price for them on the black market."

Thea's breath hitched at the beauty of the fine linen, which she would have liked to keep for herself. "This is very generous. Thank you so very much, Herr and Frau Falkenstein." Then she bid her goodbyes, inwardly seething at being fobbed off with a bunch of cloth when they could have offered her a roof over her head.

3

BERLIN, APRIL 5, 1943

Knut stood in the kitchen, heating up dinner, which the cleaning lady had prepared. She came twice a week to clean, cook and iron for him. This arrangement suited him perfectly, since he mostly ate at the canteen in the Bendlerblock anyway.

A key turned in the lock and Bernd marched inside in full uniform, his boots polished to a shine. As always when Bernd visited, warmth spread from Knut's heart into every limb in his body. They never saw enough of each other, due partly to the demanding jobs both of them held, but mostly due to the illegal nature of their relationship.

"Hmm, that smells heavenly. What is it?" Bernd entered the kitchen, pressing a kiss on Knut's mouth. During the last week Knut had asked himself many times whether being together justified the threat to their lives, but the moment their lips connected, the warmth pulsating through him pushed away all doubts.

"Goulash with potatoes."

"I'm starving. Shall I set the table?"

"Yes, please." Knut bit his tongue, not wanting to broach the disquieting events of the day just now. Selfishly, he wanted to enjoy a few minutes of bliss after Bernd had returned from a week-long secret trip with the Abwehr, where they both worked. It had been almost two years ago on Operation Barbarossa, the mission involving the attack on the Soviet Union, that the two of them had met.

Knut smiled at the memory. It had been love at first sight. After having all but given up hope of finding someone special, he'd taken one deep gaze into Bernd's eyes and his heart was lost forever. For obvious reasons, their relationship had started with difficulties and they'd needed almost six months to admit—albeit only to each other—that they were a couple.

"It was a successful week, although I'm glad to be back. I missed you," Bernd interrupted his thoughts of the past as they sat down to eat.

"Did you get the information into the right hands?" They both worked in different departments and usually weren't privy about the details of each other's individual assignments.

"I did. We had two near misses though. One agent turned up dead and with another one I got the impression he'd been turned, so I dropped him."

"Better to be careful. Our job is dangerous enough." Knut ladled a second serving into his bowl and asked, "Want some more, too?"

"Yes, please." Bernd looked at him with love. "It's good to be back. Every trip is worse than the one before. I have a terrible feeling that we'll soon be found out."

Knut frowned. The double-meaning of Bernd's words wasn't lost on him. After joining the resistance network in the Abwehr under the lead of Hans von Dohnanyi and his boss, Hans Oster, the danger of being found out and the possible consequences, had ratcheted up several notches.

It often seemed that Hitler was so paranoid about plots against him that even something as inconsequential as breathing might get someone arrested and result in dire punishment,

ranging from prison time to being shipped off to a camp, or even
execution.

"Have you heard the news already?" Knut asked.

Instantly, Bernd's ears perked up. "No. Nothing too bad, I
hope?"

Knut sighed, since there was no use in trying to hold back
the bad news. Bernd had an impeccable sixth sense tuned in to
looming danger. This talent had saved their lives more than
once during the Operation Seven they'd organized together in
1942, and apparently he sensed that something awful had
happened during his trip away from Berlin. "Hans von
Dohnanyi and Dietrich Bonhoeffer have been arrested."

Bernd hissed in a sharp breath. "For what reason?"

"Treason." Knut ran a hand through his cropped hair.
"That's not even the worst of it. Hans Oster apparently was
caught destroying some of Dohnanyi's papers. Since they didn't
have any real evidence against him, he was removed from his
position and put under house arrest."

"What about Admiral Canaris?" Bernd twirled his
moustache.

"He's above suspicion. At least for the time being."

"That still leaves the resistance without leadership."

"Exactly." Knut leaned back in his chair, mulling over the
next steps to take. "I'd say we lay low for a while. Just in case."

"Definitely. The pavement has gotten much too hot." Bernd
got up to clear the dishes and returned from the kitchen with a
bottle of red wine.

"From your French contact?" Knut moved onto the sofa,
waiting for Bernd to settle next to him.

"Yes. The job does come with some perks to make up for
the danger." A twinkle shone in Bernd's eyes. After pouring
both of them a glass, he asked, "What about you? Do they
suspect you?"

"I don't think so, or they would have arrested me right away.

Like everyone else I was searched for offensive papers when leaving the office."

Bernd raised an eyebrow, twirling the red liquid in his glass. "I should hope you were too intelligent to attempt such a stupid thing."

"You know me better than that. Even if I kept incriminating evidence in my office I wouldn't have tried to remove it under the Gestapo's noses. They have positioned their men in front of nearly every office."

"Those brutes have been itching to take over the Bendlerblock for years."

"In any case, they said that every member of the Abwehr will be interrogated over the next few days." Knut shuddered. In theory, he had nothing to fear, since the Gestapo wouldn't dare torture Abwehr soldiers before proven guilty—which didn't hold true if they found out about either of his deadly sins: his relationship with Bernd or his resistance to the Reich. "Do you think we should stop seeing each other for a while?"

Bernd rested his hand on Knut's thigh. "We've talked about this before. It would be the obvious choice, wouldn't it?"

Miserably, Knut nodded.

"But would it change anything? We'd still be at risk of being discovered for resisting Hitler."

"I know. That threat is probably the greater one. Nobody dares to treat traitors with lenience."

Playing with his moustache again in thought, Bernd mused, "I consider it a given that our resistance network will be found out sooner or later. I've been feeling the danger in my bones for such a long time; every day I wake up in the morning, I expect it to be my last day on earth. And you know what, I won't be sorry if they capture me, because I'll know I've done what's right."

Knut smiled. He felt the exact same way, even though he didn't have Bernd's talent to properly articulate his emotions.

"But I would regret every minute that I could have spent

with you and didn't." He wrapped his arm around Knut. "I've never been this happy before I met you. So, no, we shouldn't stop seeing each other, not even for a short while."

Inwardly, Knut celebrated, but he did have one last concern that he had to share with Bernd. "The Blockwart lady seems to suspect something. She never misses an opportunity to poke her nose into my affairs and ask supposedly inconspicuous questions."

Bernd guffawed. "That woman is a veritable pain in the ass. Perhaps I should properly move in, I could claim I've been bombed out."

For a moment, exhilaration shot through Knut's veins. It would be a dream come true. Then reality caught up with him. "You know that wouldn't work. Too many of our colleagues live on this street, who'd be prone to accidentally expose the lie."

The arm around Knut's shoulder squeezed him tight, before Bernd said, "Don't worry. Nothing will happen."

Then he leaned forward to grab the wine glasses and gave one to Knut, before raising his with the other hand. "To a speedy downfall of Hitler and his cronies!"

It was the trait Knut admired most in his friend, more even than his moral integrity and determination to do the right thing: his optimism.

"To a very short thousand-year empire," he answered.

4

A clinking sound rang in Roxi's ear. In a split-second she was wide awake. The cell was completely dark, not even the slightest glimmer reaching inside. Footfalls followed the clinking and she instinctively turned her head in the direction of the door.

Her inner clock told her it was the wee hours of the night, much too early for the guard to bring breakfast. She had a pretty good idea where her cell was located within the building. If the door was opened, she'd use the moment of surprise to escape. Silent as a cat she slipped from the hard cot and positioned herself next to the door, but much to her chagrin, the steps continued down the hallway.

Pressing her ear against the door, she heard softer, lighter steps all but drowned out by the guard's heavy boots. A new prisoner. Judging by the faster pace to match the guard's long strides, Roxi assumed it was a small woman—a safe assumption, since she believed herself to be in a woman-only prison.

After the *Fabrikaktion* she'd joined the Rosenstrasse protests, not so much because she considered it a worthwhile cause, because she'd never genuinely believed the Nazis would liberate the captured Jews, but because David had been there.

Her initial plan had been to find a way to get him out. From first-hand experience she knew that no building, not even the best guarded camp, was escape proof. A grin spread across her lips as she returned to her cot. Once it had become clear the Rosenstrasse inmates would be released, she'd fought with herself whether to stay and see David, or disappear.

In the end, prudence had won out over the desire to be with him. David would be fine, protected by his Aryan mother, whereas nobody was going to vouch for Roxi, so she needed to lay low for a while. A member of the Romani community, she had witnessed the disappearance of her entire extended family. Some to prisons, rightfully perhaps for petty crimes they committed, others to labor camps or medical institutions where they'd been objected to forced sterilization or died from excruciating medical experiments.

Roxi had no intention of ending up like them. She'd gone underground years ago, before the SS had cast a tight net over the country, intent on fishing out any and all undesirables. Not even David was worth risking her life for.

After her mother had died during childbirth and her father was hit by a car when she was four years old, she'd been raised by the entire traveling community, the responsibility of everyone and no one. And she fully planned to keep it that way.

On the day after the SS's first visit to the corral of wagons where the community lived, she'd left, knowing deep in her heart that her only chance to survive Hitler's reign unscathed was to be on her own. For six years it had worked just fine.

Her luck had run out in the seventh year a week ago, when a shop owner had caught her stealing food and called the police. Thanks to the stolen membership card of a sports club, she'd been taken to prison instead of being sent to a camp. At least until the police proved, or rather disproved, her identity.

That had been four days ago and she had been waiting for a chance to escape ever since. Unfortunately, the Nazis were masters in security and, so far, there hadn't been the sliver of an opportunity to escape. She sure hoped to flee before they inevitably found out her Romani ancestry and sent her on a transport to the East.

Gathering bits and pieces of information here and there, she learned that breaking out from the camps was, if not easy, at least possible. The main difficulty lay in not being recaptured in the vicinity of the camps, where every stranger raised suspicion.

She went back to sleep and was woken in the morning by the guard bringing breakfast, or so she thought. It wasn't the usual guard who opened the barred window in the door and he didn't have a tray with him.

"You. Face and hands to the wall. Legs spread apart. You'll be taken to the interrogator."

She didn't want to show him how much she feared the prospect of an "intensified interrogation" as the Gestapo euphemistically called their torture sessions, so she straightened her spine and held her head high while she moved herself into the position he'd ordered.

For a second she was tempted to dash off the moment he opened the door, but the clattering in the hallway alerted her that other guards were present and would inevitably quash her escape.

"Where are you taking me?" she asked, barely managing to stand still while the guard first padded her down and then handcuffed her behind her back.

"You'll find out soon enough. Get moving!"

She'd already learned that prison guards weren't exactly talkative, so there was nothing else for her to do than follow him through endless corridors until they came upon a metal door.

He knocked and after barking his name, it was opened from the outside. Roxi wondered whether she might be able to imitate his voice sufficiently well to gain admittance. As soon as she stepped through the door, her eyes only used to the darkness were blinded by glaring sunlight and she wavered in her step, until a sharp stab to her back, presumably by a gun barrel, prodded her forward.

Once her eyes accustomed to the light, she diligently observed every detail around her, carefully without moving her head so as not to receive another punch.

As the guard shoved her into the interrogation room on the third floor, she had to suppress a grin at the sight of treetops in front of the window.

"Sit." He left the room without taking her handcuffs off—an annoyance for sure—but also without shackling her to the chair.

Roxi waited until the sound of his footsteps had faded, before she got up and stretched her back into every direction, then curved her spine and wriggled her tied hands beneath her butt. She sat on the chair again, slipped off the clunky wooden shoes she'd been given, folded her knees and pushed her legs through her tied hands.

This time she didn't suppress her happy grin. She was as good as free. Still no steps approached from the corridor, yet she opted not to waste precious time trying to unlock the handcuffs and rather brave the escape with tied hands. Three big steps later she stood next to the window, opened it and climbed out.

The next move was critical: she had to jump the short distance to the tree, grab the trunk and climb down. An exercise she'd completed many times, although never with tied hands.

Chancing a quick glance back into the interrogation room, Roxi decided anything was preferable to waiting for what might happen in there. Even if they weren't going to torture her, she'd still end up in a labor camp, that much was sure. She'd rather not find out whether the awful rumors were indeed true.

Taking a deep breath, she closed her eyes, mentally worked through the actions of the next few minutes, carefully placing her feet and tied hands until she safely reached the ground to dash off into a side street. Then she opened her eyes and jumped.

For several seconds she flew through the air, her heart stopping its beats. Then she sensed rough bark beneath her soles and pushed her upper body against the trunk, fumbling with her hands for a branch to hold on to.

Afraid her absence might be discovered any moment, she skidded down the tree faster than she would have liked and jumped as soon as she considered it safe. Landing on her feet like the cat she was, she didn't waste time looking left or right before she dashed off across the street into a side alley.

Only when she was far enough away from the prison to consider herself safe from pursuit, did she pause to listen. Vehicles cruised down the main street, a child cried, birds chirped.

Her fist shot into the air. She'd done it again. Had snatched herself from the jaws of death. Looking down at her cuffed hands, she racked her brain how to best get rid of them—and how to hide the evidence until then.

Without a jacket or a scarf to cover them up, she opted to stay out of sight until darkness fell. It made her next move much trickier, but safety always came first. Hunkering down in a bombed-out ruin, she tipped her head backward against the wall, looking through a gaping hole into the clear, blue sky.

It was such a beautiful spring day. Her mind wandered to David. She enjoyed his company immensely, had made love to him many times. Yet, she shirked back from calling him her boyfriend, for she had been on her own all her life and wasn't used to depending on another person.

Against her own best interests she missed him with all her heart. Perhaps she could sneak into the attic... *No way*, she scolded herself. It was much too dangerous. Not only for herself, but also for him. If—God forbid—the SS found an escaped prisoner in the building, a Romani no less, they'd gladly arrest all inhabitants for treason or whatever other crime they could think of.

David's situation was tenuous as it was; she didn't need to jeopardize it. But thinking of David gave her another idea. At his former workplace, the locomotive workshop, she'd find the tools to rid herself of the handcuffs.

Back when David had worked there, he'd made sure a hole in the fence wasn't fixed and always left some of the train carts open for illegals to hide. Warmth spread through her body as she remembered their first encounter in one of those carts. She'd fallen for him right then and there, impressed by his attitude before she'd even seen his face.

A groan escaped her. Perhaps in a few months she might safely visit him again; right now she had to lay low. Her advantage was that the Gestapo didn't know where to look for her, since she'd given them a false name along with the membership card and had invented a permanent residence in a small village just outside Berlin.

Despite the pain from her scratches, she rejoiced as she imagined the wild goose chase once they found out that Tamara Gil had never lived there.

5

"That's a stupid idea." Amelie spread her hands wide, squinting her eyes at her brother.

"It's not stupid at all." He knew it was a crazy thing to do, yet he was sick and tired of his current life.

"What exactly do you think will be better if you go underground?"

"At least I wouldn't have to toil in that awful factory anymore." David had never shied away from hard work, not at the locomotive workshop under Baumann, and not during his stay at the agricultural training camp run by the Zionists.

Whenever he thought back to that time, a sharp pain momentarily took his breath away. It wasn't the lack of tedious, boring and back-breaking work he regretted, it was the lost opportunity for a ticket to freedom: sailing across the Mediterranean on a ship headed for Palestine.

"Are you even listening?" Amelie prodded his shoulder.

"Sorry, no." He ran a hand through his hair. "Living illegally I won't have to produce weapons for the Nazis' war machine."

"It sits on the conscience, doesn't it? I mean, helping our

worst enemy." Amelie wrinkled her nose. "But we don't really have a choice. Without work, no ration cards. Without ration cards, no food. How would you eat if you went underground?"

"I'll find a way." David knew it wasn't that easy. Illegals needed many helpers to stay alive.

"And where would you sleep?"

"In the attic, of course." Roxi had been hiding in the attic, so why shouldn't David do the same?

Amelie glared at him. "Under no circumstances! That's utterly idiotic. Where do you think the Gestapo will search first if you went missing? They wouldn't leave a stone unturned in the entire building. And then we'd be all on a train to the East."

"Alright. I could rough it, I mean if Thea can survive, so can I."

"Don't tell me you still fancy her!" Amelie squinted her eyes at him.

"Of course not." Even if he weren't madly, completely and utterly in love with Roxi, he wouldn't spare a single thought about getting back together with Thea, least of all marry her as she had suggested for purely practical reasons—practical for her, not for him.

His face must have given his sentiments away, because his sister suspiciously asked, "Anything you're not telling me?"

"Contrary to popular belief, you're not my parent." He smirked at her.

"I might as well be, because who else is going to keep you from plunging head first into trouble?" she said in a lighthearted tone, until suddenly her eyes opened wide and she added, "Oh my God. You have a new girlfriend! How come I don't know about her?"

"Because there's nothing to know," David snapped. He loved his sister to pieces, even though she sometimes grated on his nerves. His relationship with Roxi was none of her business.

If they still had a relationship, since she seemed to have vanished from the face of the earth.

"I'm sorry," Amelie said in a conciliatory tone. "It's just that I'm worried about you. Don't do anything stupid. You have a perfectly good home, food and protection through your status as mixed-bred. Your only gripe is the awful work." She giggled. "Sounds like a spoiled brat to me."

He had to chuckle. "I guess you're right. So what are we going to do?"

"We? As in you and me?"

"I for my part don't fancy helping the Nazis with their war efforts." Looking at Amelie he had an epiphany. "Can you organize a uniform for me?"

"Now you have lost the plot." She shook her head, her chestnut hair bobbing up and down. "Even if I wanted to, how would I go about getting one?"

"You work in a factory sewing uniforms all day long."

"That was before the raid. Now I've been assigned to Loewe Radio."

David's eyes lit up with delight as he considered the possibilities. A radio, which Jews were forbidden to own, was almost as good as a uniform. "Why haven't you told me this before?"

She grimaced. "Since when are you interested in my place of work? It's boring to the bone, bolting metal frames all day long."

"Amelie." He put his hands on her shoulders, looking deep into her eyes. "This is our chance to build a radio transmitter. I'll give you a list of stuff I need and you smuggle them home, piece by piece."

"It's a huge risk."

"But it will be so worth it. Just think what we could do with a radio. Starting with listening to the BBC—"

"Which is forbidden under the death penalty."

He waved her objection away. "To sending coded information, warning the resistance about raids, anything. This is something we can do. This is our chance!"

Very much out of character, his sister didn't outright refuse his request. Instead she took her sweet time, before she answered. "I guess it is. I'll do it. It's about time we actively resisted the Nazis."

"You're going to do what?" their mother asked as she entered the room.

"Mutti." Both Amelie and David shrunk back as if caught red-handed, which they probably were. Plotting to commit treason was punishable the same way as actually doing it.

Helga shook her head and David realized just how tired and old she looked. The week-long protest when the survival of her entire family had rested on her shoulders alone had taken its toll on her. Too occupied with his own problems, he hadn't recognized it before. Now he noticed the shuffling gait, the slumped shoulders, the listless expression, and the general aura of defeat. Just like the prisoners in the Rosenstrasse camp.

He got up and wrapped his arms around his mother's bony frame. "Don't worry about us, Mutti."

"How can I not worry?" Helga sighed. "Every minute when one of you or Vati are out, I'm afraid you won't return in one piece."

David wanted to dispel her dreary mood with a joke, but a tremor racking her shoulders changed his mind. He squeezed her harder, sending a silent plea for help toward Amelie. His sister was so much better at voicing the right words.

"Mutti. Thanks to you, we're safe." Amelie walked over, joining their embrace. "There's no need to worry."

All three knew it was a lie. There was so much to worry about, and their safety was tenuous at best. The Gestapo could take them away any day, regardless of their status as protected Jews. Or passersby might beat them up for fun, shove them in front of a rolling electric tram. Anything might be done to someone wearing the yellow star—which was the very reason why David preferred the risk of being arrested for not doing so to the constant harassment while obeying the law.

"We can't just stand by and look away while others are taken away," David said.

"I know," Helga's whispered admission shocked him to the core.

"You agree?" His heart beat faster.

"I do. The protest has taught me that we can fight the government. It has also made me realize that if everyone only looks out for themselves or their immediate family, nothing will change. So, yes, I have vowed that we need to resist the Nazis however we can and help those in need, even to our own detriment." His mother extricated herself from their embrace and gazed first at him, then at Amelie. "This doesn't mean I like what you're doing. And I implore you to be careful. Please."

"We will," David promised. It was an easy concession to make, since he fully intended to survive the Nazi reign.

6

David meticulously wrote down the pieces he needed to build a functioning radio transmitter. To minimize the risk for Amelie, he separated the things into two separate lists: one for spare parts like cables, enameled copper wire and a diode, which he was going to organize, and the other one for the specific parts that his sister had to smuggle from Loewe, namely the tubes.

The next day after work he boarded the underground train to his previous workplace, the locomotive workshop. No doubt, he'd find everything he needed to build at least a radio, if only without the sending capabilities. He scolded himself for not having thought of it earlier. Perhaps he too had acted like a sheep following the herd, instead of finding ways to resist the Nazis' stupid laws.

As he approached the vast premises, which he knew like the back of his hand, exhilaration crept up his spine, speeding up his steps. He pondered how best to sneak in, when he spotted his former boss Baumann walking toward the gate.

After a moment of surprise, Baumann waved at him. "Hey, Kessel, what'ya doing here?"

David smiled at hearing the moniker Baumann had given

him on his first day at the workshop years ago, in an effort not make the other workers privy to David's Jewish blood. Furtively he double-checked that he was wearing his reversible jacket with the starless side out, before he called back, "Good day, Baumann. Got a minute?"

"Sure. Come in." Baumann told the guard something and gave David a visitor pass.

"That's new."

"Yep, they've increased surveillance. Can't make a step without those bloodhounds on your heels. What do they think? That we're gonna steal the locomotives or something?"

Perhaps not the locomotives, some copper wire will suffice.

As they entered the factory hall, the deafening noise impeded a normal conversation. Men were dragging heavy motor blocks to different repair stations, others hammered or welded to whip the worn-out machines back into shape. *Räder müssen rollen für den Sieg*, tires have to roll for victory. A wave of nausea crept up David's throat. As much as he'd loved working here, it had turned him into a stooge of Hitler's regime. Once again, the idea of going illegal surfaced, then at least he wouldn't have to deal with his conscience.

Baumann led him to a small cubicle that was completely enclosed by thick glass panes, giving the owner both a good view over the workers and shielding him from the deafening noise.

"So, what are ya doing here?" Baumann asked as he offered David Ersatzkaffee from a Thermos that stood in the same place every day.

Biting his lip, David sized up his mentor. Baumann was beyond suspicion, had proven his trustworthiness many times, yet he hesitated; what he was about to ask would make Baumann complicit in a crime.

Baumann observed him through squinted eyes. "You're not in trouble, are you? Heard they released you."

"They did. Released everyone, but they wouldn't let us go back to our former workplaces for fear of raising undue questions."

"Rightly so." Baumann rubbed his chin. "Me and some of the old chaps joined the protests several times."

David swallowed down the lump forming in his throat. He'd never expected the bullnecked former communists to show their support in such a public way. "Thanks."

"No need to thank us. We can't let these pigs get away with everything." Baumann winked at him, giving David the courage to deliver his request.

"I was wondering if you might give me some spare wire ends."

"What for?"

David felt a slight burn climbing to his ears. "To build a radio transmitter."

"Hmm." Baumann rubbed his chin. "What exactly do you need?"

"Enameled copper wire, a diode and cables, whatever you can spare."

"Can't spare nothing, can we?" Baumann's grin took the sharpness out of the words. "But I'll give it to you anyway. It's for a good cause, I assume."

"A very good cause."

Baumann emptied his cup of lukewarm coffee, before he said, "Best if I don't know anything about your plans. There's still a hole in the fence—"

"You know about it?" David felt himself blush all over.

"You didn't believe I was oblivious to anything that happens in my workshop?"

"I thought I'd been so careful..."

"Can't fool an old chap like me. After you left, Matze took over putting water and food in the train carts."

"All this time I was proud of hiding what I was up to from

you." David looked at the other man. "Not because I don't trust you, but because I didn't want to get you into trouble."

"And that's why I don't want to know about whatever you're planning. You do you, and I'll do me. If you get caught, I know nothing. Can't snoop around the premises catching every little thing, I have enough stuff on my plate." Bauman winked at him.

"Thanks so much. I'll make sure not to get caught and only take little pieces nobody will miss."

"Good luck." Baumann escorted him back to the entrance gate, where David returned the visitor pass and then made a beeline for the hole in the fence at the back of the premises. The sun was about to set, casting the most beautiful orange and pink hues across the sky. He walked across the railway tracks leading to the repair shop, biding his time while scouting the terrain for any changes since he'd last been here.

Once darkness had fallen he squeezed through the hole in the fence and crossed the yard, which he knew like the palm of his hand, in pursuit of the material needed to build a radio transmitter. True to his word he took only offcuts nobody would miss. Finding a suitable diode was a bit tricky, since they were kept in a locker inside the huge factory hall.

When he found the back door unlocked, a grin spread across his face. Baumann must have *forgotten* to lock it before going home for the night. Inside it was almost completely dark, lacking the faint moonlight to guide him.

He stayed still, perking up his ears and listening for unusual sounds. The last thing he wanted was to encounter a guard. A violent shiver ran down his spine. Or a guard dog.

Fighting hard against the burgeoning fear, he listened for a few more minutes until he was certain he was alone. Then he fumbled for the flashlight in his pocket and made his way to the closet with diodes and other electric stuff.

He took what he needed. Then his hand hesitantly hovered

over a battery. The radio could be operated straight from the socket, although a battery would make it much more versatile. After fighting with himself for a few seconds he removed his hand. Batteries were always scarce and if one was found missing it would surely alert not only Baumann, but also the penny-pincher in the bookkeeping department.

Outside he thought he saw a shadow crossing the yard. Squinting his eyes, he made out the silhouette of a person. His heart drummed fiercely against his ribs, recognizing the familiar way the shadow moved. He almost called out her name, before reminding himself that neither one of them was supposed to be here.

He turned toward the area where the train carts were parked to intercept her there, but much to his surprise she walked toward the shed with the tools. Perhaps it wasn't Roxi after all, but a common thief?

Goosebumps spread over David's skin as he realized the imminent danger. The shed door screeched horribly when opened. It would certainly alarm the night guards and SS would swarm out and cordon off the premises. Frantically gazing toward the fence in the distance, David calculated the time to reach it. It was too late to flee. So he followed the intruder. Just before the other person reached out to grab the shed's door, he hissed, "Don't open it or we'll both be caught."

The intruder swung around, her mouth agape as she whispered, "David."

"Roxi." He stood stunned in front of her, relieved to see her alive and well. His gaze travelled down her body until it stopped at her strangely cradled hands. Taking a step forward, he noticed the handcuffs around her wrists. "What happened?"

"I was arrested. Help me get rid of them first, then I'll tell you the entire story." Again she turned toward the shed.

With one stride he was by her side, whispering into her ear, "Don't open the door. It screeches like hell."

Roxi leaned into him and he seized the opportunity to wrap his arms around her. She wasn't the cuddly type and often shrunk back from physical contact, apparently considering it a threat to her independence. Thus David was surprised to find her pressed hard against him and tipping back her head for a kiss. Despite their precarious situation he took his sweet time to explore her mouth with his tongue, a multitude of emotions washing over him and pooling deep in his loins.

"I was so scared you were gone," he whispered when he came up for air.

"Me too." Her eyes spoke of dread, but he knew better than to ask.

"Let's get rid of your handcuffs. Follow me." For the second time that night, David entered the factory hall. There, he led her to one of the workstations and grabbed a pair of pincer pliers to cut off the handcuffs. Once she was free, he scrutinized the meandering angry red marks on her wrists.

Roxi followed his gaze. "They didn't torture me. This must have happened when I escaped."

Swept away by love for the petite woman standing in front of him, he wrapped her into another embrace, but this time, she pushed against him. "Let's get out of here. This place gives me the chills."

He pointedly gazed at her bare and dirty feet. "Shoes might help."

"Oh, come on, you should know me better than that. There's almost never a need for shoes." She snuck her hand into his, suggesting, "Let's go to one of the train carts."

He nodded, his heart jumping with joy. "You can't imagine how happy I am to see you again."

"I missed you too. Although you hug too much." Her grin told him she didn't really mind him cuddling her at all.

7

Roxi was hovering a few inches above ground. She chalked it up to finally being free and rid of the handcuffs, which had not only impeded her movements, but also hurt her wrists.

Perhaps a tiny bit of her delight might have to do with meeting David. She quickly shrugged off the thought. She was very capable of taking care of herself and didn't need a man to watch over her. If he hadn't shown up, it might have taken longer to dispose of the handcuffs, but she would have managed anyway.

Still, her heart fluttered in his presence and desire rushed through her veins. In reality she yearned for his embrace, a disturbing development, because she was so used to fiercely protecting her independence.

They found an unlocked cart and climbed inside, availing themselves of the Thermos of soup and the water bottle left there.

Between eating she told him the events that had transpired over the past weeks, starting with meeting his mother at the Rosenstrasse protests, her arrest for stealing food and ending with her escape this morning.

"You must be the only person in the world capable of pulling that off." David gazed at her full of admiration. "Escaping through the window on the third floor with your hands cuffed."

She laughed. "If Houdini were still alive, there'd be two of us."

"Don't sell yourself short. It was quite a feat. And I for one am so happy you managed to free yourself."

Unused to receiving praise, she quickly hedged. "It was more difficult than I thought and I have the scratches to prove it."

"Want me to have a look?"

"What for? Are you going to somehow miraculously heal me?"

"Unfortunately I can't do magic, but I can clean the wounds so they won't get infected."

"If you insist, why not?" She pulled her blouse over her head, exposing her naked torso to his gaze. Even in the dim torchlight she saw his pupils dilate with desire.

"Umm. It doesn't look too bad. Does it hurt?"

"A bit." Sliding down the tree, Roxi had ripped open big chunks of skin, which had hurt like hell. Right now, the desire rippling through her body pushed every other feeling away.

David fumbled a clean handkerchief from his pocket, drenched it with water and gently cleaned the scratches. Roxi gritted her teeth as the burning seeped deep into her skin. Closing her eyes, she blocked out the pain, instead concentrating on the touch of his fingers.

"That should do it," David said in a very breathless voice.

When Roxi opened her eyes, she caught him staring at her naked breasts, visibly holding onto the last thread of his self-control. Without uttering a word she unbuttoned his shirt and let her hands wander from his bony shoulders down to his tight stomach.

"Are you sure? I don't want to hurt you," David murmured.

"I couldn't care less about my scratches, just take me already, will you?"

David willingly obliged and it was almost dawn when their bodies and minds were satiated.

"We should leave, we don't want to be caught by the morning shift coming to work," David said as he lazily stretched his limbs.

Roxi opened the blackout curtains to fetch her clothes and get dressed. Then she looked down at her feet. Personally she preferred to go barefoot, but since she wanted to blend in, shoes were needed.

David followed her gaze. "What size do you wear?"

"Thirty-six. I could fit both feet into one of yours."

He chuckled. "That would be a funny sight. I wasn't thinking of my shoes, but perhaps Amelie's or Frau Falkenstein's."

"You're not going to steal a pair of shoes from your family, are you?"

"Of course not." While David was buttoning up his shirt, she cast a last look at his muscled front. "I'd ask them."

Instantly her muscles tautened. "You can't tell them about me!"

"No need to worry. I'll say the shoes are for an illegal." He put a hand on her arm, but an alarm was sounding in her head and she jumped away from him.

"I'm sorry." David looked contrite.

Taking another step backward until her back came flush against the compartment door, she felt for the handle. Her escape literally in her hands, the rush of adrenaline subsided and she gazed into his eyes, shaking her head. "No, I'm sorry. It's an old habit. I panic when someone tries to grab me."

"I don't want you to be afraid of me. Ever." His eyes shone with honest concern.

"I'm not afraid of you." Roxi was angry at her own stupid reaction. David had never staked a claim on her or tried to turn her into a possession. It was unfair to mistrust him. Despite knowing this on a rational level, she simply couldn't shed those ingrained reactions. "I'll try harder."

"While I'd love to keep you close by at all times, I understand how much you value your independence. I will never try to cage you." He cast her a lopsided grin. "Just like your feet feel better without shoes, you feel better on your own."

"Not really. I do like being with you." She wrinkled her forehead, trying to sort through her emotions. "It's just... this feeling is so new and so... scary. I don't want to wake up one day to find out I lost myself and have become your... sidekick, or something."

"I wouldn't want it that way either."

"You wouldn't?" Roxi was taken aback. Every other man she'd met, especially those in her community, considered women and children their possessions just as their wagons and the horses that drew them. The Nazis weren't much different either, Hitler always touting that 'Women took care of the small world at home, so men could accomplish big things in the big world outside the home.' It surely wasn't a life Roxi envisioned for herself. She'd grown too fond of her liberty, even if sometimes it got lonely. Deep in her soul she yearned for another human being with whom she could share good and bad times.

"No. It's much better to have a girlfriend who stands on her own feet and shoulders part of the burdens we face in daily life." David mirrored her own thoughts.

She mulled over his words for several seconds, before she responded. "It might be worth a try."

"A try at what?"

"At being a real couple." Even considering the possibility of going official with him felt like a heavy weight pressing down on her.

"Gee whiz. I surely hadn't expected that."

"If you don't want to…" Roxi backtracked on her offer.

"No. I mean, yes, I absolutely want to. I just wasn't prepared for this. I always got the impression you wanted to keep our relationship without strings attached."

Roxi recoiled at the image of ropes strung around her wrists and ankles forcing itself upon her mind. That was exactly what she was afraid of. Being forcibly tied to another person. She struggled to put her feelings into words. "I hate the idea of strings shackling me to a man."

"I don't—" She put a finger to his lips to stop him from speaking.

"Let me explain. I do want to be with you, a lot more than I find comfortable. It pains me to be separated from you, especially when I don't even know if you are safe. You might find it hard to believe, but I was positively out of my mind with worry when they kept you in the camp. I'd been planning ways to break you out."

"How sweet." David was visibly moved.

"Every day for a few hours I joined the other women to protest. It was a wonderful feeling of community, something I didn't know I'd missed ever since my own tribe was taken away."

His hand shot forward to land on her arm, but he stopped the movement midway, for which Roxi was grateful. His touch always clouded her mind, making clear thinking all but impossible.

"Long story short, I want to be with you, I just don't want to be trapped. Instead of strings shackling me to you, I want it to feel like a rubber band, which ties us together, while at the same time allowing each one to go our own way, returning to the other person whenever we want. Knowing we belong together, but can still do our own thing." She observed his face keenly for his reaction to her rather unconventional suggestion.

Much to her surprise, his face lit up. "I love the way you see us. And... I love you." He took a slow step forward to wrap her up in an embrace and this time she didn't shrink back. On the contrary, she leaned into him, letting the warmth of being loved seep into every cell of her body.

After a while he stepped back, saying, "We really need to get going or we'll soon be shackled together with iron cuffs."

"And neither of us would like that," she chuckled.

8

Sick and tired of hiding out in more or less filthy conditions, Thea decided to splurge on an opera ticket. Back when she'd still lived with her parents, she had regularly taken off her yellow star and bought the cheap standing room only tickets. More often than not she and her friends had snuck down to the pit during the break and settled into unoccupied seats they'd spotted from above.

The memory of those relatively carefree times warmed her inside, before goosebumps pushed the cozy feeling away and anguish over the well-being of her parents sent icy shivers into her limbs. She hadn't been able to contact them, although she knew from reliable sources they were being held in the transit camp at Grosse Hamburger Strasse.

Shaking her head, she sent thoughts of support toward her mother, who must be terribly frightened at the prospect of being sent eastward. Thea stomped her foot to dispel her dreary mood. As long as her parents remained in Berlin, there was hope. The war couldn't go on forever and once Germany had won, Hitler would ease up the restrictions against assimilated Jews like her and her family.

Tonight, she was going to block out all unhappy thoughts and enjoy her evening out to the fullest. For one night she would pretend not to know a sorrow in the world, as she mingled with other Berliners. Exhilaration took hold of her, sending a fine blush to her cheeks. She retrieved her finest dress from the suitcase she'd been dragging from place to place during the past months and slipped into a knee-length blue dress with white polka dots and a white belt showcasing her slim waist.

Her eyes widened in horror when she noticed the beautiful garment hanging loose around said waist in addition to crinkling unattractively at the bustline. She urgently needed to get her hands on more food, or she'd soon be as thin as a rake.

Her good looks weren't simple vanity, they were her life insurance. A soldier smitten by a beautiful girl's ample cleavage rarely asked for identification papers, and if he did, he never scrutinized them too closely, his eyes busy looking elsewhere.

If only she might convince one of these soldiers to shelter her at his place, touting to the world she was his girlfriend, an Aryan like him and not a filthy Jew. But for that plan to come to fruition she needed better papers. Not the falsified ones she'd paid an extortionate amount for, but true, legitimate papers previously owned by an existing person, preferably a foreigner, perhaps a Norwegian or Danish woman who'd got stranded in Germany at the outbreak of war.

Those passports were the coveted ones every illegal dreamed of, since they all but guaranteed a carefree life right under the Nazis' noses. Unfortunately, they were even scarcer than they were popular and costs ranged from five to ten thousand Reichsmark, an amount her father used to earn in an entire year—before Jews had been squeezed out of their professions.

She waved her current host goodbye—a kind lady she'd met through mutual acquaintances—and walked to the opera house. For a moment she was tempted to take the tram, then decided against it, because she'd rather invest the fare on food. After half an hour of brisk walking she reached the venue just in time for the second bell, which allowed her to settle into the standing space without loitering in the foyer.

As much as she used to enjoy strolling about to observe the other patrons, it wasn't advisable for an illegal like her. Just when she was about to enter the staircase to the upper balconies, she bumped into none other than her missing husband, who seemed as aghast as she was.

"Thea? What are you doing here?"

Her eyes furiously glaring daggers at him, she quipped, "Watching the opera, of course. The more urgent question is what are you doing here? I was told you'd been sent on a transport."

His face was an awkward mask. "I was about to be sent away... when they changed their plans."

"So why didn't you call on me to let me know? I was worried to death about you!" she snarled at him, full of right-eous anger.

"I couldn't just go and visit," he said lamely.

Thea changed her approach. "It seems you're free to go wherever you want and you don't wear your badge." She looked pointedly at the space on his chest where the yellow star was supposed to be.

"Same as you." His lips pursed. "Look, Thea, what we had was never love. We both know that. Do yourself a favor and forget you saw me. Go away and never return."

"What? You're abandoning me? I'm your wife, if you care to remember." It took all her composure not to raise her voice and shout at him—but she couldn't risk drawing any attention to herself.

"Doesn't matter. I don't want anything to do with you, ever again. Now get lost. Go home and cry to your mommy. Make it quick, too." He put himself straddle-legged between her and the staircase, a menacing glint in his eyes.

Goosebumps broke out on her skin. She hadn't pegged Ralf as a violent man, but now she was afraid of him. With deep regret—both at her terrible choice of husband and the money spent for a performance she wasn't going to attend—she turned on her heels and walked out of the foyer. Her head held high, she waited until she passed through the entrance, before she let the tears fall.

Too occupied to deal with the inflicted humiliation, she didn't pay attention to two small vans parked in front of the theater. Only when she heard the telltale heavy footfalls trampling up the stairs behind her, did she turn around, her eyes tearing wide open.

A bunch of SS men raced into the theater building, their intention clear to every observer: chasing after illegal Jews hiding among the audience.

Thea staggered when the full force of it hit her, right between the eyes. Then, she gathered herself and walked away from the opera house as calmly and natural as she could muster. Just before turning around the corner, she glanced back and saw SS men manhandling several people—no doubt Jews gone underground—to the parked vans.

She ran until fierce stitches in her side forced her to slow down. Trembling like an aspen leaf, she sunk to the ground, not caring that her best dress was getting dirty. There, she stayed for several minutes, frozen in fear while her brain shouted that this time it had been much too close, her escape much too narrow.

9

Upon Knut's arrival at the Bendlerblock the secretary called out to him, "Leutnant Hesse, Oberst Luger is expecting you in his office."

Oberst Luger was the new man replacing the arrested Hans von Dohnanyi as head of Abwehr Overseas. He came highly recommended by Admiral Canaris as a man with the same political convictions as his predecessor, which patently meant he was eager to work for the resistance.

Knut remembered as if it had happened yesterday how he'd come to join the network. He'd been disillusioned with Hitler's politics for quite a while, following the invasion of Poland and the attack on Russia. However, the real impetus had been the farewell party for his sister Edith when she wanted to emigrate. Back then, he had caught David Goldmann hiding an illegal. He had felt deeply ashamed of his own passivity, and walked for hours to clear his head. The following day, he made a momentous decision and approached a well-known opponent of the regime, who in turn had recommended him to Hans von Dohnanyi, who also worked for the Abwehr. He'd been over the moon with joy to find Bernd was a resister, too.

Once Knut had joined the network, he was amazed at the number of resisters. Starting at the top from Admiral Canaris, there were dozens of men who actively engaged in sabotage, espionage, relayed war-critical information to the Allies and other clandestine activities.

"Oberst Luger," Knut greeted as he entered the office through the open door.

The bald man in his fifties with bushy dark eyebrows pointed at the chair in front of his desk. "Take a seat." Then he called out to his secretary, "I don't want to be disturbed. By anybody." As soon as the door closed, he disconnected the telephone to prevent the Gestapo from listening in.

"Have you heard about Operation Valkyrie?" Luger asked without preamble.

Taken aback by the question, Knut needed a few seconds to sort out his thoughts. "Vaguely. I'm not privy to the details. All I know is that it is a plan designed to quell an uprising instigated by the civilian population, prisoners of war, or concentration camp inmates.

"As far as I know, soldiers of the reserve army are intended to occupy war-critical points in Berlin as well as other major cities and to take swift action against the insurgents. Only Adolf Hitler personally, or the commander of the reserve army, can give the triggering code word."

"I see you are well informed." Oberst Luger nodded, his lips slightly tipping up at the sides, before he launched into a completely unrelated topic. "Admiral Canaris has commended you and Leutnant Bernd Ruben for your stellar work on Operation Seven."

Knut's heart hammered against his ribs, even as he carefully scrutinized his superior's face for a hidden clue. Operation Seven had been a rescue mission to spirit away several Jews disguised as Abwehr agents. He and Bernd had led the operation.

"Thank you, sir. I do what I can to serve our country."

"Our country, but not necessarily our Führer?" Luger asked in a cool voice.

Knut's blood ran cold. People had been convicted for treason for saying lesser things. "I always put duty to my country first."

"Well said." Luger stapled his hands on the desk. "Personally I'm about to commit high treason, and I'm asking you, are you willing to follow me?"

Knut relaxed. "Oberst, I'm willing to do anything it takes to save Germany from obliteration."

Luger nodded slowly. "The admiral spoke highly of you." He tipped his head, raising his bushy eyebrows and scrutinizing Knut, who sat completely still under the perusal. "You and Leutnant Ruben are friends?"

For a second time, Knut was caught off guard. Bernd was so much more than a friend, although that was what they pretended to be in the eyes of everyone but a very small group of like-minded men. "Yes, sir. We are colleagues and consider ourselves friends."

The slight movement in the corner of Luger's mouth gave Knut the impression that his superior knew more than he let on. "As of today the two of you will work together on a top-secret assignment." Then he laid out the plan to adapt Operation Valkyrie in such a way that it could be used to overthrow the government after Hitler's—untimely—demise, by implicating the SS and other organizations in the Führer's death and subsequently seizing control of the state organs via the reserve army.

When Knut left the office, he was equally elated and frightened. Finally, someone was taking control and making a plan that was worth the paper it was written on, instead of empty talk.

He couldn't wait to get home and discuss the new developments with Bernd, who must be equally excited at the prospect of turning the wheel around and saving the nation, before it was too late.

10

AUGUST 1943

Thea's summer dress was drenched with sweat as she waited in the sweltering heat. She had resorted to running errands, or rather standing in line, for several well-off families. Her usual excuse was that she had been bombed out and lost everything including her parents, and now needed to provide for herself doing odd jobs.

It was a humiliating occupation, even worse than toiling in the munitions factory, since she sensed the eyes of everyone upon her, silently wondering why a young, healthy woman like her didn't do her bit for the war effort like everyone else. The only other people standing in line were old women, invalids, or mothers with little children.

After she'd delivered the groceries to the big mansions in the affluent suburbs, she sorely needed to refresh herself. Not a huge fan of nature, she pondered whether to spend the money to go to a public swimming pool or rather cool down and wash for free in one of Berlin's lakes.

Given that living illegally was highly expensive, she pursed her lips and bit the bullet. Defying dirty earth and spiky stones, unwelcome insects and slimy grass, she opted to go to a nearby beach to wash herself as well as her clothes. In a secluded area she undressed down to her undergarments and entered the water. After the first shock, she soon enjoyed the cool water and scrubbed away the sweat and grime of a hot summer day from skin and hair.

When she was done, she washed her summer dress with a few flakes of curd soap she had scratched off the bar she'd bought for one of her employers and laid it out to dry in the sun.

She allowed herself to doze off for a while. About an hour later she slipped into the almost dried dress. In a much better mood, she returned to the city center, where she'd found a place to sleep for a few nights. But first, she wanted to do something nice to spruce up her dreary routine. Therefore, she headed for one of her favorite cafés and ordered a lemonade. Sometime later a former neighbor came inside and noticed her.

"Thea," the Jewish woman greeted. "I had no idea you were still around. When your parents moved, I assumed you'd moved with them."

Thea pointedly gazed at the empty spot on her neighbor's chest. "Nice to see a like-minded person. How are you doing these days?"

"It's tough, but one has to make do." Frau Kuppa sat on the chair next to Thea as if the two of them were best friends. In a low voice she asked, "Any tips where to find a place to sleep tonight?"

Thea wasn't about to give away her sources to a woman she barely knew, so she smiled sweetly and whispered back, "I'm trying to find a place myself."

"Good luck." Frau Kuppa got up and walked out of the café, leaving Thea to finish her lemonade. Seconds later three SS men strode through the door, walking up to Thea's table. As always, she cast them her brightest smile, expecting them to be mesmerized by the attention of a beautiful blonde.

Today though, the young man didn't smile back. "Thea Dalke, née Blume?"

Her eyes widened with shock, which he took as a yes. Putting his hand on her shoulder, he said, "You better come with us. You're under arrest. Don't make a scene or you'll regret it."

Frozen with fear, Thea somehow managed to get up and follow him outside to the waiting van. So many of her friends, relatives and neighbors had entered one of these vans and nobody had ever seen them again. Panic clouded her mind, pushing every thought away except for escape.

As soon as her muscles tensed to make a run for it, she felt the soldier's heavy hand on her shoulder. "Don't try anything or I'll shoot you on sight."

For a second she hesitated, musing whether a quick end by a bullet to the back of her head was preferrable to the unknown fate awaiting her. But the will to live triumphed over fear and she continued forward.

The van's sliding door opened as if by the hand of a ghost, exposing a black, menacing hole. Before she comprehended what was happening, the SS man gave a shove to her shoulder and she stumbled into the black void. A second later, the door slid closed, effectively capturing her in the darkness as the motor roared up and the vehicle sped away to an unknown destination.

When the door opened again, she squinted her eyes against the sunlight, stumbling behind a different SS man leading her, together with several other captured people, toward the building of the former Jewish boy's school at the Grosse Hamburger Strasse, which had been transformed into a holding camp.

It was the same place where her parents supposedly were detained. She immediately stood a bit straighter as she hoped for a chance to find her parents here. Whatever she was to face, it would be easier in their company.

After a lengthy wait in a sweltering holding cell, she was brought upstairs. On the office door hung a plate with the inscription "Director, SS-Scharführer Walter Dobberke".

Inside sat a tall, beefy man in his late thirties with a pinched, pithy face. Wearing his dark hair in a military short style, he was neither handsome nor ugly. Definitely not the usual type Thea went for, but given the circumstances she would make an exception and flirt with him. It wouldn't be the first time she had coquetted her way out of a dicey situation.

"Frau Dalke, or do you prefer Fräulein Blume?" He gave her a sarcastic wink.

She decided to feign innocence. "My husband is missing presumed dead, therefore I took on my maiden name again."

"Well, well." Dobberke observed her with keen eyes in his chubby face. "You must be an intelligent woman, having evaded capture for such a long time."

Unsure how to answer, Thea remained silent.

"You must have had plenty of helpers, too." He seemed delighted. "Now, you surely agree with me that I cannot in good conscience let the illegal Jews run wild across the city."

She certainly didn't agree. Luckily he didn't seem to expect an answer, because he continued to speak. "You will understand that I must punish you for breaking so many laws for such a long time." A shudder racked Thea's frame as she gazed into his cold eyes. "It pains me to know that such a beautiful, intelligent, young woman is actively working against the well-being of our beloved nation. Therefore,"—he grinned with delight—"I'm giving you the opportunity to redeem yourself."

Doing what? At the last moment she kept herself from blurting out the question.

"You see, we can conduct an amicable discussion where I ask the questions and you answer them."

"So far you haven't asked any questions," Thea interjected, signaling to him she was open to his suggestion.

"Slowly. We'll get there soon enough. First I want to warn you that our little chat might get a bit more unpleasant if you don't give me the answers I want to hear." Again he smiled at her as if he'd just extended an invitation to a coffee party. "So, shall we begin?"

Thea nodded despite the goosebumps popping up on the skin of her arms. If Dobberke had noticed them, he didn't comment. He leaned back in his chair, grabbed a fine fountain pen and poised it at the top of a blank piece of paper.

"I'd like to know the names and addresses of the people who helped you."

She felt all blood drain from her face. If anyone found out that she'd betrayed the underground community, her days were numbered.

"I'm sorry, I didn't have any helpers. I toughed it out all on my own." Thea widened her eyes in an effort to convey innocence.

"Now, see, this is what I was warning you about. You're lying to me, which makes me very sad." He crunched up his face into a puppy-like grimace.

"It's the truth. I was very careful not to tell anyone about my true identity."

Dobberke tapped on the white paper in front of him. "I need names and addresses. Give me the names of ten helpers, or..." He paused to give her a once-over, causing a violent shiver to run down her spine. Clearly enjoying her panic, he let the unspoken threat linger in the room.

It seemed to become more menacing with every passing second, sucking the oxygen out of the air, weighing heavily down on Thea's chest until she was barely capable of breathing.

"... or other illegal Jews."

The tension snapped like a rubber band, causing Thea to sit

upright, staring at the man in front of her, while the horrific fear slowly dissipated, because he hadn't threatened to torture her.

Having lived in Berlin's underbelly for close to six months, she knew many people in the same situation, knew their gathering places, their favorite haunts, knew the people who falsified identity cards, the Gentiles who slipped ration cards to those in need or offered a place to stay for the night.

Her train of thought came to a violent stop. She wasn't going to betray ten people for nothing.

"What happens if I don't know any names?" she asked with a tiny voice.

"We'll have a different kind of conversation, after which I can guarantee you'll give me everything I want." Dobberke seemed delighted by this suggestion.

"And if I do give you the names?" Her voice was but a whisper.

"Then you and I part amicably."

It seemed much too easy. Suspiciously she asked, "What will then happen to me?"

He made a dismissive gesture. "You'll go the way all Jews go."

Said in a light tone, it still carried a finality that made Thea cringe with terror. Whatever she did, that pig would ultimately send her on a transport, where incomparable hardships awaited her. She could as well not tell him a word.

"I appreciate your honesty." Thea tried to charm him with a mesmerizing smile, but he seemed immune to it, his face unmoved. "I would absolutely tell you everything, but unfortunately the only Jews I know have been arrested long ago."

"That is very unfortunate indeed." He picked up a bell on his desk and rang. Seconds later two orderlies arrived, whom he ordered, "Take her to an isolation cell."

Before Thea comprehended what was happening, one man

was by each side and put his arm beneath her shoulder, hauling her away into a damp and dark cell in the basement.

There, she was all alone.

But not for long.

Walter Dobberke strode through the door, his uniform jacket unbuttoned, holding a multi-tailed, leather bullwhip in his right hand.

11

SEPTEMBER 1943

Most evenings, the Falkensteins and Goldmanns gathered in the living room in a circle around the forbidden radio David had built, listening to the equally forbidden BBC.

Everyone knew that being caught would inevitably get them arrested and possibly executed or sent to a labor camp. Yet, even for Helga, who'd strictly opposed keeping the radio in their apartment, the broadcasts had become a source of hope.

Tonight, she listened with bated breath for news about the situation in Italy following the Allied landings in Sicily two months prior and the subsequent arrest of Il Duce, Benito Mussolini. It was a topic the German radio stations that she overheard when at work cleaning the managers' offices rarely touched upon and, if they did, it was only to sneer at the weak and treacherous Italians.

Facts about the Allied advance were impossible to get, except on the BBC broadcast in German. Herr Falkenstein often asked David to tune in to the English program as well and then translated the gist of it, comparing the information to the one given in German.

Helga was well aware that both the Nazis and the Allies

kept their cards close to their chest and never divulged critical war information to the public. It was carefully curated information sent over the ether. Still, she took heart at the steady advance, because it meant that the tide of the war had turned against Hitler and hopefully soon they'd be rid of his regime. How soon was the topic of many heated discussions in the privacy of their apartment.

The crackling transmission made it all but impossible to understand the words. Amelie, who had the superior auditory abilities of a dog, seemed to crawl into the radio, wanting to decipher what was said.

Suddenly her eyes became wide and she shouted, "Italy has signed an armistice!" The next moment she slapped a hand over her mouth. Six pairs of panic-stricken eyes turned to stare at the door, fearing her cry had somehow reached the street three stories down and alerted the Gestapo.

Nothing happened.

After a while, Helga whispered, "That is good news. Having lost Italy as an ally must surely shorten the war."

"It may or may not." Herr Falkenstein moved his head from left to right. "Hitler will not give up. I reckon the Wehrmacht will disarm and arrest the Italian soldiers fighting alongside Germany on the different fronts."

"But that *is* good news," Edith objected. "Surely less soldiers mean faster defeat."

"If the bottleneck is men, which I doubt. Hitler's most pressing problem is the scarcity of armaments. If the new Italian prisoners of war are forced to work in the munitions factories, it might actually have a positive impact on the German war effort."

David shook his head. "It won't. Our main problem is the scarce raw materials, especially steel. No number of prisoners can replace the missing metal."

"And the untrained workers oftentimes do more harm than

good, at least when fiddling with the delicate wiring of a radio," Amelie said.

Helga looked suspiciously at her daughter, who seemed much too happy about this fact. "You wouldn't know anything about sabotage, now would you?"

"Me? Never!" Amelie put up her hands, giving her mother the impression that she was knee-deep into illegal activities.

But who wasn't these days? And who cared anymore? Not Helga. Laws by an unlawful regime didn't require following, although she often wished her children would be more prudent.

Everyone had to get up early for work the next morning, so one by one they said goodnight and retired to their rooms, except for David who mumbled something about having to check the alarm wire put in place at the front door. He frequently disappeared after dinner and didn't return until late at night, believing his mother didn't notice.

Helga never mentioned his absences, yet she was increasingly worried and never slept well until she heard him sneak into the room he shared with Amelie.

When they lay in their bed, she told Heinrich, "I wish Hitler would sign an armistice."

"That will never happen." He wrapped his arm around her shoulders and squeezed her against his body, his lips seeking hers.

"Why not?" Helga turned her head away. Her mind was too anguished to enjoy her husband's advances—something that never used to happen.

Heinrich picked up on her mood and loosened his grip. "On the one hand, the Allies won't accept an armistice, they are after an unconditional surrender. On the other hand, Hitler would rather burn the entire nation to the ground than accept defeat."

She sighed deeply, too disheartened to answer him.

"Don't worry so much, my darling." Heinrich stroked her upper arm with his hand.

"How can I not worry?"

"Does it change anything?"

"What?" She looked at him, confused.

"Does your worrying change the reality?"

"Of course not." She furrowed her brows at the stupid question.

"Then, don't do it. If it won't help, it just wears you down."

"I wish I could." She kissed him on the cheek and snuggled into the warmth of his shoulder. "I'm tired. Let's get some sleep."

But she didn't find peace, as she listened to Heinrich snoring softly next to her. Her ears perked up at every sound, waiting for David to return home, while she mulled over her inability to take a more logical approach instead of constantly fearing for her family's well-being.

12

When David returned home from watching a movie with Roxi, he frowned. Something did not look right. He carefully opened the entrance door and sniffed. The air smelled of cigarette smoke. Instantly alert he checked the alarm wire on the first stair, but it was intact.

Possibly one of the residents had left the house in the evening. All of them knew to step over the wire so as not to set off the alarm. Sniffing again, he ruled out that possibility. The smokers in the household, except for Julius, used cheap self-rolled tobacco that left a much more acid, burnt smell. And Julius Falkenstein was too frail to leave the house at night—unless something awful had happened.

Driven by a sudden urge to make sure everyone was alright, David raced up the stairs, taking three steps at once, almost tripping on the alarm wire. When he arrived in front of the apartment, he lit up his torch. Everything looked exactly as usual, except for a brown envelope stuck in the door frame.

He approached it with suspicion, half-expecting the thing to explode any moment, until he read the word "Kessel" on it.

His eyes became big, since only Baumann and his former colleagues at the workshop used that moniker.

Still cautious, he grabbed the envelope and decided to enter the apartment before reading it. He tiptoed to each of the bedroom doors, listening for anything out of the ordinary. But the only sounds were heavy breathing or snoring. Relieved, he walked into the kitchen, checking the blackout curtains, before he lit his torch again and unfolded the note inside the envelope.

There's someone I want you to meet. Tomorrow at 7 p.m. at our usual pub. B.

A smile crept on David's face. The note was written in Baumann's handwriting, there was no doubt about it. He just wondered whom his former boss wanted to introduce him to.

After memorizing the time and location, he opened the coal stove and put the note into the embers, watching how the paper caught fire before closing the lid. There was nothing incriminating or illegal written on the note, yet it was better to be safe than sorry. Nobody needed to know that David kept in touch with an Aryan co-worker.

He drank a glass of water from the tap and then sneaked into his bedroom, quietly undressing in complete darkness so as not to wake his sister, since he had no intention of making her privy to either Roxi or Baumann.

The next day at work, David barely kept his curiosity under control. As soon as the siren announcing the end of the shift sounded, he dashed toward the underground station to catch the train before everyone else got onto the same one. Even as his feet clattered down the stairs, he used the unobserved moments to reverse his jacket to show the good side out. Glimpsing back to make sure none of his co-workers followed on his heels, he mingled with the other waiting passengers and a minute later stepped into an incoming train, just as he saw a young man from another department walking down the stairs.

Luckily, the doors closed before he could get inside, but just in case, David put an arm in front of the empty space on his chest until the train had left the station. After changing lines twice, he finally arrived in Wilmersdorf. He didn't have to wait long before he discovered Baumann, standing on the opposite platform, smoking. Baumann acknowledged him with a barely visible nod.

Pointing toward the exit, Baumann walked away and David followed suit, catching up with him as they emerged on the street.

"Good to see you," Baumann said. "Come with me."

Itching with curiosity, David chanced a look over his shoulder. Baumann noticed and preempted him. "We're going to church."

"I thought you were an atheist?" Like most communists, Baumann didn't care much for religion.

"Changed my mind." Baumann winked. "Just you wait and see."

It didn't take long until they stood in front of a nondescript redbrick building, behind which a church tower pointed upward. Baumann knocked on the entrance door, which was soon opened by a friendly young woman, who smiled when she recognized him. Then her gaze wandered toward David and back to Baumann.

"This is Kessel. He works with me."

Apparently this introduction was good enough, because she stepped aside to let them walk through the door. "Welcome, Herr Kessel."

"We wanted to see Pastor Perwe."

"He's in a meeting with the countess. It shouldn't take long. Would you like a glass of water, while you're waiting?"

"Yes, please. I can get one myself, I'm sure you have plenty of work to do," Baumann said.

"I always do." The woman gave a sweet smile and hurried away.

Before David could ask who she was, Baumann beckoned him to follow. He seemed to be well acquainted with the church, because he moved through the corridors without hesitation until he reached the kitchen, where several women and older children were chopping vegetables. This place resembled a canteen more than a church.

Baumann greeted the women, chatting with them like an old friend. David's curiosity increased with every minute and he gazed inquiringly at his boss, who just shrugged, signaling that David should wait. Mulling over who might be the mysterious countess and Pastor Perwe, he listened with one ear to Baumann's conversation with one of the kitchen helpers.

"You remember the three children you brought to us in March?"

"I remember them well," Baumann responded. "Such a tragedy when their parents were taken, but they took it in their stride, I've rarely seen more resilient children. Especially the oldest, Holger."

David perked up his ears at the name. "Are you by chance talking about Holger Gerber?"

Baumann squinted his eyes at him. "You know him?"

"Well, yes, they used to live in our..." Unsure how much he should divulge about their relationship, he said, "...apartment building. We were extremely worried for them after their parents didn't return home from work one day."

"They were lucky." The friendly woman with braided, chestnut-colored hair turned toward David. "Frau Lemberg, God bless her, took them in and Baumann brought them here."

David knew his mother and Frau Falkenstein had been

riddled with guilt about not keeping the siblings with them, so he asked, "Are they still here?"

"No." The woman cocked her head. "By the way, I'm Frau Perwe, the pastor's wife. And you are?"

"Kessel," Baumann said before David could open his mouth. "I thought he'd make a good helper for the pastor."

Confused by the strange exchange, David simply nodded. "Pleased to meet you, Frau Perwe."

"As I was about to tell your friend, we finally got word that they arrived safely in Sweden and are diligently studying our language."

"You are Swedish?" David wondered why a foreigner, from a neutral nation no less, would choose to stay in war-ridden Berlin.

"Yes, and as you may have gathered already"—she cast a questioning glance toward Baumann, waiting for his nodded approval to continue—"we've stayed here to help those in need. Your friend is one of our supporters. But best let my husband explain everything to you. He's the heart and head of the operation."

David was stunned for words. He'd never once considered Baumann to belong to the resistance... although, why not? His former boss hated the Nazis with all his heart, despite putting on the façade of an obedient citizen. But a Swedish pastor?

Just then, a murmur went through the kitchen helpers as an elegant woman appeared at the door.

"Countess Borsoi," Frau Perwe greeted her. "Can I talk to you for a minute, please?"

"Sure." The countess let her gaze travel across the room, acknowledging Baumann and frowning at the sight of David, before she turned toward Frau Perwe again. "Shall we go into the gardens?"

David couldn't stop marveling at her. Countess Borsoi belonged to a wealthy noble family, her sister was married to a

Field Marshal. How could someone like her become a resister? Perhaps not all hope was lost.

Baumann elbowed him. "Stop gawking and follow me."

After another long walk past endless corridors, Baumann knocked on a door.

"Come in," a deep voice prompted them to enter. "Baumann, I've been wanting to—Who's this young man?" asked the dark-haired man in his late thirties with thick, round glasses.

"This is Kessel. I thought he might be of help to your network."

Apparently Baumann's words were a good enough introduction, because the pastor's eyes lost their guardedness and he extended his hand. "Welcome, Herr Kessel. I'm Pastor Perwe." After shaking hands he invited them to take a seat. "You must be very curious."

"Indeed." David was dying of curiosity. "Baumann hasn't told me anything."

"And that's good. We don't want news spreading to the wrong kind of people. Therefore I must warn you: nothing that you see or hear on these premises can make it to the outside."

"Understood."

"I gather the two of you would rather talk alone." Baumann stood up. "I'll have a chat with Jens meanwhile."

"Now, Herr Kessel—"

David interrupted him. "Just David, please."

"David. Please tell me a little bit about yourself."

Something about this man's appearance made David trust him implicitly. So he began to relay his story as a mixed-bred Jew and how he'd sworn to resist the Nazis in any way he could after being released from the Rosenstrasse camp.

"Well, I think there are plenty of opportunities for you with us." The pastor's friendly face grew serious. "But I must warn you. Our work is dangerous."

"I don't care." David relished the idea of doing something meaningful.

Perwe put up a hand. "Hear me out, first. My predecessor Birger Forell was under Gestapo observation and had to return to Sweden on the insistence of the German government. As his successor, I'm a thorn in their side, too. Even though I'm protected by my diplomatic status, I fear repercussions every time I leave the premises." Perwe observed David's reaction carefully. "For a German citizen, it is much more dangerous. Normally I wouldn't allow a half-Jew into our network, because due to your precarious status, the Gestapo doesn't even need a reason to arrest and murder you. I don't enjoy exposing someone to danger." Perwe pushed his glasses up his nose. "But for several reasons I'm inclined to make an exception in your case, not least of all because Baumann recommended you. He's a key person I can always count on to keep his word and I implicitly trust his judgement of people. So, if you're willing to risk your life to help others, I'm happy to have you."

"Just tell me what I can do." David didn't need to think twice. This was the opportunity he'd longed for. Finally, he'd found someone who didn't just utter empty words, but backed them with actions—although he doubted the pastor would go as far as raise weapons and fight against the Nazis like the Jews in the Warsaw Ghetto had been doing during their Uprising in April and May this year.

"For the moment, lie low and wait. I'll send someone to your house if we need you. The messenger will reveal himself by showing you one of these." The pastor produced a cheap leaflet with the image of a pair of folded hands on one side and a Bible verse on the other side.

"Thank you. I'll wait for your messenger." Exhilaration rushing through his veins, David hoped he wouldn't have to wait too long. Pastor Perwe showed him the way into the yard, where his wife stood chatting with a few women. When she saw them, she came over and said, "I'm sorry, Baumann couldn't wait. Can you find your way back to the station on your own?"

Disappointed, David nodded. He'd hoped to grill Baumann for further information. But on second thoughts, it was probably better if the two of them weren't seen together.

Back at home, the others were gathered at the dinner table. As soon as he stepped into the room, his mother jumped up. "Thank God, you're back."

"I'm sorry, there was a problem with the underground," David lied.

Even though his mother raised an eyebrow, the tension in the room dissipated.

After dinner, David waited until his mother was alone in the kitchen, washing the dishes. Without saying a word, he grabbed a towel and dried them. Once he'd checked nobody was near enough to eavesdrop, he said in a low voice, "The Gerber children made it safely out of the country."

Helga stopped her work and turned to face him, holding the sponge in her hand like a weapon. "Who told you this?"

Since he wasn't supposed to divulge anything that went on in the Swedish parish, he shrugged apologetically. "I can't tell you."

Pursing her lips, Helga fixed him with a stare. "Was that the reason you came late?"

"Perhaps." David took up a bunch of plates and stored them in the cupboard to avoid her gaze. "Please don't ask."

A glint of fear flickered through her eyes. "Take care, won't you?"

"Always."

13

Thea was huddled in the dark room, every cell in her body screaming with pain, when the door opened and two orderlies walked inside.

"Get up!"

She scrambled trying to get to her knees, every movement sending piercing stabs of pain through her tortured body.

"I can't," she whispered through cracked and swollen lips, wishing the pain would end.

"Not again," the taller one murmured, taking several strides toward her, grabbing her around her waist and throwing her over his shoulder.

She screamed at the top of her lungs.

"Shut up. Or I'll have to gag you."

Instantly, Thea gritted her teeth, involuntarily retching at the notion of a gag in her mouth.

The younger man looked at her with pity in his eyes, as she was carried past him and whispered, "If I were you, I'd give him what he wants."

If he'd intended to comfort her, his words had the opposite effect, causing chills colder than ice freezing the blood in her veins as she tried to fight the burgeoning panic. The vibration with every step her captor took sent new, excruciating stabs through her flesh, making her wish she would die already and get it over with.

He finally dropped her into the same chair she'd been sitting in earlier. She had lost track of time since her first encounter with SS-Scharführer Dobberke a day or possibly a week ago. Thea groaned with the wave of agony shooting through her body.

"Don't move," the orderly said with an audible smirk.

Thea didn't acknowledge him. Even if her limbs still obeyed her, she had no intention of going anywhere, since she was fully aware of the hopelessness of her situation. There was no way to escape from this place, certainly not in her current condition.

After a lengthy wait, Thea heard soft steps entering the room, yet she was too bruised to even turn her head. Inwardly she shrugged. What difference did it make who it was?

Much to her surprise a woman in a nurse's uniform stood in front of her, offering a glass of water. "Here, drink this."

"Thanks," Thea croaked.

The nurse looked at her with pity in her gaze. "He gets really upset when people lie to him."

Oh, now the whipping was her own fault?

The nurse waited for Thea to empty the glass and took it away. Before she walked off, she said, "If I were you, I'd tell him what he wants to know."

Then she was gone, leaving Thea with more anguish than before. She could not—she would not—survive another flogging. Just thinking of the excruciating pain stiffened her limbs. Overwhelmed by her emotional turmoil she closed her eyes, trying to will the pulsating pain away. Suddenly she sensed fingers around her chin, raising it up. In panic she opened her eyes and stared directly into Dobberke's wide face, smiling at her.

In an attempt to dispel the hallucination, she blinked several times, without success. He was still there. Smiling.

"Good, you're awake." He seemed pleased. Then he shook his head and sorrow entered his gaze. "I must say I hadn't expected you to last this long. Such a shame. I strongly dislike hitting a beautiful woman."

Her eyes shot open with disbelief. For all she remembered he'd never wavered a second before any of the dozens of whip lashes he'd given her. He had not flinched at her screams, or shown sympathy when her flesh had torn, spilling blood onto the stone floor.

He walked around his desk and settled behind it, staring at her from a safe distance. "It's disgusting. Why must Jews always lie? Why can't your ilk tell me the truth for once?"

Thea's head swirled, not comprehending what he wanted.

"Was I wrong to think you an intelligent young woman?" He looked at her with a hopeful expression, comparable to that of a mother imploring her child to admit it had done wrong.

But Thea hadn't done anything wrong, apart from the fact that she'd gone underground and evaded arrest for several months, of course. Her mind stumbled over the notion. Did he expect her to regret wanting to stay alive?

"Have I?" His voice had taken on a sharpness, clearly waiting for her answer.

"Have you what?"

"Been wrong about you? Are you scum like the rest of your ilk?"

Somehow the insult revived her spirits. "I'm not scum."

"See? That's what I thought." He scribbled something on a sheet of paper, seemingly forgetting about her presence. After a while he looked up again, surprise settling into his features. "You're still here. That's good."

Thea bit back a groan. Had he expected her to run away

and give him an excuse to flog her again, or shoot her in the back?

"I'm going to offer you a deal. There's no need to answer me right away. Take your time and sleep on it. I'll call for you tomorrow to hear your answer. Are you interested?"

She would have agreed to anything if it meant no more pain. "Yes."

His face lit up like a Christmas tree. "Here's the deal: we forget our little disagreement and you start working for me."

"What do I have to do?" Her toenails rolled up with anxiety, even as she tried to sound nonchalant.

"Really not that much. You'll still live here, but you may come and go as you please. Take up your old life. Go to the theater, visit the movies, have a drink in a café, mingle with friends, do everything a beautiful young woman enjoys."

Suspicion raised the hair on the back of her neck. "What do you expect in return?"

"As I said, nothing much. A hint here and there if you happen to recognize someone evading justice."

The air seemed to swoosh out of the room, making it hard to breathe as she understood his plan. "Illegal Jews you mean?"

"Criminal subjects, yes."

She was about to bluster that she absolutely would not betray her former friends, but he preempted her, raising a hand. "As I said, there's no need to answer right away."

Then he rang the bell on his desk and told the two orderlies, "Take her to the sick bay and see that her wounds are tended to."

Just as Thea was about to hobble through the door, Dobberke raised his voice again. "If it helps your decision, your parents are here. Depending on your answer they may or may not go on a transport by the end of the week."

14

BERLIN, OCTOBER 1943

Knut walked toward the impressive Prinz-Albrecht-Palais, about to meet his brother Joseph, who was on an official trip to Berlin from Theresienstadt, where he was the camp commandant.

A shudder racked Knut's shoulders as he reflected on his older brother's radicalization over the years into complete infatuation with Hitler and his ideologies. It had caused a rift in their family, beginning with disavowing Edith due to her mixed marriage.

Over the years Knut and Joseph had seen each other less and less, the last time being almost a year ago at Christmas, when Joseph and his wife Liesel had introduced their firstborn to the family. Everyone had been enthralled by the cute little bundle with a fluff of white-blonde hair and the brightest blue eyes.

Of course, his mother had seized the opportunity and asked Knut when he was *finally* going to get married and make her a grandmother. As if close to a dozen grandchildren by Carsta and Joseph combined weren't enough.

He sighed. He'd been tempted a thousand times to confess

to his parents that he was never going to get married, but each time he thought better of it. They had driven Edith away for the crime of staying married to her Jewish husband; they would do the same with him if they ever found out that he loved another man.

If it had been up to him, Knut wouldn't have met with Joseph again, feeling the brother he knew had turned into a beast unwilling to show sympathy to anyone outside the Nazi volk community. Thus he'd been utterly surprised to receive a written invitation to meet up. He and Bernd had discussed the matter at length, rather heatedly.

"What if he has changed?" Bernd had asked.

"Joseph? Never? He's truly and completely lost to humanity."

"That's a rather stark thing to say about one's brother."

Knut had shaken his head. "You don't know him the way I do. He's always been like that: single-minded, pursuing what is right. The problem is, somewhere along the way his sense of justice got twisted so far that he cannot conceive a reality different to the one he's made up in his mind."

"Let's assume you're right and he truly has turned into a monster. What if the realization that the tide of the war has turned has sown doubt in him about Hitler's other convictions?"

"My brother isn't capable of doubt. He's either in or out, never in between," Knut had responded.

"Right now, you're the stubborn one." Bernd gazed at him. "What do you have to lose?"

"A beautiful afternoon, maybe?"

"That's a small price to pay for the chance to drum a bit of sense into your brother. Just think of the many ways he could help our cause, if he saw how damaging the war is for the German people."

Knut had sighed, since he was running out of arguments. Mulling over the implications, he had finally agreed. "Well, then. I'll go and see Joseph. Perhaps you're right and he wants to break with the Nazi ideology."

As he now looked at Joseph striding down the majestic driveway, where the Reich Security Main Office resided, a glimmer of hope kindled in his soul. Perhaps not all was lost. Perhaps his brother had issued the invitation to voice even a slight discomfort with Hitler's regime.

"There you are, punctual like a clock." Joseph looked impressive in his spotless black SS uniform and the polished-to-a-shine boots.

"Congratulations," Knut said as he spotted the oak leaf on the collar patches, signaling Joseph had been promoted to SS-Standartenführer.

"Thank you." Joseph beamed from ear to ear. "I received the promotion just last week. Don't tell our parents yet, I want to surprise them."

"No worries, I'm not going to spoil your surprise." He wasn't going to visit them anyway, since he was neck-deep in work and rarely had a day off, which he preferred to spend with his partner.

"Shall we celebrate my promotion with a good dinner at the officers' club?"

"I thought we were going to your place?" Knut wasn't particularly fond of Joseph's second wife, Liesl, but he enjoyed horsing around with his little niece and nephew.

"Liesl stayed in Theresienstadt with the children. The trip would have been too strenuous especially for the newborn."

"Considering that the Allies shower us with their gifts on a regular basis, it was probably a wise decision." Knut tipped his face toward the sky.

"Our Luftwaffe will crush them in no time at all, they can't keep this up for long," Joseph protested, his lips pressed into a thin line.

"One would hope so." Knut thought it better not to mention

that there was a running joke among the population calling Air Marshal Hermann Göring *Hermann Meier* following his alleged quote that he wanted to be called Meier if a single enemy bomber showed up in the German skies.

Joseph turned his head to squint at Knut. "Be careful with such defeatist talk."

"You know me, I would never." Knut raised his hands in an appeasing gesture, feeling how the glimmer of hope was dying. Apparently Joseph was sufficiently deluded to believe the war could still be won.

After a few minutes' walk, they arrived at the officers' club, where the watchman greeted Joseph by name. "Standartenführer Hesse, a pleasure to have you."

"This is Leutnant Hesse, he's my guest today," Joseph introduced Knut, who then had to sign into a book before he was let inside.

"Quite heavy security," Knut commented as they steered their way toward a table in the middle of the room. It was typical of his brother to want to sit where everyone would see them. "Who is the SS afraid of—subversives?"

"One can never be too careful." Joseph raised an eyebrow. "You of all people should know that."

"Me? Why?"

"If you care to remember, your own boss was arrested earlier this year."

Hot and cold shock waves raced down Knut's spine. So far the Gestapo hadn't connected Hans von Dohnanyi and Hans Oster to the broader conspiracy within the Abwehr, planning to eliminate Hitler. "For a mere currency offence? That's hardly worth fretting over."

The waiter brought a bottle of wine, pouring two glasses.

Joseph picked up his glass. "To a victorious Germany under the leadership of our beloved Führer!"

"To our Führer!" Knut answered with a wry smile and added, "Congratulations on your promotion, Standartenführer."

Joseph leaned back, tasting the premium French wine. "Sometimes I wish for a posting in Paris."

"Who doesn't?"

"Yes, who doesn't." Joseph sighed. "You have no idea how disgusting Theresienstadt is. Be grateful you don't have to deal with the Jewish scumbags day in and day out. Unfathomable how dirty, infested with lice, stinking, lazy and plain out deplorable these subjects are."

Knut seized the opportunity to worm some classified information out of his brother. "I thought it was a home for the elderly, privileged Jews."

"Don't believe everything you hear in the news." Joseph smirked. "But enough of this. You don't genuinely expect me to spill the beans about top secret issues now, do you?"

"Can't blame me for trying." Knut smirked back.

Joseph swirled the red wine in its glass, inhaled like a connoisseur and then downed it in one swig.

"More?" he asked.

"No, thanks." Knut shook his head, gazing at his own half-full glass.

"Back to the topic of your previous boss." Joseph stapled his hands on the table and stared intently at Knut. "There's rumors he did much worse than shift currency."

"What are you insinuating?" Knut feigned indignation, while he carefully observed his brother's face. Apparently the true reason for their reunion was Oster's arrest, which was worrying to say the least.

"It's an open secret that senior Wehrmacht officers have been criticizing Hitler's military strategy and are advocating for peace talks with the Allies, especially after Italy's surrender." Technically Italy hadn't surrendered, but had signed an armistice.

"Idle talk." Knut wiped the argument away. "Understand-ably, the generals are nervous after the defeat in Africa and now the loss of our ally. But I can assure you, there's no treasonous motivation behind any activity in the Bendlerblock."

Joseph swigged down his second glass of wine, before he answered. "Never forget that you have sworn an oath on our Führer's life. If you learn about a real or perceived act of resis-tance, you must notify the Gestapo."

"I can assure you, nobody in the Abwehr wants to cause harm to our Fatherland." Knut kept his voice strong and clear, hoping his brother wouldn't pick up on the small but important difference between Fatherland and Führer.

"You're my little brother and I feel responsible for you, therefore I'm going to warn you. Hitler has a divine mission to lead Germany to greatness. Anyone opposing him will be punished with the full force of the law. If it ever turns out that you're working for the wrong side, I won't let emotions cloud my logic, even if it means I must hang you myself."

The blood froze in Knut's veins as he looked into Joseph's eyes, realizing he meant every word he'd said.

"Don't worry about me, Joseph. I'll do what is right." Suddenly feeling sick to his stomach at the revelation that his beloved brother was a soulless monster with no recourse, he looked at his wristwatch. "Sorry, but I need to get going. Thanks for the wine. And, good luck."

Then he strode out of the officers' club without looking left or right, only stopping when he was several blocks away. A single tear rolled down his cheek as he realized that, from this moment on, he didn't have a brother anymore.

15

NOVEMBER 1943

As every year, the trees had lost their leaves. This year though, the bleak twigs exuded a finality that made Edith shiver. She wrapped her shawl tighter around her shoulders, brushing the skin of her cheek against the soft angora wool, remembering the day when the Gerber children had brought home several angora rabbits.

Helga had relayed the good news that the three siblings had successfully been spirited away to a foreign country. At least some members of the three-family household didn't have to worry about Nazi persecution any longer. A sad smile spread across her lips. While the children might be safe, they had paid a huge price. Their parents most likely wouldn't survive the war, if they weren't dead already. And the children might never return to see their home or family members ever again.

"Edith!" Knut waved at her, long before she reached the side street leading to his apartment building.

She increased her pace and came to a stop in front of him. Unexpectedly she found herself wrapped into a tight embrace. "Stop that. You're going to crush my bones," she protested half-laughing.

"Sorry. I'm so happy to see you." He released her. "Shall we take a walk?"

"To enjoy the November drizzle, while stumbling through the soot leftover from last night's air raid?"

He broke out into laughter. "Sounds romantic, doesn't it? Actually, I need to talk to you away from prying ears."

"Has something happened?" Her skin instantly tingled with alarm.

"Yes and no." When he noticed her frightened face, he soothed her. "It's nothing to do with you."

After walking briskly for ten minutes they reached a park. Out of habit, Edith hesitated to enter, until she remembered that Julius wasn't by her side. Without him she was not only allowed to enter green areas, but also to sit on a bench.

"Aren't you afraid to be seen with a woman who is married to a Jew?" Most of her former friends had either completely cut the contact or kept finding excuses not to meet up with her for fear of being denounced as a Jew-lover.

Knut looked at her, his face serious. "I'm afraid of many things, my sister is not one of them."

Her heart warmed with gratitude and she linked arms with him. "So, what did you want to tell me that mustn't be overheard?"

He sighed long and hard, burying his hands deep in the pockets of his thick gray Wehrmacht coat. "Joseph."

A horrible sense of foreboding made her feel sick to the stomach. Ever since Joseph had visited her during the Rosenstrasse protests, accusing her of ruining his career with her obstinate refusal to divorce her subhuman husband, she had given up hope that he'd one day recognize his delusion and come round to being a kind-hearted person again. Hardly daring to breathe, she prayed feverishly that Knut's next words would belie her gut feeling.

"He's become a soulless monster."

She almost laughed out loud. "We came all the way here for you to tell me this?"

Knut's face was a grimace of pain. "I met him last week. He's been promoted to Standartenführer."

"Are congratulations in order?" she quipped, happy when she saw a smirk appear on her brother's face before it grew earnest again.

"He's drinking too much. And spewing a lot of hate. It's such a shame..." Knut mumbled something unintelligible, before he stopped to look into her eyes. "He threatened to personally execute me should I conspire against the Führer."

Edith swallowed. She wasn't so much shocked at Joseph's threat against his own brother, but at the insinuation that Knut might be engaged in the resistance. "Are you serious?"

"Unfortunately, yes."

"I mean..." she said, glancing over her shoulder, "are you involved in subversive activities?"

"Is that what you worry about?" He seemed disappointed.

"Yes." She put a gloved hand on his arm. "Not because I believe it's a bad thing, but because it's extremely dangerous and I care about you."

He visibly relaxed. "You have enough problems of your own, so I'm just going to say that everything I am doing is for the good of our country."

...but not for our Führer. She squeezed his arm to show him she'd understood. "Good luck with everything. I love you."

"It's a sad thing, isn't it?" He bit his lips, clearly unwilling to bare his soul to her.

"Whatever happens, I'll always be proud of you."

"Thank you." He seemed tempted to tell her something else, then shook his head and continued his march. "I didn't tell Joseph that I decided never to contact him again. He's not my brother anymore."

"He used to be such a wonderful man." Edith felt the pain

of losing her oldest brother deep in her gut. To dispel the dreariness she said, "On a more positive note, do you remember the Gerber family?"

"Your tenants?"

"Yes. We got word that their children made it out of the country. We don't know where and how, just that they are in safety."

"Now that is good news." Knut turned around to head in the direction from which they had come.

"If the war lasts much longer, Julius might not make it." She sighed full of sorrow. "He has become very frail. There's never enough food, and we have to save on coal, so the apartment is cold and damp, aggravating his arthritis. And then the long and arduous shifts. Every day when he returns home, he's looking worse and worse."

"For what it's worth, this war will be over sooner than we think and everything will be better."

"That would be nice."

Edith said goodbye to Knut, sensing he was warring with himself whether to tell her something or not. Since he'd always kept to himself, she knew it wouldn't help to ask, it would only cause him to close up. "Always remember: I'll be on your side, whatever you do."

"Thank you, Edith." His eyes shone with emotion. Then he turned around and walked away, leaving her with a horrible foreboding in her gut. She was tempted to call out after him. *Don't do anything dangerous! I couldn't endure losing both of my brothers!*

Taking a detour, because she needed to be alone with her sorrows, she arrived home when the sun settled behind the horizon. Julius was sitting on the sofa, a book she'd gotten for him from the library on his lap, softly snoring. Her heart hurt for him, because he'd become so frail. Every day he seemed to vanish a bit more, until the once imposing man literally would disappear in front of her eyes.

She quietly hung her coat on the rack, along with hat, gloves and scarf, put her shoes on a rag that served as draining board and tiptoed into the living room.

He started, pretending to have been reading when he recognized her. "You're late, Edith, where have you been?"

"I met with Knut."

"How is he?"

"Seemingly fine." She bit her lip, wondering how much she should tell him, since she didn't want to burden her husband. "He told me the war might last shorter than we all think."

Julius' body might be decaying, but his mind was as sharp as ever. He tipped his head, searching her face for clues. "Does he know anything we do not?"

"If he does, he didn't tell me." Edith settled on the sofa next to Julius. "He met Joseph."

"Now that is a reason to worry. What is Hitler's puppy up to?"

Edith had to bite back a giggle at the images filling her head. "He threatened to kill Knut with his own hands, should he engage in subversive activities." She involuntarily shuddered. Joseph's threat certainly extended to her as well, if he ever found out they were helping illegals to hide.

"I didn't expect anything different from him." Julius squinted his eyes. "He's been running down the abyss for decades, there's no way he's capable of pausing to ponder his path now."

She nodded slowly, her heart hurting. Julius had pointedly put into words what she'd been feeling for a while now. Whatever evidence to the contrary, Joseph would never doubt his only true love—Hitler. "I'm worried about Knut, though. He seemed on the verge of telling me something several times. The poor man, he must be caught up in really nasty work. I wish I could help somehow."

In an unusual show of affection, Julius reached out for her, rubbing his thumb across the back of her hand. "Each of us has to fight our own battles."

Her brain knew that, though her heart refused to accept this truth. After sitting silently for a while, she asked, "Would you like coffee?"

"I'd love coffee." For a few seconds, his face lit up and he licked his lips, then he seemed to remember that the liquid they called coffee these days had nothing in common with the real thing both of them used to enjoy so much. "Actually, I'd prefer a mint infusion, if we have some left."

"I'll have a look." Edith walked into the kitchen, where she searched the cabinet for the herbs Amelie had collected and dried during the summer. There was still a bunch of mint leaves. She took three and while she waited for the water to boil in the kettle, she mused about Knut and what kind of illegal activities he might be engaged in.

A few minutes later, she stepped into the living room with two cups in her hands to find Julius sagged against the sofa, his eyes closed. He looked devastatingly vulnerable. Her hands began shaking so hard, she spilled the infusion into the saucer. Short of a miracle, Julius would not survive much longer.

16

For the past few months David had been running the odd errand for Pastor Perwe. This week they were finally planning something big. The entire plan was shaky at best and the possession of a uniform was going to make or break the operation. Someone had organized a Wehrmacht uniform, unfortunately it was much too small to fit David.

"I urgently need a uniform," he told Amelie, who'd been helping with the odd errand for the Swedish parish.

"Again? We talked about it. Firstly it's too dangerous, secondly I can't organize one." She rolled her eyes at him.

"Perhaps you have an idea where I could get my hands on one?" He glanced at her hopefully. His sister was resourceful.

After a while she shook her head. "Sorry, no idea. I don't usually liaise with men in uniform."

"What did you just say?" David's ears perked up.

"That I don't have an idea."

"No after that."

She looked at him as if he'd lost his mind. "That I don't know anyone in uniform."

"But we do." Exhilaration singed his skin, causing him to jump up and down.

"Who?" Amelie wasn't impressed by her brother's excitement.

"Frau Falkenstein's brother."

"We met him once. And despite him seeming like a decent guy you can't just seek him out and ask to borrow his uniform. He'd have you arrested on the spot."

"Or maybe not." David worried his lower lip.

Amelie raised an eyebrow. "Do you know something I don't?"

"After the farewell party for the Falkensteins he returned to our place, because he'd forgotten his scarf. I was the only one home." David didn't mention that Knut had caught him red-handed climbing down from the attic with an illegal he'd been hiding there. "In confidence he told me that he didn't agree with many of Hitler's policies and that he'd help me if I ever was in need. He even gave me a way to contact him." David kept the business card Knut had given him in a drawer with other important things.

Amelie's eyes widened with surprise. "Damn! And it took you two years to tell me about it!"

"You don't need to know everything." David smirked. "It's safer for you that way."

"Ach, now you're suddenly worried about me? Two minutes ago you wanted me to steal a Wehrmacht uniform for you." Her voice was dripping with sarcasm.

"Don't be a sorehead. Rather admire how brilliant your big brother is."

"Ha. Ha. I'm in awe." She rolled her eyes. "He might have offered his help, but I doubt that will extend to loaning you his uniform."

"I'll never know if I don't ask him. What do I have to lose?" David wasn't about to give up this easily.

"Your life. Which is more or less the only thing you still own."

Amelie's wry words sent shivers down his spine. She was right. In a time when soldiers and civilians died like flies, an individual life, especially if it was a half-Jewish one, was a dime a dozen. Yet, he refused to believe that Leutnant Hesse would turn him in. The worst outcome was that he'd say no to David's request in a less than amicable way.

Amelie keenly observed his expression and then added, "Look, David, you're probably right and Leutnant Hesse won't denounce you to the Gestapo. I'm actually more worried about him loaning you the uniform than him refusing your request."

David looked up with surprise. "You are?"

"Yes. Contrary to popular belief I do love you to bits and would like to keep you around just a little while longer."

"I love you too, sis. But you do understand that there's more at stake here than just the two of us?"

"I know and that frightens me."

"I'll ask him." David got up, retrieved the business card and grabbed his coat.

"Wait! What? Now?"

"There's no time like the present." He grinned at her and walked out to find the nearest public phone, where he dialed the number Knut had given him and told the telephonist, "I have news for Herr Hesse from his sister."

The next day, David told his boss he needed to go to the registration office during his lunch break and rushed away to meet Knut in front of the elephant enclosure in the Berlin Zoo. Despite the constant threat of bombing there were quite a few visitors, since the zoo was one of the few pastimes still available to Berliners.

Just as David anxiously wondered whether Knut would show up, he saw him striding toward the enclosure. David looked at him, acknowledging his presence, and then waited for

Knut to sidle up to him. They didn't look at each other, both pretending to be interested in the elephants.

"What do you need?" Knut asked, taking out a camera and snapping a photo of the majestic animal without even looking in David's direction.

"A uniform."

If Knut was surprised, he didn't show it. "What kind of uniform?"

"Any Wehrmacht officer is fine." David furrowed his brows. "Although SS would be even better."

"Let me see what I can do."

Flummoxed at how easy the exchange had been, David asked, "Don't you want to know what I need it for?"

Again, Knut didn't as much as glance in David's direction, as he answered with a smirk in his voice, "Never ask if you'd rather not know the answer."

"Sorry," David mumbled, scolding himself for being stupid. Naturally a Wehrmacht officer did not want to be privy to what exactly a resister was going to do with an illegally obtained uniform.

"Wait a few minutes before you follow me to the monkeys." Knut left, before David fully comprehended the order.

Taking a detour to watch the hippo with her baby, David strode into the monkey house. A good dozen animals were performing all kinds of shenanigans, hunting each other, jumping from branch to branch and swinging in the air. Since he didn't see Knut, he watched the monkeys, a huge smile spreading on his lips.

He regretted not having brought Roxi, she'd love to be here; she was so much like a monkey, a free-spirited being, never boring, never sitting still, and most of all not conforming to rules.

"Ask your sister to pass by this laundry tomorrow to pick up a package for Leutnant Hesse. She can tell them she's standing in for my housekeeper who has the week off." Knut handed him a piece of paper with an address scribbled on it.

"Thank you." It took all his willpower not to look at the man who was going to risk his own life by organizing a Wehrmacht uniform. How and why, David didn't dare ask.

"I probably won't need it back."

That struck David as odd, and he turned around just to find an empty space where Knut had been seconds earlier. Shaking his head, he rushed home to tell Amelie the exciting news.

17

"Well done!" Dobberke said with a pleased expression. "You'll realize this was the best decision of your life."

Thea swallowed hard. It hadn't been easy, but the prospect of another flogging had been too much for her, so she'd told him that she would collaborate. There was one thing she wanted to ask him in exchange. Gathering her courage she asked, "And my parents won't be deported, right?"

"They won't," he promised.

"Can I see them, please?"

He wagged a finger at her. "That's a bit early, isn't it? How about you prove yourself first and then you ask me again?"

It wasn't what she had hoped for, but what other choice did she have than to agree? Dobberke held all the cards in this game.

"I have another surprise for you," he said, ringing the bell on his desk.

Moments later none other than her husband Ralf stepped into the room. Thea stared at him and then back to Dobberke, not comprehending what was going on.

"I thought you might like to work with someone you trust."

After the way Ralf had treated her at the opera house, trust was the last word she would have used to describe her feelings for him.

"You'll learn from one of the best."

It took a while for the revelation to seep into Thea's brain. "You're working for the Gestapo?"

Ralf shrugged. "Sure do. I'm glad you're on our side."

Dobberke clapped his hands. "You can catch up later, love-birds. There are Jews to catch. Out you go. I'm expecting results very soon."

"Come." Ralf took her hand and pulled her after him to a corridor with a sign on the door. *Entry prohibited. Staff only.* When he opened the door to lead her through, a violent shiver racked her frame.

He led her to a spacious room with a broad bed and said, "This is our room. Do you have a suitcase with clothes hidden somewhere?"

"Yes, why?" Thea answered without thinking.

"We'll go and get it." He gave her a once over, a disgusted expression spreading on his face. "You'll agree that you can't go out wearing this grimy dress."

"I can't?" Her limbs felt numb and her thinking was much slower than usual.

"Ach, Thea, I remember you being more astute. We represent the German government now and have to look our best."

Finally, her mind seemed to take up its work again. "That day we met at the opera house, were you the one who alerted the SS?"

Ralf nodded, pride shining in his eyes. "Yes. It was my biggest catch so far. Half a dozen illegal Jews in one fell swoop."

"Was that the reason you pushed me away?"

"I didn't want you to get hurt." He stepped closer, putting a hand behind her neck and gently pulling her toward him. "I'm sorry about the way you were treated. If I'd known you'd been arrested, I would have asked Dobberke to spare you."

"That would have been nice."

His face hovered so close to hers, she could feel his warm breath on her cheek. "Let's forget the unpleasant events; they are behind you. I'm so glad the two of us are working together. You'll see, it'll be worth it. Dobberke is very generous to those who support the Reich." The next moment, Ralf put his lips on hers and devoured her mouth in a passionate kiss.

She tried not to flinch when his fingers stroked the flayed skin on her back, slowly trailing down to her behind.

"I've missed you, my darling," he said, his desire for her evident in the bulge pressed against her front.

Despite her entire body hurting from the treatment she had received, Thea gritted her teeth and bore it. Since she was going to live with her husband, she had better get on his good side from the first day onwards. After all, he was supposed to show her the ropes in her new position as Gestapo employee.

Once he was finished, he showed her where to wash up and then urged her to hurry. "The earlier you are seen out on the streets, the better." He stroked her cheek with his thumb. "Don't tell anyone about your arrest, or they'll become suspicious why the Gestapo let you go. This will only hinder our work."

Thea nodded, despite the queasy feeling in her stomach.

Ralf must have picked up on her hesitation, because he added, "Don't worry, my darling. We're doing the right thing. Once the war is over, we'll be rewarded for our service to the Reich."

For a fleeting moment, David's face crossed her mind. He'd be disgusted by her decision. She brushed the image away. If David had found himself in her shoes, he would have done the same. Dobberke had made it clear what awaited her if she refused to cooperate, so what choice did she have?

She shrugged. Everyone wanted to survive. There was nothing wrong with that.

18

NOVEMBER 23, 1943

Knut was packing his suitcase when the bedroom door opened and Bernd came in.

"You're determined to do this?" Bernd asked.

"Someone must do it."

"Why don't you use a bomb with a chemical detonator, which would give you enough time to get yourself to safety?" Bernd put an arm around his shoulder, sending shudders down his spine.

"We've talked about this. It's too unreliable. In the ten minutes between priming the bomb and detonation, too many things can happen. With Hitler's long record of narrow escapes, I'm almost sure the assassination attempt will fail once again. This is the most reliable way. Once I pull the hand grenade, it'll be over in five seconds. Too little time for him to be snatched from the jaws of death."

Bernd sighed. "Why does it have to be you?"

Knut hadn't taken this decision lightly. After a lengthy discussion in the Bendlerblock, he had offered himself for the suicide mission to kill Hitler during a presentation of new uniforms for the soldiers on the Eastern Front. As a soldier he'd sworn an oath to put the needs of his country above his own. Currently, Germany's acutest need was to rid herself of the Führer who had brought so much suffering to his people.

"I love my life, I want to survive the war, find happiness... with you." He felt sadness bubble up in his heart as he imagined a small house in the suburbs, a garden with blossoming flowers, him and Bernd sitting on the veranda, wrinkled faces, gray hair, holding hands. It was a dream he held dear to his heart, which regretfully would never come to fruition. Certainly not if Hitler had a say in it. "The way the war is going, there'll soon be nothing left but scorched earth. Nothing worth living for. Someone has to stop this insanity."

"Looking at it from a logical point of view, I understand that. Just in here." Bernd tapped on his heart. "It feels wrong. It hurts more than I can put into words."

"You'd do the same if you were in my position."

"I would absolutely knock you unconscious and embark on the mission in your stead, if I worked in your department."

He stepped into Bernd's embrace, kissing him deeply. "I know that and it makes me happy. I really couldn't have wished for a better partner than you."

Bernd jutted his jaws, his eyes shining treacherously. "Me too."

"We're both soldiers. We knew what we were getting into when we signed up for the job. Once Hitler is dead, our country can escape the death grip he has on it and recover."

"I'm proud of you, I just wish there was another way."

"Believe me, I do too." Knut looked around the familiar apartment a few blocks away from the Bendlerblock that he'd moved into a few years ago. It was small, but cozy. It was a place of joy and peace away from the bedlam in the outside world. Here, he returned after work to forget the war, to recharge his batteries, and to be happy with the man he loved so much. His soulmate, his lover, his everything.

They looked at each other silently for several minutes, Knut's heart growing weary until he was ready to blow off the mission, because all he wanted was to stay in Bernd's arms for the rest of his life.

Bernd seemed to pick up on his mood, because he squeezed his hand, before he broke the silence. "You're so very brave—and you're doing the right thing. Our country is at war and we could die any minute by a bomb falling on the city, or because our resistance activities are found out, or we could be sent to the front and be killed by an enemy bullet. None of us knows whether we will survive this night or the next day. We can only enjoy every minute given to us."

Knut was deeply moved, unable to speak for a while. He took several deep breaths, before he finally was able to say, "Let's make the most of our last night together."

In the morning, he woke long before the alarm sounded and watched Bernd's sleeping face. Fond memories sprung to his mind, from the day they first met during an Abwehr meeting, Bernd's mischievous smile coupled with his warm brown eyes had captured his heart immediately. The way he twirled his moustache whenever he was in deep thought still caused Knut's heart to flutter, even after years of being together.

He was grateful for the many happy moments they'd shared and at the same time mourned what they never had: a normal life like any other couple. A life where they didn't have to hide their love for each other to everyone but a very close group of like-minded friends.

His fingers itched to trace Bernd's strong jawbone, to feel the pricking morning stubble on his skin. But it was better to leave without waking him, it would make it so much harder still. They had said goodbye to each other last night; there was nothing left to say.

Knut bit on his lower lip as his gaze traveled one last time over the familiar form beneath the blanket, before he grabbed his uniform and tiptoed into the living room to get dressed. Several times he was tempted to call off the operation.

But every time his sense of duty won over. Germany's future depended on him. His sacrifice would prevent millions of other deaths. After Hitler's demise, Edith and Julius would finally live in peace again. His parents, Carsta, and her children, they would come round once all of the Nazis' cruelties were exposed. His mind wandered to David. A handsome young man with his heart in the right place. He deserved a chance at a better life, as did countless other men and women of the younger generation whom the Führer cold-bloodedly offered for slaughter at the frontlines and back home in the hail of bombs. Yes, he definitely was doing the right thing. With that thought, he rushed out the door, before he could change his mind and crawl back into bed to stay forever in Bernd's arms.

At Rangsdorf Airport a plane waited for the delegation to be flown to the Führer's headquarters, Wolfsschanze in East Prussia. Once Hitler was dead, an insider would alert the Bendlerblock and Operation Valkyrie would be set into motion, assuring the resisters took over the key positions in the leaderless nation, arresting Hitler's loyal allies along with SS and Gestapo. Once they had secured Berlin, the rest of the country would follow.

When Knut arrived he handed his co-conspirators, Major Kuhn and Oberst Stieff, the secret documents titled *Operation Valkyrie*, a step-by-step instruction on the measures to take after Hitler's death was confirmed. Once again, Knut had to swallow down the lump forming in his throat, because he wouldn't be there to witness a better world. Yet he felt no regret for offering his sacrifice. All other eligible officers had wives and children depending on them, whereas for him just Bernd would mourn.

"We'll see that everything goes according to plan once we

hear the explosion," Oberst Stieff said. "Good luck, Leutnant Hesse."

"Thank you." Knut walked away, taking residence in the guest house and waiting to be summoned. Hitler was finicky with security concerns and often changed schedules or locations at the last moment, so one was never sure whether a meticulously planned meeting would actually take place. Oftentimes it happened hours or days later, sometimes not at all, or with a completely different topic, which none of the officers had prepared for, inevitably causing the Führer to lash out at them for their utter incompetence.

Knut spent his time writing a letter to Bernd, which he would never send as not to compromise him. It was already late in the afternoon when Oberst Stieff showed up in the guest barracks with an earnest face.

"Leutnant Hesse, we just got news that the train cart with the demonstration uniforms has been destroyed during an Allied air raid on Berlin."

Contradictory emotions welled up in Knut's chest, choking him to the point that he was barely able to speak. "Understood."

The Oberst seemed to understand Knut's inner turmoil, because he respectfully left the room after saying, "We can talk about the consequences for your stay here during dinner tonight."

As soon as Oberst Stieff had left the room, Knut sank to his cot, his limbs trembling with exhilarated relief. Looking out the window, the sun suddenly shone brighter, the fall foliage on the trees exploded in a sinfonia of vibrant colors and the gray-clouded sky had lost its dullness, instead glowing with delight. Even as Knut relished in being alive, a shadow crept into his soul as he mourned the missed opportunity to free the world of a tyrant.

His personal salvation came at the cost of many thousand innocent lives. For a long time, Knut sat perfectly still, staring out the window at the ever-changing sky, where one cloud chased the next one, until finally the corners of his mouth tipped upward. A lost battle didn't decide the war—a saying that couldn't be truer.

When it was time to join the others for dinner, he freshened up, put on full uniform and walked to the officers' mess, where Oberst Stieff was waiting with more news.

"It seems the replacement of the demonstration uniforms will need at least until January. Thus unfortunately your presence isn't needed here anymore and you are to fly out first thing in the morning."

"Thank you." Knut slightly bowed his head as he tried to hide the tears welling up in his eyes. Tears of relief that he was still alive, but also of profound sadness that the Führer was too. "We may try again in January. My superiors will be in contact with you."

19

Amelie had retrieved the uniform from the laundry without a problem and done a few minor alterations until it fit David perfectly. Knut hadn't skimped and a day later the matching uniform cap had lain in a box in front of the apartment door.

Fully dressed, David stepped in front of the mirror at a friend's house, amazed at how authentic he looked. A slight shiver rumbled through his bones as he realized that he would be a soldier—dead or alive—if it weren't for his Jewish heritage.

"You look so real, it gives me goosebumps." Roxi was sitting cross-legged in the corner of the room. Her aversion to men in uniform was no secret.

"Let's hope everyone else is as impressed as you are." The success of their mission depended on people kowtowing to David's perceived authority and not questioning his orders.

"It'll work just fine." She wriggled around, clearly uncomfortable in his presence.

He loved her all the more for it, because she, too, was going to play an important part in the rescue operation.

"Salute!" Jens, a co-conspirator and genuine Wehrmacht soldier commanded.

"Heil Hitler!" David had practiced the greeting dozens of times under Jens' tutelage to get it perfect. Every little detail had to be correct to assure a successful operation.

A friendly policeman had alerted Pastor Perwe that a Jewish family in hiding had been denounced by their neighbors and his colleagues had arrested them. He'd been *too busy* to call the Gestapo to have them transferred to the holding camp, but would have to do so in a couple of days at the latest in order not to raise suspicions.

"Finally, you've got it." Jens grinned. "Let's go."

Adrenaline rushed through David's veins, alerting his senses. He nodded his agreement.

"Just follow along, doing everything I do and for God's sake never waver or hesitate."

"*Jawoll!*" David clicked his heels in the painfully small boots Jens had loaned him—another thing he'd practiced for hours to transform himself into a believable Wehrmacht soldier. They had opted to demote David, both to protect Knut and to make Jens—who was a Feldwebel—his superior, since he had much more experience.

They opened the back door to the nondescript gray van, organized by another helper, to let Roxi climb into the back. Jens positioned himself behind the wheel and sped away to the police station.

"What if something goes wrong?" David didn't fear so much for himself, but for Roxi and the Jewish family.

"Don't worry, I'll be fine," Roxi answered through a window between the driver's cabin and the back.

"You can't think this way," Jens admonished him. "We went through the operation several times. There's no backup plan. If things go awry, it's everyone for himself. Under no circumstances are you allowed to try and save anyone else."

The harsh words stabbed David's heart, since he couldn't bear the thought of Roxi being hurt.

Again, her soft voice came from behind. "Jens is right. If we're caught red-handed, it's better to save at least one or two of us, instead of all three going down."

David so wished he could squeeze her hand through the small opening. Since that wasn't possible, he took a deep breath, rehearsed the plan in his mind once more and assured himself, *Everything will work out just fine.*

About fifteen minutes later, Jens parked the van in front of the police station. David followed him inside, where Jens approached the policeman sitting behind the reception and announced with a loud voice, "Heil Hitler!"

The elderly man got up laboriously to return the salute.

"Feldwebel Kaiser, we're here to retrieve the captured Jews," Jens said.

"I was expecting the SS."

A chill froze David's expression, while his heart hammered against his ribs.

"I know." Jens stayed absolutely calm. "They're short on men due to a large-scale operation. That's why they sent us."

"Alright. You know where to take the prisoners?"

"Holding camp Grosse Hamburger Strasse," Jens responded without hesitation, clicking his heels for emphasis.

"You have to sign here," the policeman pointed at the list.

After Jens had put his signature next to the entry with the names of the prisoners, the policeman beckoned them to follow him to the back of the police station.

There, they found a frightened couple with two middle-school-aged children huddling in a cell. David forced himself not to wink or smile, since Jens had drummed into him to always exude authority, and even disdain for the prisoners, however much his heart desired to do otherwise.

"Get up. Fast!" Jens barked at them, making David flinch at the prisoners' fearful faces. It took all his willpower not to reach out and squeeze a hand or utter a comforting word.

"I don't have all day." Jens prodded the man forward.

David's job was to make sure the others followed in line.

Thankfully the woman and children were too frightened to do anything stupid, because David would have hated to hit them. They didn't know he and Jens had come to their rescue, and it was better to stay that way. If they should be recaptured they wouldn't be able to tell the Gestapo anything of value.

After shoving the family into the back of the van, where Roxi waited, pretending to be another prisoner, Jens started the motor and drove toward a forest area. There, he turned off the motor and said unnecessarily loud, "I need to go for a pee and a cigarette."

"I'll come with you," David answered, equally loud. They tossed the doors shut and stomped away.

Meanwhile, Roxi seized the opportunity to pick the prepared backdoor lock and make off with the prisoners into a safe house on the other side of the forest patch.

Standing a few dozen meters away, their backs toward the van and smoking their cigarettes, David perked up his ears until he heard rustling leaves. Inwardly he crossed his fingers that Roxi would lead the family to their next station without a hiccup, while he engaged in idle chit-chat with Jens, who seemed not to have a care in the world.

Once they'd smoked up their cigarettes, Jens grinned. "Now, let's return the van."

Despite the successful conclusion of their mission, David's tension didn't ease up until the next day when he visited Pastor Perwe to hide his uniform.

"Congratulations, that went very well. I heard Roxi delivered the 'packages' unharmed."

Finally, David allowed relief, pride and joy to wash over him. "Anytime you need me again."

"Not for a few weeks."

David's euphoria crumbled. "How can you know there won't be another opportunity?"

"I don't. But if there is, it won't be you who I send."

"Why? Have I done something wrong?" A stab of disappointment hit David.

"No, your work was perfect and I couldn't be prouder of you. In order not to attract attention, you can't go twice within a short time. By now the Gestapo must have realized there are prisoners missing and wonder who Feldwebel Kaiser is."

"I see." Despite understanding the logic behind the pastor's action, David was disappointed. Just when he'd finally done something useful, he was sent to the sidelines again.

"From your face I can tell how eager you are to do more, but heed my warning and don't become reckless. Caution must always be your primary concern. It doesn't help our cause if you get arrested and possibly end up betraying the network."

"I would never!" David bristled.

"Under torture almost everyone does. Some earlier, others later. Therefore it's best not to get caught in the first place." Pastor Perwe winked at him.

20

Thea enjoyed her freedom. Instead of changing location every two or three nights she shared a comfortable bed with Ralf in the staff area of the holding camp. Gone were the days of hustling for food, because they joined the other staff at the canteen for hot meals. She and Ralf often ambled along the Kurfürstendamm, stopping in a café for a drink. In the evenings they attended theatre performances, movies or operas. Her life was better than it had ever been since the beginning of the war.

Thea sipped Ersatzkaffee, her eyes wandering around the location, taking in the patrons, when the door opened and a young man with blond hair and round glasses came inside. He carefully scrutinized the place before he settled at a table close to the exit, unfolding a newspaper in front of him.

Thea elbowed Ralf and whispered, "The man who just entered. I know him."

"You sure?" Ralf didn't turn his head to look at the newcomer.

"One hundred percent. He sells ration cards." Goosebumps spread across her arms. This was her first find.

Ralf picked up on her nervousness and wrapped an arm around her shoulder, pulling her toward him. His mouth close to her ear, he whispered, "Go and say hello. If it's really him, sit down and engage him in chit-chat, while I call the Gestapo."

Her heart drumming wildly, she walked over to the man from whom she'd often bought ration cards, intent on keeping him distracted until the Gestapo arrived. Depending on the circumstances, officers would either ignore her or pretend to arrest her as well—she hoped for the former, since she'd rather not relive that experience.

"Good afternoon, Jakob," she greeted him.

"Thea? How are you doing?"

"May I sit?" She smiled sweetly at him.

He glanced at his wristwatch. "I don't have much time though."

"I won't stay long." Most illegals had developed a sixth sense for danger living in the underground, which was the reason Ralf wanted her to sit with Jakob; to keep him from bolting before the Gestapo arrived. Since he was going to be her first catch, she wanted to do everything right.

"Well then." He gestured at the empty chair next to him. "How have you been? Haven't seen you in a while."

Thea gulped. Ralf had thought of everything, except that she needed to continue frequenting the places she used to go for ration cards, black market food, etc. "It was getting too hot and I had to resort to other places."

Jakob nodded pensively. "Best to always be on the move."

"How about you? Still working with food?" Out of the corner of her eyes she noticed Ralf returning, supposedly having alerted the Gestapo. Her nerves were strung so tight, she barely managed to suppress the tremble in her hands.

"Yes. You need something?"

Thinking on her feet, she agreed. "In fact, I do. Can you recommend a contact closer to Nikolassee?"

"That's where you found a place to sleep?" Jakob's eyes widened at the mention of the rather affluent quarter in the outskirts of Berlin.

"Yes, just for a few nights a month, but who am I to complain?" She gave a false giggle, while inwardly waiting to get it over with. The more she chatted with him, the more she felt sorry for Jakob.

Luckily, just a minute later two SS men stepped through the door and headed toward their table. Thea saw the shock cross through Jakob's eyes, before he regathered his sangfroid and busied himself with the paper, apparently hoping they'd pass him by. But he had no such luck.

"Papers!" the SS officer demanded.

With trembling fingers, Jakob showed them a fake identity card. "Here you go."

"Jakob Weiss, you are under arrest." The SS man's voice boomed through the café causing the other patrons to intently study their fingernails, since nobody wanted to become the center of attention. Then he ripped the fake identity card into pieces. "Arrested for evading justice, not wearing the yellow star, black market activities and possession of a fake identity card."

All blood drained from his face, Jakob got up and walked out of the café with his hands in the air. He didn't glance back at Thea, for which she was grateful. At least she didn't have to see the pain and fear in his eyes.

"You were fantastic," Ralf congratulated her on their walk back to the holding camp.

"Really?"

"Believe me." He wrapped an arm around her waist, affection shining in his eyes. "I'm so proud of you, my darling Thea."

For a second, Jakob's anguished expression entered her mind. Thankfully Ralf didn't give her time to reminisce. "There's no reason to feel bad. Those Jews aren't like us.

They are a threat to Germany. We're doing our country a service."

"I guess we are." She wasn't fully convinced, but who was she to bother with these issues when much more intelligent people had decided already.

Back at the camp, Ralf took her to Dobberke's office to report.

The Scharführer was extremely pleased. He clapped his hands and called the nurse who doubled up as his secretary— and probably his mistress. "Bring us some wine, Ingrid, we have reason to celebrate."

Dobberke raised his glass and toasted. "To Thea's first catch, may there be many more!"

Blushing at the praise, Thea played down her feat. "I didn't do all that much."

"If Ralf is to be believed," Dobberke said with a wink, "you comported yourself perfectly. It was your calm demeanor that made the operation a success."

Sipping from her wine, she felt warmth spreading through her body. After living in the shadows for such a long time, finally her accomplishments were appreciated. Between the four of them, they emptied two more bottles of wine.

Dobberke brushed his hand over Thea's hair. "You are incredibly beautiful, the epitome of a German woman."

At a loss for an adequate answer she smiled at him, which he took as an encouragement and squeezed her hand. "I'm so happy to have you in my team. And I want to apologize for hurting you on your first day here. You must understand that I had no choice. If you'd told me the truth right away, you could have spared yourself the unpleasant treatment."

Thea gulped down the anger snaking up her throat. It wouldn't do her any good to bite the hand that was feeding her.

"I'll make it up to you," Dobberke whispered into her ear.

"Continue the good work and I'm going to ask Hitler to make you an honorary Aryan. Wouldn't you like that?"

"Indeed, I would." All the doubts, the pain and the sorrows were forgotten as she relished in the promise of becoming a valued member of the German nation once more.

21

SPRING 1944

It was another of those nights in the basement, suffering through an air raid alarm. The walls trembled slightly as the bombs detonated around them. Helga huddled tight against Heinrich, praying it would be over soon. Ambivalent feelings kept her awake. A part of her hated the bombs for the threat they posed to her life, another part welcomed them, hoping they would shorten the war and liberate the Jews from the Nazi yoke.

"It's coming nearer," Edith, sitting opposite Helga, commented. During the early days, the basement had been overcrowded with people up to a point when, after several hours, the lack of oxygen made it difficult to breathe. Back then, David had announced it was much too claustrophobic and he'd rather stay in the apartment during an alarm.

These days though, they had the shelter to themselves, since the other inhabitants of the building had long been deported to an unknown fate, and Aryan families were not desperate enough yet to move into a Jewish house.

Which was pure serendipity, because Helga had no illusions that they would be forced out then, so as not to pollute the purity of the air the Aryans breathed.

Suddenly, the sturdy stone walls seemed to become liquid, moving back and forth like waves in the ocean. A deafening roar cut through the room and Helga jumped into Heinrich's arms.

"What was that?" Amelie squeezed her mother's hand so tight, Helga feared the bones might break.

"It must have been a direct hit." Herr Falkenstein's surprisingly calm voice announced. "I'll go and have a look."

"You can barely climb the stairs," Edith said.

"I'll go." Heinrich readied himself to stand up, just as the door crashed open, a sooty face peeking through.

"An incendiary bomb hit the roof. The attic is on fire. I need help." David didn't wait for an answer, instead sprinting away as soon as he finished speaking.

For a moment, Helga stared into the dark void behind the open door, wondering whether it had been a dream. But no, next to her, Heinrich and Amelie hastened upstairs to help David put out the fire with the prepared buckets of sand.

Finally, the danger registered in her brain and she followed her family. As she reached the uppermost floor, the attic was ablaze, voracious flames guzzling the wooden construction. Here and there, the fire attempted to leap into the apartment beneath.

"Water, we need water!" someone shouted.

Automatically, Helga rushed into the apartment, just to recoil at the heat and smoke attacking her. Putting her scarf over her mouth and nose she hastened into the kitchen to fill every receptacle she could find with water. Unfortunately, just as Amelie snatched the first bucket from Helga's hand, the tap petered out with a soft sizzle.

Frantically she rushed into the bathroom, where the same thing happened.

"Blankets," a shrill voice screamed that she recognized as Edith's.

It pained Helga's soul to destroy the few blankets they possessed, but anything was better than losing the roof over their heads and becoming homeless, since no landlord in Berlin would rent out to a mixed Jewish family.

"You get the blankets, I'll find more water." Helga ran downstairs and threw herself against the apartment door. At the third attempt, the lock gave out and she stumbled into the strange place. All possessions of the previous residents had long been looted by upright German citizens, except for the heavy furniture and the built-in kitchen.

Here, it was much cooler and water flowed from the tap. Helga filled up the bowl she'd brought with her and returned into the staircase, shouting upstairs, "Here's water. Bring more containers."

Moments later, Amelie arrived with a bunch of bowls and pots from the Falkenstein's kitchen. "Here you go," she said, passing them to her mother and grabbing the full bowl, vanishing as quickly as she had appeared.

An hour or so later, they managed to put out the fire. Everyone gathered in the apartment to examine the damage. Helga gasped as she noticed the huge hole in the ceiling of her and Heinrich's bedroom. Judging by the yelp coming from Amelie, the same must be true of the room she and David shared.

"We can't possibly stay here. The risk of the roof collapsing on us is too great," Heinrich's deep voice cut through the room.

"But where else shall we live?" Edith brushed a loose strand of hair behind her ear, smearing soot across her cheek in the process. Helga had to bite her tongue to prevent herself from laughing.

"Downstairs." David looked like a coal miner after a day's

work. He'd done the brunt of the work extinguishing the fire, while the others constantly replenished his supply of water, sand and blankets.

"In the basement?" Amelie shrieked. Nobody liked the long nights down there during the air raids, although Amelie seemed to be most affected. She absolutely loathed the damp darkness along with the claustrophobic feeling. More than once she'd snuck out to join David upstairs.

"Of course not. Who'd want to live down there?" David himself never joined them in the shelter, presumably to be on fire watch instead.

"Then where?" Helga looked at her son, sensing in her guts that he'd come up with an outrageous suggestion.

"Into the empty apartment on the ground floor, of course."

All heads turned toward him, four pairs of eyes staring at him in disbelief. Helga sensed something amiss, but didn't have time to follow that train of thought, because David answered as if it were the most natural thing in the world. "The residents have long since been deported."

"But... but..." Edith cleared her throat and started again. "But that's illegal, the apartment isn't ours."

David scoffed. "We're in the throes of a war, fighting for our very lives, do you really still care about laws?"

Seeing Edith's shocked face, Helga quickly added, "We will vacate the apartment as soon as the former owners return to claim it." They all knew that neither the former owners nor the tenants would return—at least not as long as the Nazis stayed in power.

"Well, perhaps..." Edith's voice trailed off, an awkward expression on her face.

"I agree it's a rather bold decision, but in our current situation, it's the only possibility," Heinrich chimed in. His calm intervention seemed to soothe her, because Edith nodded.

A small smile tipped up her lips, before she craned her neck in all directions, shock entering her eyes. "Where's Julius? Has anyone seen my husband?"

Confusion appeared on each face as one after another shook their head.

"Oh my God! What if he—"

Helga put a hand on Edith's shoulder. "Stay calm, we'll look for him. I'm sure he's fine." She turned toward her children and ordered, "David you look upstairs in the attic, Amelie and Heinrich you check the lower floors and the basement."

Ignoring the soaked mess, Edith sank down onto the sofa. "I should have checked for him earlier, what if—"

"Shush. We had to extinguish the fire, it's perfectly understandable that this was foremost on your mind." Normally, Helga would have gotten up to make coffee. Since that wasn't possible for several reasons, she simply sat next to Edith, murmuring soothing words.

It didn't take long before Amelie raced through the open door, wheezing heavily. "We found him... He's alive..." She paused to take a couple of breaths before she explained. "Herr Falkenstein fell and it looks like he has broken his leg."

"Oh dear!" Edith jumped up, leaving in a hurry.

"He really is alright, Mutti," Amelie assured Helga. "But he couldn't get up by himself. We found him lying on the stairs to the basement."

"Better go get your brother. He and Heinrich shall carry him..." Helga thought for a moment. "Or rather, tell your brother to break the door of the ground floor apartment before carrying Herr Falkenstein upstairs."

Once Herr Falkenstein had been settled in their new place, the rest of them spent the remainder of the night carrying their personal belongings to the downstairs apartment. As Helga glanced at Julius, she noticed in how much pain he was, his face pale and sweaty.

By morning, he didn't seem to be any better, so Helga told Edith that she would pass by the Jewish doctor on her way to work and ask him to have a look at Julius' leg.

22

Edith leaned against the door jamb scrutinizing Julius' face as he slept. A week had passed and there was nothing she could do to stop his decline. Helga had not found the Jewish doctor—presumably deported or gone underground. Short of a miracle, she feared her husband was going to die.

A knock on the door cut her musings short. These days nobody knocked anymore. Nobody ever visited. Even if someone showed up, the door hung on its hinges, giving free passageway.

"Come in," Edith called out, not caring who it was.

A young woman with straight blonde hair and carrying a huge briefcase stepped inside. "Are you Frau Falkenstein?"

"Yes, I am." Edith was too downtrodden to ask what the stranger wanted or how she knew her name.

"I'm Anna Klausen. David sent me to have a look at your husband."

"Are you a doctor?" Hope flared up in Edith's chest.

"Not quite. I'm a nurse."

Edith stared at the young woman, observing there was no yellow star on her coat. God only knew how David had coaxed her into risking her reputation by visiting a Jewish house.

"Where is he?" Fräulein Klausen asked.

"Please, excuse my manners." Edit shook off her lethargy. "I'll show you the way. May I take your coat?"

It wasn't exactly warm in the apartment, but Edith had never gotten used to wearing a coat inside.

"That would be very kind of you." Fräulein Klausen set the briefcase atop the table, before she shrugged out of her coat, handing it over to Edith. Beneath it, she wore a nurse's uniform. Her gentle kindness soothed Edith.

She resisted the urge to ask the nurse how she knew David and why she risked her career to attend to a Jewish patient. "Herr Falkenstein is not well, he's delirious, talking in his sleep, and I'm afraid his broken thigh is not healing well."

"I'll see what I can do. Can you boil water for me?"

"Certainly." Edith rushed off into the kitchen. Despite the apartment having roughly the same layout as hers on the upper floor, she still found it difficult to get around and bumped into a cupboard. As she entered the bedroom with a bowl of boiling water, she found the nurse bent over Julius' leg.

"I can't do much about the broken femoral, it must heal by itself. Currently, I'm more worried about the scratch. It's infected." Fräulein Klausen turned toward Edith, looking like a veritable angel with her halo of blonde hair. Then she rummaged in her oversized briefcase and retrieved an envelope.

Edith gasped at the sight of the printed words *Sulfate* and *Charité Hospital*.

"Don't tell my boss," Fräulein Klausen said, as she turned again and went to work on Julius' leg. He woke up, his face a grimace of pain. "Relax, Herr Falkenstein. I'm going to put medicine on your wound, so it will heal."

His eyes clouded by fever, he asked, "Is this how angels look?"

"You're not yet dead, if that's what you're asking. And you won't die anytime soon, either."

Edith felt the tension in her shoulders dissolve at these words, not caring whether they were true or merely meant to calm down an agitated patient. Several minutes later, Fräulein Klausen finished her work and beckoned for Edith to follow her into the living room.

"Your husband has a good chance, since the infection hasn't settled into the bone yet. I'll leave the sulfate here. You must apply it to the wound every twelve hours and be meticulous that the dressings are clean."

"I will." Edith nibbled on her lip, wondering how to tell the nurse that they didn't have money to pay.

She seemed to read Edith's mind. "Don't worry about money. David told me about your plight. I just ask you not to tell anyone that I was here."

"Of course. That's the least I can do. I would never compromise you."

"I'm afraid I won't be able to visit a second time. But if you're stringent about keeping the cut clean, that won't be necessary."

"Thank you so much."

Then, the nurse was gone and Edith returned to the bedroom, where Julius was lying with his eyes closed. She was about to leave him to sleep when he asked softly, "Who was that?"

"I don't know her. She seems to know David, who asked her to look after you."

"He's a good man, and she must be an angel sent to work miracles. I already feel better."

Edith smiled for the first since his accident. "She said you'll get well soon if I keep pouring that powder over your wound."

He sniffed. "Is that sulfate I'm smelling?"

Edith nodded.

"I guess I'd rather not ask how and where the miracle nurse got it."

"That is right." Edith was one hundred percent sure Fräulein Klausen had stolen it from the hospital.

"I'm tired." Julius yawned.

"You concentrate on healing. It'll work out just fine." She wiped his sweaty forehead with a cloth, her heart lighter than it had been in weeks.

23

MAY 1944

Knut arrived at the Bendlerblock for a meeting with Oberst Luger, Oberleutnant Graf von Stauffenberg and General Olbricht. He winked at Bernd who approached at the same time from the other direction. They always took different routes to the office so as not to give away their relationship.

After the failed assassination attempt in November there had been others, all aborted because Hitler either had not arrived at the meeting, changed the location, or left before the bomb could be detonated. With every passing day the situation in Germany became more dire and countless people on both sides were dying unnecessary deaths. The urgency to rid the nation of its demonic leader and begin peace negotiations with the Allies weighed heavily on the souls of the conspirators.

"We're running out of time," Luger said.

"Operation Valkyrie is ready to be set into motion and usurp power, but we need Hitler dead for it to work," Bernd answered. Over the past months he'd become Stauffenberg's right hand.

Embarrassed silence permeated the room, every attendant reminiscing about the aborted and failed assassination attempts.

If they didn't succeed soon, there would be neither country nor people left to save.

After a lengthy discussion, General Olbricht decided to promote Stauffenberg to a position in the headquarters of the reserve army under Generaloberst Fromm. There he would have access both to the reserve army and Hitler. The next assassination attempt should be done by Stauffenberg.

Despite having offered to sacrifice his life for his nation, Knut felt a burden lift from his shoulders when that task fell on another man. He secretly sought Bernd's gaze, the same relief apparent in his partner's eyes. Their relationship had intensified since Knut had returned from the Wolfsschanze unscathed. Being forced to say goodbye had driven home that either one of them could die any day. For the past five months they had never taken the other one for granted, maximizing the time they spent with each other. However long or short their lives were, they wanted to savor every moment.

At home that night, Bernd opened a bottle of red wine.

"Are we celebrating something?" Knut asked.

"Just that we're both still here." Bernd grinned. "Isn't that enough reason to celebrate?"

"It absolutely is." They settled on the sofa, putting a record with classical music on the gramophone. After a while, Knut's mind returned to the topic of the meeting this afternoon. "Do you think it will work this time?"

"It has to. I'm afraid another failed attempt will be the end of our conspiracy."

Knut groaned, the weight of his own shortcoming pressing heavily on his chest.

"Don't beat yourself up." Bernd put a hand on Knut's thigh. "It wasn't your fault the meeting was cancelled."

"I keep thinking that I ought to have tried to meet Hitler under a pretext and detonated the bomb." Knut frowned slightly.

"It's selfish to think that way, but I for my part am quite happy your suicide mission didn't work out."

"Me, too. Though I still keep thinking what I could have done differently."

"Nothing."

"That man is slippery like a fish, always sliding away when you want to catch him."

Bernd chuckled. "That's a fitting comparison. Just don't let anyone hear it."

"Don't you sometimes wish we could just walk away and leave the war and everything behind?" Knut closed his eyes, dreaming of a better place.

"But where would we even go? Is there a place on earth where they'd let us live in peace?"

"I don't know. South America, perhaps? On a finca deep in the middle of nowhere without nosy neighbors or overzealous government officials. Just the two of us."

"Well, dream on. I for my part will go to bed, because I have to get up early tomorrow morning. Stauffenberg wants me to accompany him to visit the leaders of several administrative districts—forging alliances, you know."

"Go ahead, I need to finish some paperwork. We can't leave anything to chance."

"Goodnight." Bernd got up and went to sleep, while Knut revised the plan to usurp power after Hitler's demise for the hundredth time, making sure every tiny detail was taken care of. They couldn't afford even the smallest oversight if the attempt to take over the country was going to be successful.

24

It was Sunday, the blue sky cloudless and the linden trees were in full bloom—at least the ones that had defied the constant hail of bombs. David shaved and left the bathroom whistling.

"Hey, brother, has the war ended and nobody told me? Why are you so happy?" Amelie had been waiting for her turn in the bathroom.

Being caught red-handed doing something illegal, which technically speaking he was going to do, he went onto the offensive. "Why can't a man enjoy what little happiness this life offers without being waylaid by his annoying little sister?"

"Ooh la la." She raised her eyebrows. "Is that aftershave I smell?"

"That's none of your business." He pushed past her, escaping into their shared room, but not before hearing her sing, "David is in love. David is in love."

"I'm not," he growled, despite her being right. He was madly in love with Roxi. Today he was going to take her out to a café on the Kurfürstendamm—a street forbidden for Jews and probably for Romani too. He and Roxi would amble leisurely under the Nazis' noses. A small victory over the constant oppression, and another reason to be happy.

As he arrived at the arranged meeting place, he spotted her coming toward him from the opposite direction in her inimitable panther-like gait. As always when he saw her, his heart swelled with joy. He barely managed to keep himself from running toward her and wrapping her up in his arms, which would only cause unwanted attention.

A big smile appeared on Roxi's cute face and she greeted him with a quick peck on the cheek.

"Where do you want to go?" he asked.

"A lemonade first. Then a stroll through the Tiergarten Park after?" she suggested.

"Sounds like a plan. And I know just the perfect café. I used to go there a lot." He grabbed her hand and steered her toward his favorite café, a place that usually milled with people. The perfect spot to see and be seen, while sipping a soft drink.

But when they drew up in front of the location, David slowed his pace. Unpleasant memories created a lump in his throat. Here, Thea had told him she'd married some random guy, seconds after admitting she was still in love with David. He'd thought he was over all of that, yet it pricked his insides once more.

"What's wrong?" Roxi asked, always perceptive to unspoken things. Her unparalleled intuition was one of the traits which had kept her alive against all odds.

"Just bad memories. I'd rather go someplace else, if you don't mind."

"Not at all. I just want us to have a lovely day together, it doesn't matter where." She gave his hand a quick squeeze.

He glanced gratefully at her. The moment they steered past the café, two SS men walked out through the door, two men with their hands held above their heads between them. David recognized one of the arrested men as a former classmate at the

Lemberg school. Since he wasn't wearing a yellow star, David concluded that he must have gone underground.

Roxi grasped the situation at the exact same second and he sensed her entire body tightening.

"Keep on walking," he whispered, just to feel his jaw dropping to the floor moments later, when Thea stepped out of the café with a tall, dark-blond man. Without thinking, he readied himself to come to her aid, but Roxi dragged him away.

"We need to get away from that woman," she mumbled, holding his hand in an unforgiving grip.

"She might need our help," David answered listlessly. True, Thea had hurt him by betraying him with another guy and then marrying a third one, but she still held a spell over him and he didn't wish her anything bad.

"You can't be serious," Roxi scolded him, not allowing him to stop or turn around until three blocks down the street. "Don't you know who she is?"

"I do." He shrugged embarrassed. "From a long time ago."

Roxi squinted her eyes at him. "What kind of nonsense are you talking? She's the Blonde Poison."

"Don't you think that moniker is a bit harsh? I admit, Thea flirts shamelessly with every man—"

"So you know her personally?"

David gave an awkward smile. "We used to date for a while."

Roxi's eyes widened with shock. "Tell me that's not true!"

"It was long before I met you." A sting of annoyance hit David at her insistence. She must have had other boyfriends before him, too.

"You honestly have no idea that she's turned and has become a prolific catcher of Jews?"

"No. No." He shook his head. "Thea may be selfish, but she's not a bad person."

"Oh, David. It seems her charms have clouded your brain.

This woman has earned her nickname with the blood of dozens of Jews she has betrayed to the Gestapo."

David refused to believe it. It couldn't be true. Thea had rescued Julius Falkenstein from being run over by a van, hadn't she? And she'd tried to get him to hide with her during the *Fabrikaktion*. She'd come to their house to thank him for covering up for her. Could she really have turned? Was she betraying her own people?

25

The camp in the Grosse Hamburger Strasse had recently been evacuated and everyone, including staff, had transferred to the Jewish Hospital in the Schulstrasse. One tract still served as a hospital, whereas the majority had been transformed into a holding camp.

Thea and Ralf returned to the camp after another catch, finding Ingrid waiting for them. "Thea, Dobberke wants to see you."

Instantly the hairs on Thea's neck stood on end as she racked her brain to see whether she'd done something wrong. "Right now?" she asked.

"No need to worry. He's in a good mood. Now hurry." Ingrid shooed her away. "I'll help Ralf with the report."

"Alright." Thea nibbled her lip. Ingrid was Dobberke's mistress and at the same time the camp's good soul. She always had a smile, an encouraging word or a glass of water for the prisoners, especially after they'd been subjected to Dobberke's floggings. He possessed a volatile temper, appearing sweet and caring one moment, just to shout viciously at anyone who didn't do his bidding a second later.

A shudder ran across her shoulders. Fortunately he never took out his whip to punish the people working for him, but a dressing-down, especially if one was alone with him, was also savage.

"There you are." The smile on Dobberke's face indeed indicated a good mood. "My best catcher. I must say, I'm proud of your flawless work."

Thea's face flushed hotly at the unexpected praise. "Ahh... thank you."

"How many successful operations have you had? Several dozen? And each one better than the one before. I heard today was especially fruitful."

"Yes, Herr Scharführer, we managed to catch two subjects who'd been on the black list for quite a while." She swallowed. If she was honest with herself, she suffered pricks of conscience, despite the exhilarating flash of adrenaline during each chase.

"Please, call me Walter." He cast her a disarming smile.

"Thank you. Walter." She tasted his name on her tongue, overwhelmed by the honor to be on a first name basis with the man who held the lives and deaths of several thousand prisoners in his hand.

"I couldn't be prouder of you, Thea." He approached her and took her small hand into his soft, beefy fingers. "Since you've turned out to be the pick of the bunch, I have a gift for you. Come with me."

Curious, she followed him through the long corridors until he stopped in front of a door with an expectant gaze. "You have thirty minutes. Go inside." Then he turned on his heel and walked away, leaving her wondering what or who was waiting behind that door.

Her knees trembled slightly and for a second she considered following Dobberke's example and walking away. But then she straightened her shoulders and turned the doorknob. It was dark in the room, only a few rays of light shimmering through the boarded-up windows, so she didn't immediately recognize the two scrawny figures crouched in the corner.

"Thea! Is that really you?" The croaking voice unmistakably belonged to her mother.

"Mother!" A lump formed in Thea's throat. She'd dreamt of being reunited with her parents every night, and now that it had really happened, she had no idea what to say or do. Hesitantly she stepped further into the room. She had no sooner let the knob go, than the door clicked shut behind her with a finality that sent icy chills down her spine. The doors in the prisoner tract could only be opened from the outside.

The joy of seeing her parents mixed with fear that Dobberke had tricked her and wouldn't keep his promise to return in half an hour.

"So it is true, they've captured you," her father said.

"Unfortunately, yes." Thea thought it better not to mention that she was working for the Gestapo. "I'm so happy to see you. How are you coping?"

"It's not the Ritz." It was a good sign that her mother hadn't lost her sense of humor.

Finally, Thea composed herself and walked toward her parents, who laboriously got up to embrace her. For several long minutes the three of them stood entwined in silence, until she spoke. "I have missed you so much. Every single day I was thinking of you, praying you were alright."

"We are. We are." Mother squeezed her shoulders.

Her father cleared his throat. "Several months ago, our names stood on the infamous transport list, until one of the orderlies told us we'd stay. Without further explanation we were transferred to a different part of the old camp and when it was evacuated, they brought us here."

"I'm so happy." Goosebumps broke out all over Thea's skin despite the warm temperature. So, Dobberke had kept his word and spared her parents from going on a transport in exchange for her agreeing to work for him. In this very moment a warmth settled in her heart, slowly spreading into her limbs. The ordeal had been worth it. She had saved her parents.

After bringing each other up to date on friends, relatives and acquaintances, her mother put a hand on Thea's. "My sweet darling, we've heard rumors that you're working for the Gestapo. Tell me, is it true?"

One look at her mother's lips pressed into a thin line told Thea the truth would not be appreciated.

"Of course not, Mother. Would I be here if I did?" she answered as nonchalantly as possible.

"It's just... people around here call you the Blonde Poison. Why's that?"

Thea flinched at the mention of the loathed moniker. "They're just jealous of my good looks."

Despite having yearned to see her parents for months, she suddenly wished for the meeting to end, since she feared an inquisition of her role in the camp. Neither of her parents would appreciate the sacrifice she was making to keep them alive.

Inwardly counting the minutes, she sagged with relief when the door opened and Dobberke's face peeked through. "Time's up."

Thea hastily hugged her parents, whispering, "Keep your chins up!" Then she left the cell. Outside in the corridor, her knees trembled with emotion.

"Did you enjoy the time with your parents?"

"Very much. Thank you for keeping them here."

"Don't mention it. It's the least I could do for my best catcher, and, if I may say so, the most beautiful one too."

His genuine admiration flattered her equally as much as it surprised her. But then, she'd worked hard to become the efficient catcher she was, always tweaking her methods and discussing with Ralf new angles where and how to find Jews gone underground.

"Would you do me the honor and drink a glass of wine with me to celebrate your latest success?" Dobberke asked as they reached the staff-only floor.

"I'd love to."

Instead of entering his office, he steered her toward his private quarters, consisting of three adjacent rooms. She'd never been there before and gasped in awe at the stark contrast of his exquisitely furnished home to the staff quarters' functionality or the somber prisoner tract.

"Welcome to my modest home." He made a grand gesture, beckoning her to enter the living room. Ingrid was sitting in the wingchair reading a book and looked up. "You're early, Walter."

"I have invited Thea for a glass of wine to celebrate her latest catch. Would you mind getting a bottle for us?"

"Of course not." A glance of understanding passed between the two of them.

"Please take a seat," Dobberke prompted Thea. Several minutes later, Ingrid returned with a bottle and two glasses.

"I'm afraid I have to look after a patient in the hospital," she apologized, before she walked out the door.

Again, Thea sensed a finality as it clicked shut, even though the staff rooms had doorhandles on the inside as well.

After the third glass of wine, Walter took her face in his hands and kissed her. "I've been wanting to do that ever since I first set eyes on you. You're such a beautiful woman."

Thea was too surprised to react. His kiss wasn't unpleasant or rough.

"Ralf doesn't deserve you. He doesn't admire you the way I do," he murmured next to her ear, his hands moving beneath her blouse. "You'd be so much better off with me. I'd lay the world at your feet." His lips suckled on her earlobe, even as his hands continued their move upward until they cupped her breasts, sending a sharp tingle through her body.

Guilt mixed with pleasure. Ralf wasn't an accomplished lover and she'd grown tired of him. Dobberke—*Walter*, she corrected herself—could do so much more for her. Being his mistress, even if only second in rank to Ingrid, had many benefits. Thea didn't need to think twice before she gave herself to him.

Shooing away a stab of conscience, she told herself this was a small price to pay for her survival. None of this was her fault. Not the betrayal of her compatriots and certainly not sleeping with the man who held the fate of every single Jew in Berlin in his hands.

26

THERESIENSTADT, JUNE 23, 1943

Joseph put on his dress uniform to welcome the important visitors. The entire camp—SS and inmates alike—had worked meticulously for several months to prepare everything for the International Red Cross' visit.

Die Stadtverschönerung, city embellishment, had left no stone unturned. No effort, no money, no work, no incentives and no rewards were spared to complete the makeover.

Deeply impressed with the results, Joseph called for his aides, Mayer and Helm, looking splendid in their immaculate SS uniforms. Pride warmed his heart as he strode down the recently repaired and cleaned main street of *his city*, past the town square that had recently been opened up to the prisoners, the fence torn down, the ground plowed, a magnificent lawn laid out. The highlight was the freshly planted twelve hundred rose bushes.

"The city does us proud," Joseph told his aides. Making a good impression on the visitors was the first directive. The International Red Cross commission, consisting of one Swiss and two Danish officials, had instigated the visit after consistent rumors about the dreadful treatment of Jewish people in the camps.

Joseph's initial reaction had been to sneer at the request and tell the Red Cross to shove it up their behinds, but the Führer, in his omnipotent wisdom, had come up with a brilliant plan: invite a delegation to visit Theresienstadt, woo them with stellar conditions to silence the uncalled-for badmouthing once and for all. The perfect opportunity for a smashing propaganda victory.

Today, Joseph would make his Führer proud.

He nodded at Dr. Eppstein, chairman of the Jewish Council in Theresienstadt, arriving in frock-coat and top hat to show the visitors around. While Joseph disliked the man, he realized that he was invaluable for the smooth running of the camp. Eppstein so far had proven to be a good councilor, always eager to please his German masters, while at the same time purporting to be a spokesperson for Jewish interests. Today he would represent the city's Jewish population, who obviously weren't allowed to talk to the visitors. Eppstein himself, despite being a faithful enforcer of directives, had been warned only to speak to the Red Cross delegates in the presence of the SS.

The guests arrived by passenger train first class, a stark contrast to the usual arrival of inmates crammed into third class wagons or cattle cars.

"Standartenführer Joseph Hesse, I'm most pleased to welcome you to Theresienstadt, the city our Führer has gifted the Jews. These are my aides, Mayer and Helm, but as you will see for yourself, we're only in a supporting role. The entire city is under Jewish self-administration."

The visitors introduced themselves and Joseph gave them a short overview of Theresienstadt's history, whereby he carefully avoided the word *camp* and only referred to it as *city* or *town*.

"Approximately ten thousand Jews live and work here, along with fifteen Aryans, whose main responsibility is administrative liaison with the Reich." He did not mention that the fifteen Aryans were SS men, and neither did he expand upon the fact that in the run-up to the delegation's visit half of the inmates had been transported to Auschwitz, as not to give the impression of overcrowded living conditions.

"For now, I will leave you with the Chairman of the Jewish Council, Doctor Eppstein. He'll give you a tour around the city." Joseph smiled at the visitors, then sent a warning glare toward Eppstein, reminding him of the consequences should he talk out of line.

Dr. Eppstein led the delegates to a vehicle that was going to drive them back and forth through the camp, showcasing the beauty of Theresienstadt. The first stop was the Jewish Council. Eppstein gave his prewritten and rehearsed lecture on the self-administration departments, housing conditions, nutrition, youth welfare, and care for the elderly and sick. He reported on the factories, the stores, as well as the city's rich cultural life. Much to Joseph's delight, the counselor never deviated from the rehearsed script. His description of life in Theresienstadt sounded plausible and normal.

Joseph carefully studied the delegates' expressions. They were falling for the sham without recourse. Perhaps he should reward Eppstein for his stellar performance, or should he dispose of him once the Red Cross people had left? Better not to leave witnesses who could contradict the glowing reports Joseph was sure would be written, he supposed. Once again, Hitler had excelled himself and devised the perfect plan.

A pleased smile on his lips, Joseph invited the guests to stroll along the newly planted flower borders edging the main street. It was a sight to behold, much too beautiful for the subhumans living here. They came to a halt in front of a "laundry collection point" with attached steam laundry.

"This has been a necessary implementation to counter war-related shortages and make sure every inhabitant has adequate, and clean clothing." Under Joseph's keen eye, Dr. Eppstein preempted any questions that might arise as to why the house-holds weren't doing their own laundry.

"Would you like a tour through the steam laundry?" Joseph asked, happy when the delegation agreed, because he'd prepared a special highlight for them.

Inside, a group of well-dressed young women—the new uniforms had cost a fortune—worked to music from the radio.

"What a lovely sight," one of the delegates murmured.

Joseph barely bit back a chuckle as he followed the man's gaze to the bustline of one of the girls. His aides had chosen the prettiest women in town, who'd been given extra rations for the past few months for this exact reason. Apparently it had worked.

Behind the delegates' back he shot a glance at Dr. Eppstein, reminding him of his task to woo the Red Cross commission. Instantly, sweat drops showed on the man's forehead, as he eagerly sprung into action.

"We do take pride in our younger generation," Dr. Eppstein said, perhaps not as enthusiastically as he could have done. Though he redeemed himself with the transition to the next action point. "If you'll please follow me, the children's choir has prepared several songs for you."

The children, too, had been decked with new clothes and fattened up with extra rations. Even Joseph had to admit, they sung surprisingly well.

"Well, thank you," the Danish delegate said as a pre-school girl bestowed him with a bouquet of daisies. "Do you like it here?"

The girl shyly nodded, and then, catching a glimpse of Helm's dark glare, quickly dashed off to seek shelter among the other children.

Joseph clapped his hands. "That was a beautiful perfor-mance. Let's continue on our tour." Young children were diffi-cult to handle, and he'd rather not risk them letting slip an honest opinion. He gave the choir master a sign to lead them away from the visitors.

Once more the commission boarded the vehicles and drove across the city, past freshly painted workers' barracks, restaurants, and a music pavilion erected opposite the café to evoke the atmosphere of a health resort.

The Red Cross delegates were duly impressed.

"I believe the rumors were unfounded," one of them murmured.

Wisely Joseph left the remark uncommented on, simply smiling to himself. Hitler's plan was working nicely. By the end of the day, the delegation members were going to be converted to the most fervent advocates for the Jewish city of Theresienstadt.

Perhaps all the money spent for this ridiculous performance was going to be worth it, when the remainder of the Jewish scum begged to be taken here instead of subsisting in the underground of Germany's cities.

At lunchtime they stopped in a restaurant, where waitresses in white aprons served them food, each one coaxed to sing from the rooftops about the camp's benefits. With these young women Joseph didn't have to worry about a false word. They had been carefully selected, their families taken into protective custody for the duration of the visit. None of them would risk their loved ones' lives by uttering a critical word.

Invigorated by the hearty meal and home-brewed beer, Joseph prodded the delegation onward. There was a strict schedule to follow. He whispered an order to Helm. "Go ahead and check whether everything is ready at Südberg."

"No problem, Standartenführer," Helm whispered back. "I'll make sure everything goes according to plan."

Joseph breathed deeply, content that he could trust his aide implicitly. The delegation arrived just in time—no coincidence—at the vast grass area, to watch a soccer game in full swing.

The players were privileged, often famous inmates, who paid for extra rations. None of them looked famished.

Dr. Springer, the main surgeon, extolled the virtues of exercise for body and mind. Just as he finished his lecture, one team scored a goal, resulting in a happy celebration on the field.

"Isn't it a joy to watch these virile young men?" Joseph asked the Swiss delegate.

"I must say, I'm truly impressed," he answered.

"I'm afraid we can't watch the entire game, we're expected in the community center, where children will be giving a performance of the opera *Brundibár*."

"An opera, you say? I've never heard of it, and I consider myself something of an expert," the Danish delegate said.

"The composer is Hans Krása, a Czech. He happens to live here and has graciously agreed to rehearse his piece." Joseph arranged his expression into one of warmth and kindness. "Please be lenient with your judgement, the actors are children living in the orphanage and not professionals."

"Certainly. I find it a laudable effort to give these children something to look forward to."

"It is our deepest desire to make life in Theresienstadt as pleasurable as humanely possible to all inhabitants," Joseph lied without batting an eyelid.

"Due to time constraints we won't be able to attend the entire performance," Mayer warned the delegates before ushering them into the first row of the audience.

So far the visit had run like clockwork. Joseph couldn't be more pleased. He furtively glanced at his wristwatch to make sure they didn't miss the *chance encounter* with the bread distributors, who'd been issued new and shiny white gloves for the duration of the Red Cross visit.

After that, the trickiest part was coming up: a visit to Danish inmates in their homes. Despite having mollycoddled them for months, and having bribed them with the promise to be spared from the weekly selections to go on a transport to Auschwitz, there was a risk they'd tell the truth. None of the SS men spoke Danish, which might encourage the inmates to slip their compatriots a few honest words about Theresienstadt.

Joseph hovered in the background, biting his lip, watching the facial expressions of the inmates with eagle eyes, straining his ears to catch a critical or disdainful tone. Fortunately, nothing appeared to have gone wrong. He left the Danish homes feeling as light as a feather, knowing that from this pivotal point onward, nothing could spoil the delegates' pleasant experience.

The tension leaving his shoulders, he actually enjoyed visiting the bakery, the orphanage, the pharmacy, the post office, the store and the butcher's shop.

Exhausted after an eventful day, the delegates gladly accepted the offer of a ride to the train station, where they embarked on their first-class carriage to be returned to the airport.

"Herr Standartenführer, I want to thank you for taking the time to show us around, since you must have other pressing issues to attend to," one of the Danish delegates said.

Joseph slightly bowed his head. "Not at all, I'm always eager to serve my nation. It was the Führer's wish that you saw for yourself how well Jews are treated in the so-called camps."

"I was surprised indeed," the man answered, clearly not having expected such a beautiful place.

"Hopefully positively." Joseph grinned inwardly, imagining the mask of horror should the delegate ever find out that every single moment he'd experienced today had been part of a carefully rehearsed performance—and had as much to do with reality as any other theatre piece.

"Definitely. I'll write my report to the International Red Cross Headquarters in Geneva as soon as I return home."

Again, Joseph bowed his head. "Thank you for coming."

"Thank you for having us."

Then, the locomotive whistled and the delegates hurried to board the train. As soon as the train was out of sight, Joseph ordered, "The charade is over. Back to work. We have people to deport."

27

JULY 20, 1944

Knut was sitting in his office, biting his nails in suspense. Early in the morning, Bernd had accompanied Oberleutnant Stauffenberg to the Wolfsschanze. It had been yet another difficult farewell.

Stauffenberg had a bomb in his suitcase, in an attempt to assassinate Hitler, and several of his highest staff, in one fell swoop. Since the Oberleutnant had lost one hand during combat in Africa, he needed help to prime the bomb—and the person chosen was Bernd. The mission was highly critical, and so much could go wrong.

Several hours ago Stauffenberg and Bernd had landed in Berlin again, calling the Bendlerblock to let them know that Hitler was dead. Then, Operation Valkyrie was set into motion like clockwork. The conspirators quickly gained control over Berlin and the other districts in Germany, and had even begun arresting high-ranking Nazi officials, including Goebbels, when conflicting news came in that there had indeed been an explosion in the Wolfsschanze, but Hitler wasn't dead.

Knut was willing to ignore the disturbing rumors and forge ahead with the planned coup, when suddenly the radio crackled and the current broadcast was interrupted by an emergency announcement. As soon as he heard the familiar voice, Knut felt the blood drain from his face.

It was Hitler himself, addressing the German population. "Fellow Germans! I do not know how many times an attempt on my life has been planned and carried out. When I speak to you today, it is for two reasons: First, so that you can hear my voice and know that I myself am unharmed and healthy. Second, so that you can also learn more about a crime that is unparalleled in German history."

His heart sank. Dropping his head to the desk, Knut groaned with desperation, only half listening to Hitler promising to ruthlessly persecute and punish everyone involved in the coup lead by Stauffenberg. The speech ended with the Führer saying, "I also see this as a sign from Providence that I must continue my work and, therefore, I will continue it!"

"It's over," Knut whispered to himself, desolation taking hold of him. Hitler was alive. Germany was doomed. Then the realization struck and shock froze his limbs. What was going to happen to Bernd?

The door to his office flew open, a messenger poking his head in. "Have you heard the radio message?"

"I did." Not knowing whether the messenger was friend or foe, Knut squared his shoulders and asked, "You have any other news?"

"Stauffenberg has been arrested, General Olbricht and Generaloberst Beck, too."

Knut hissed in a breath, asking as nonchalantly as he could master, "What about Stauffenberg's adjutant?"

"Leutnant Ruben you mean?"

"Yes."

"Not sure. I reckon he'll be arrested soon, there's no way that man isn't guilty, being Stauffenberg's right hand and all."

The messenger dashed off to spread the news through the long corridors at Bendlerblock.

Slumping into his chair, Knut stayed motionless for several minutes, trying to cope with the devastating anguish he felt about Bernd's fate. Once he finally regained his composure, he got up, put on his tunic and cap, then strode down the hallway into the office of Generaloberst Fromm's, the commandant of the reserve army. A shot echoed through the corridor. Knut froze in his tracks. A second shot rang out, setting his feet into motion, he hastened in the direction of the sound. Just as he reached Fromm's office, a third shot rang out.

Knut grabbed his own pistol as he carefully opened the door and stepped into the room. A ghastly scene greeted him.

Generaloberst Beck lay dead in a puddle of blood.

"Down with the weapon!" came the order. At the same time Knut felt a rifle stabbing into his shoulder.

He let the hand with the pistol sink, gazing at Fromm. "Generaloberst, I heard shots and came to help."

Fromm squinted at him. "That might be true. Nonetheless, I'd rather have you disarmed until I'm sure on which side you stand." The former co-conspirator seemed to have switched sides for his own benefit. He knew about Knut's involvement, but arresting him would mean implicating himself in the crime too.

Knut bent down to lay his pistol on the ground and kicked it toward one of the SS men guarding the conspirators. His gaze was drawn to Beck's corpse. A thin thread of blood seeped from his mouth, a dark spot formed on his chest.

"He tried to commit suicide," Fromm explained.

Tearing his eyes away from the dead man who'd been designated to become the Chancellor of an interim government after Hitler's demise, Knut got up, his eyes wandering over the group of arrested conspirators. His breath hitched in his chest as he recognized the fourth one to be Bernd. Their eyes locked, the pain in Bernd's eyes piercing through him like a sword.

"Let's get it over with," Fromm said. "The traitors shall be executed."

"Shouldn't we wait on Hitler's orders?" someone asked.

"Much too dangerous. We must eliminate them immediately."

Knut realized that Fromm was trying to cover his tracks. As an accessory to the conspiracy, albeit not an active member, he was at risk of being arrested himself.

Darkness engulfing his soul, Knut followed the others down into the backyard, where the first man was put against the wall. The shot pierced his eardrums, the sound ricocheting from the walls. Here and now all hopes for a quick end to the war dissolved into spilled blood.

He used an unobserved minute during which the next victim was led toward the wall to sidle up with Bernd and quickly squeeze his hand.

"Don't despair. You must continue our work," Bernd whispered through gritted teeth.

Blinking a tear away, Knut gave an almost imperceptible nod. Then, when the next fusillade of shots indicated the end of yet another righteous man, he used the background noise to say, "I love you so much. You will stay in my heart for as long as I live."

"Don't make me cry," Bernd was barely able to speak. "I don't want to give them the satisfaction of thinking it's because of them."

In spite of the dreadful situation, Knut had to smile. "It was an honor to know you, Leutnant Bernd Ruben."

Then, the henchmen came for Bernd. He cast one last gaze at Knut, whispering, "I love you, too. Take care." As one of the SS men grabbed his arm, he straightened his shoulders and said with a firm voice, "I can walk on my own."

Fromm declared him guilty of high treason, punishable by execution. Bernd heard the verdict, raised his fist into the air and yelled, "Stand up and do the right thing!" No sooner had the last word left his mouth than the firing squad pulled their triggers. Several bullets hit their target and Bernd's lifeless body fell to the ground, his blood mixing with that of his co-conspirators already gone.

Knut bit hard on his lip to prevent himself from bursting into sobs.

28

David arrived at the photographer's shop where he was to pick up a set of passport photos to issue fake identity cards for illegals hiding at the Swedish parish.

"Is Herr Schiller here?" he asked the young woman helping out with the sales.

"He's in the darkroom, you'll have to wait." She cast him a terse smile.

Just as David pondered whether he should leave or not, he sensed eyes boring into his back. Looking around, he didn't see anyone. Yet, his neck hair stood on end, warning him something was amiss.

"I'll return later," he announced, turning on his heel to leave the shop, just as someone stepped out from behind the curtain, leading to the darkroom.

"Not so fast," the SS man ordered.

David, though, had no intention of finding out what he wanted and dashed off, directly into the arms of two more SS men, who were positioned outside the shop and pointed their weapons at him.

Shit, David cursed silently.

Seconds later the first man stepped outside, an earnest expression on his face. "Papers."

David handed over his *Kennkarte*, bracing himself for the inevitable.

"A Jew," the SS man sneered. "I knew you had dirt on your hands. Where's your star?"

Thinking on his feet, David decided it was preferable not to admit that he was wearing his jacket inside out. Even on the off chance that they believed he'd innocently put it on the wrong way, they'd still arrest him.

"I'm sorry. I wanted to buy a photograph for my girlfriend's birthday." David gave a guilty smile, hoping to soften the officer's resolve, while at the same time his body snapped into alert, frantically searching for a way to escape.

"Ach. Illegally entering a shop forbidden for Jews, not wearing your star and resisting authority, that's a whole lot of offences for one dirty Jew."

"I'm a *Mischling*." David hoped for lenience. The opposite happened. A second later a fist connected with his jaw.

Yelping with pain, he rubbed the spot.

"You're arrested," the SS man said and his colleagues unceremoniously grabbed David by his elbows to haul him away.

Gritting his teeth so as not to give them the satisfaction of screaming, David stumbled along, never quite getting to his feet to alleviate the agony in his shoulders. He almost rejoiced when they shoved him into the police car. His arms freed from their grip, he rubbed his aching shoulders. The vehicle careened through the streets, devoid of the usual traffic congestions before the war.

To keep himself from succumbing to panic, as well as clinging to the slim chance of finding a way to escape, he looked through the window. Left and right there was scenery of utter devastation. Since the Americans had joined the RAF in their air raids, it wasn't only at night that the bombs fell. When the

Tommies returned home with the first sunlight it didn't take long for the Americans to arrive and unload another shower of unwelcome gifts onto Berlin's population.

Along the city center not a single building stood unscathed, charred ruins lining the streets. David wondered where all the residents had gone. Not everyone was lucky, or unlucky, enough to be able to move into the lower floor apartments of their deported neighbors.

The vehicle stopped in front of a building that David recognized as the Jewish Hospital, which had been transformed into a holding camp. His gut twisted viciously at the sight of the place he'd spent a few months in at the beginning of 1941 with a severe infection. Once he had recovered enough to leave the hospital, his ship to Palestine had sailed and he'd been stuck in Germany.

David snorted. It looked as if he'd be able to leave the country after all—just not the way in which he'd planned. He was under no illusion what would happen to him, since his status as *Mischling* had ceased to protect him from deportation the very moment he'd been arrested for not only one, but many crimes. This time he couldn't count on his mother to get him out. This time he was truly and utterly doomed.

Manhandled out of the police car, David gritted his teeth to not cry out loud, when another, even more somber thought crossed his mind. The photographer! Despite not being an actual member of the resistance network, he must have suspected something, since it was David's third time to pick up passport photos in as many months *for a friend*.

If he had shared his suspicion with the Gestapo, the entire network was in danger. A shudder racked his frame, as his mind went down that train of thought. Perhaps David's arrest hadn't been bad luck, but deliberate action after a report—then he was in for a lot of pain when they started interrogating him.

His eyes wide with fear, David swore not to give his friends away, or at least hold on for a day or two. Pastor Perwe expected him back within the hour and was surely going to raise the alarm if David didn't show up. Protected by diplomatic immunity Perwe would somehow manage to spirit the implicated persons away. At least David hoped so.

The queasy feeling in his stomach all but hindered him from breathing as he stumbled behind the SS men into the Jewish Hospital. *Roxi.* Whatever the Gestapo did to him, he would not mention her name. Ever. Under torture he might betray everyone else, but not her. Swallowing hard, he hoped his determination not to talk wouldn't be tested.

At long last, the SS men shoved him into a cell, where many others already sat, presumably waiting to be processed. The time seemed to slow down, while panic settled deep into his soul. David felt relief, when finally an orderly came for him. Whatever awaited him, he just wanted to get it over with.

He was ushered to an office with the inscription, "Director, SS-Scharführer Walter Dobberke".

David's courage evaporated. Behind the desk sat a balding man with a chubby face and pudgy fingers, holding an expensive-looking fountain pen.

"Another illegal Jew?" Dobberke said in a bored tone, not even looking up from his writing.

While David pondered whether he should make his status as half-Jew known, the orderly answered in his stead, "No, Herr Scharführer. This one has valid papers."

Dobberke's head shot up, his eyes widening in disbelief. "That's not possible. Berlin is free of Jews. He must be illegal."

"I'm half-Aryan, my mother—" David began, causing Dobberke's face to turn beet-red.

"You speak only when asked a direct question. Do you understand?" The droning voice was laced with fury.

"Yes, Herr Scharführer," David dutifully responded, bowing his head. He'd learned not to antagonize a Nazi official, although he sincerely doubted it would make a difference in his current situation.

"Hmm," Dobberke scoffed. "So, why is he here?"

"I... I don't know... I assumed..." The orderly backed away like a caged animal.

"Blighter. Why am I surrounded by clueless good-for-nothings?" Dobberke shouted before he fixed his gaze on David. "Why have you been arrested?"

David seized his chance with both hands, pushing out his lower lip in an attempt to appear riddled with guilt. "I was trying to buy something in an Aryan-only shop."

Dobberke glared daggers at the orderly. "I have more important things to do than chit-chat with a petty Jewish criminal, get him out of here!"

"You don't want to interrogate him?" the orderly asked.

"Haven't you heard what I said, idiot? He's not an illegal, so he doesn't know anyone in the underground. I'm not going to waste my time trying to beat information he doesn't have out of him. Take him away."

Just as David was about to sigh with relief, Dobberke added, "And put him on the next transport, lest his Aryan parent comes here begging for mercy."

A cold chill froze David's limbs, making it difficult to force his legs into motion. About halfway down the long corridor, David summoned up the courage to ask, "Excuse me, when is the next transport leaving?"

"Can't wait to get away, can you?" The orderly smirked.

"If it were my choice, I'd rather return home."

The brash answer earned him a painful punch with the end of a truncheon. Given that reaction he didn't dare ask the question he was dying to know: what the ominous transport's final destination was. For the moment he contented himself with having avoided torture and the risk of betraying everyone dear to him.

As they reached the cell where David had been before, the orderly paused to unlock the door. Just in that moment, a blonde woman flanked by two SS men stepped through the main entrance into the building. The breath hitched in David's chest as he recognized Thea. Much to his surprise, she seemed to be chatting in a friendly manner with the two men.

In the meantime the orderly had opened the door and pushed David through. Out of the corner of his eyes, David saw Thea waving at the two men. "See you guys later."

Shocked to the core by the ghastly revelation, he tripped and fell flat on his face. By the time, he'd picked himself up, the door had been closed behind him, locking out the traitorous woman.

David crouched in the corner of the almost empty space, shaking his head time and again, trying to cope with his ex-girl-friend's incomprehensible perfidious behavior. "I don't believe it, she's betraying her own kind," he mumbled.

"The Blonde Poison got you?" A young man sidled up to him.

"Can't believe it. I just can't." David was too distraught to properly answer.

"Don't beat yourself up, you're in good company."

"Me?" Finally David raised his head to peruse the other man, about his own age, with dark hair and sharp eyes.

"Yes, you. So you fell for Thea's innocent smile and she turned you in?"

"Actually—" David stopped himself. He had no idea whether the young man could be trusted. He wasn't going to tell him that, indeed, he had fallen for Thea's magnetic smile years ago, but she wasn't the reason he'd been caught. "Thea is the one they call the Blonde Poison?"

The other man shrugged. "Yep. Dobberke's top catcher, must have turned in at least a hundred Jews. Perhaps two hundred, but who's counting?"

"I am." Strong determination surged through David's veins. "Once the war is over I'll make her pay for every single person she's harmed."

Admiration shone in the other's eyes. "That's a pretty bold thing to say, since you probably won't make it out alive. I'm Zim, by the way."

"David." They shook hands. "Have you been here long?"

"Long enough to know how everything works." Zim narrowed his eyes at David, "You're not a plant, are you?"

Breaking out into a chuckle, David answered, "I wouldn't tell you if I were one, would I?"

"You're right, that was a stupid question. I'm just wondering, you weren't away for long. Dobberke mustn't be here."

"Is that the chubby, red-faced, balding SS officer barking commands at everyone?"

"That's him. So, you were in his office?"

David nodded.

"And came out unharmed? That must be a first. Every prisoner who goes in there is introduced to Dobberke's bullwhip. He loves wielding it. I've seen people with their skin peeling off in a thousand shreds."

"Eek." David recoiled at the image forming in his head, once again thanking the stars for saving him from that fate.

"You can say that again. Not all victims have survived." Zim cocked his head. "I wonder, why did he let you go? It's not at all like him. Or... did you just rat out all your helpers? Everyone does, eventually, but you must be the first person to do so without the boss laying a finger on you first."

"Shut up already!" David snapped, regretting his harsh tone immediately, since he didn't want to make enemies. It was hard enough as it was. "I didn't rat out anyone and I certainly was prepared to keep my mouth shut for as long as humanely possible. Luckily, it wasn't necessary." He narrowed his eyes at Zim. "If you must know; I'm a privileged Jew. My mother is Aryan. I never went underground and don't know anyone, helper or illegal. So Dobberke let me go, because I couldn't have told him anything of value anyway."

"Clever. I like that." Zim's expression softened.

"It's not clever, it's true." David didn't fully trust his new friend yet, so he had no intention of admitting that despite living legally himself, he'd been part of a resistance network.

"So, why did they arrest you?"

Again, David made a show of appearing embarrassed. "I got caught entering an Aryan-only shop."

"Must be the most stupid move ever," Zim sympathised. "I bet you've been regretting it ever since."

"Indeed." David seized the opportunity to get more information. "Dobberke ordered that I should be sent onto the next transport. Do you know where it's going?"

Zim rolled his eyes at the naive question. "To Auschwitz, of course."

David shivered as his worst fears were confirmed. Even if only half the rumors were true, he certainly had no desire to become acquainted with that place.

"Do you know when it leaves?"

"It used to be every Friday. These days, if there aren't enough people to fill a train, it's cancelled and you get to live for another week."

"You're not dead just because you step on the transport," David said it more to instill courage in himself than to counter Zim's statement.

"But most likely when you step off the train. In Auschwitz people are selected to go through the chimney, straight off the ramp."

David's head was swimming as images of witches burnt alive at the stake attacked him. He could already feel the flames licking at his feet, when Zim's voice broke the bad spell.

"Although able-bodied men like you are normally sent to toil in the quarry."

"How do you know all this stuff?" David clung to the notion that none of this was true. Zim's suggestions were too horrific to even contemplate.

"It's an open secret. You must have led a very sheltered life if you've heard nothing about Auschwitz."

Suddenly, David felt ashamed. "I have heard rumors, but nothing substantial. Honestly, I struggle to believe that hundreds of people are burnt alive upon arrival there."

"Make it thousands," Zim commented wryly. "By the way, only your corpse is cremated if that comforts you. Don't ask me how exactly the Nazis are murdering a vast number of people in such a short time. You'll have to go there and see for yourself, if you want to know."

"No, thanks. I was rather thinking of escaping before they send me on a transport."

Zim chuckled. "You sure are something else. Tell me when you've found a way."

Thinking on his feet, he answered, "I just might. Together we'll have a better chance."

29

When David didn't return from his errand, Pastor Perwe alerted the network, ordering the members to cease all illegal activities for a while. Roxi couldn't care less about the pastor's orders; remembering her own time in prison, she feared David was going to be tortured to death or sent on a transport—which ultimately amounted to the same result.

She grappled for close to twelve hours with herself until she said, "To hell with lying low. To hell with staying safe." Then, she packed a few utensils into the pockets of her dungarees, stashed her shoes in a hiding hole and took off in the middle of the night to find the man she loved.

Her inquiries with helpers in the underground ascertained that David had been taken to the Jewish Hospital. There he most probably was kept in a cell on the first floor, his name on the list to go on the next transport to the East.

Gnawing on her lip, she decided to try the easier target first, directing her steps toward the holding camp. Despite her dark complexion, her skin shone in the moonlight, so she stopped to smear earth on her face, feet and hands, before she snuck up to the Jewish Hospital.

No guards stood in front, which was both a good and a bad sign, because it meant the prisoners were locked away and she had to find David first. Since she didn't want to alert anyone to her presence, she had to be very careful.

A wave of adrenaline washed over her, sending her senses into high alert. After losing her parents and later her entire extended family, she'd perfected the talent of stealth, stealing for her upkeep. In the beginning she'd loathed the transformation into the very stereotype of a "dirty, lying, cheating gypsy" as the Nazis called her people, just because they didn't understand the Romanies' way of life. As the years passed, she'd found peace with the actions forced on her to survive. These days she found immense joy in putting one over the detested ruling party.

The moon lit up the night. The ground and first floor windows were boarded up, but that wasn't the case for the upper floors. It didn't take long for her to spot a cracked-open window on the third floor. The corners of her mouth tipped upward. *There you go*, she thought as her eyes wandered along the façade to find the best path to get there. Façade climbing was her specialty and this building with its balconies, ornaments and protruding structural elements posed no challenge for her.

An exhilarating rush of adrenaline spread through her body. She waited until it reached her fingers and toes, flooding her with awareness. Then she wiggled her hands and toes to loosen them and pressed herself against the wall, feeling for an unevenness to put her fingers into.

The first step was always the hardest. Once she found suitable spots for her fingers and heaved herself up by the strength of her arms, her surroundings faded away, her entire focus on the wall she was about to climb. The sensation of unbridled freedom never got old. Her nimble toes fumbled for the tiniest crevice, and when they found it, she dug them into it, shifting

her weight onto that foot, while stretching the knee in a determined, flowing movement.

This way she climbed up to the third floor without pause
until she arrived at a projection in the wall. There she stilled,
waiting for her pulse to settle into a steady rhythm again. The
hardest part was done. Usually she loved to pause and look
down to the ground, taking in the beauty of the world from
above. Tonight, though, she didn't have the leisure to idle.

As soon as her heart stopped drumming against her throat,
she continued her way along the ledge, parallel to the ground,
until she reached the cracked-open window. Carefully peering
inside, she swung it fully open and jumped from the windowsill
inside, quiet as a squirrel.

Suddenly deprived of the moonlight, she waited until her
eyes accustomed to the almost complete darkness. The room
must serve as an office, evidenced by the huge desk and the file
cabinets. With three large steps she reached the door, listening
intently to sounds from the other side. When she was satisfied
there was nobody, she turned the doorknob, a wave of relief
washing over her when the door sprung open into an empty
corridor. For a second the bright light blinded her. Once her
eyes had adapted, she realized that she was standing directly
beneath the only switched on light bulb.

Next, she had to find the cell where David was held. Even
half a year ago, this would have been almost impossible, but
these days most of the cells stood empty, since there simply
weren't enough Jews left in Berlin to fill them.

Roxi snuck into the empty corridor and down onto the first
floor, since her contact person had said David was being held
there. The cell doors had been fitted with small windows
through which the guards peeked or passed a tray of food.

She approached the first door, pressing her ear against it,
before she opened the flap. A sharp sound cut through the
silence, echoing off the empty walls, permeating through the air,

until it drifted to the ground. Roxi hissed in a breath. She knew the noise had been loud only to her own ears, since every cell in her body had been strung tight listening for it. Still, she didn't dare to breathe for fear someone might have heard and had pricked up his ears.

Poised against the steel door, a shadow becoming one with the cold material, she waited for a full minute before she dared peek through the opening. A couple was sleeping on the cot, pressed tightly against each other. Closing the flap, she moved on.

On the fourth attempt a smile crept into her face as she recognized David's familiar silhouette. The joy was followed by dismay when she realized that she'd come without a plan of how to get him out. Even if she managed to pick the cell door's lock, they couldn't simply walk out through the—bolted and guarded —entrance door, and unlike her, he wasn't capable of climbing down the façade.

Silently cursing herself for her snap decision, she clicked her tongue, followed by a low hiss, "David."

The body on the cot moved slightly.

"It's me, Roxi."

Instantly he sat up on the cot, throwing the threadbare blanket off him. His pale skin shone surprisingly bright in the dim light filtering through the barred window in the door.

"Are you for real?" he asked suspiciously.

"I sure am." She recoiled at the slight giggle in her voice, ricocheting off the walls, filling her ear with loudness.

David must have sensed the same, because he whispered in a barely audible tone, "Where are you? I can't see you."

"Come to the door."

She could practically smell his mistrust. "It's really me and I'm alone. Promise."

Gingerly he felt his way to the door. The moment his eyes locked with hers, a huge grin spread from ear to ear. She went on her tiptoes pressing her face against the bars, at the same time as he raised his hand, his thumb caressing her smeared cheek. "Roxi."

They stood mesmerized, gazing into each other's eyes for almost a minute, before he broke the spell. "You shouldn't have come. It's dangerous. What if you get caught?"

"I won't." She cocked her head, intently listening for footsteps. "How often are they patrolling at night?"

The grin on his face intensified. "Once or twice per night, at most, but we can't just walk out of here."

"Have they hurt you?"

"No. They don't know anything. I was accused of entering an Aryan-only shop while not wearing the yellow star."

The strength of relief that washed over her at learning David hadn't been tortured, surprised herself.

"I'm earmarked to be sent on the next transport."

His words felt like a punch to her gut. "When?"

"Friday. This one or the next."

"I'll get you out." Roxi pressed her jaws together, racking her brain how to liberate him.

"How did you get in anyway?"

"Climbing the façade, naturally." She shook her head at the obvious question. "How else?"

"Perhaps through the door, like any other person would." He stretched his hand far enough for his middle finger to touch her throat. A delicious tingle covered her skin.

She bit back a giggle. "The door was locked."

"You don't expect me to climb the wall like a cat burglar, do you? I'm sure to plummet to the ground like a ripe apple."

"Now that would be nice. I'd pick you up and sink my teeth into your juicy flesh." The sound of a vehicle driving along the street caused her body to tense, sobering her immediately. Once it had passed by, she relaxed. "Enough chit-chat. Tell me everything you know about the building."

David filled her in with all he knew, which wasn't much. In the end he concluded, "It's impossible."

"It's not!" The authority in her voice was clear, despite being nothing more than a murmur.

"You'll need help."

"Pastor Perwe said it's too dangerous. We cannot risk the entire network for one person." Everyone knew this and had agreed to it when joining the clandestine operation. Any other time Roxi would have heeded Pastor Perwe's orders without blinking an eye, but not where David was concerned. He was her first true love, the one man who understood not to cage or dominate her, who'd given her the freedom she needed to feel safe with him. And whether she wanted to admit it or not, she'd fallen for him lock, stock and barrel. She would not allow the Nazis to take him away from her too, the way they'd done with her entire community of sixty-plus members.

"Don't risk your life for me," David whispered. The gentleness in his voice engulfing her, sending a marvelous warmth into her soul. It was a sensation she'd missed for so many years, the feeling of belonging, of being at home. Family.

Roxi shook her head. "I won't stand by and let them send you away. If Pastor Perwe isn't going to help, I'm going to find someone else."

David sighed, knowing her well enough to be certain she wouldn't budge once she had made up her mind. "Is there anything I can do or say to make you drop this insane plan?"

"No." She pouted. "I'll get you out of here whether you agree or not, but it would be much easier if you helped me make a plan."

"I don't want to endanger you. I love you, Roxi."

His admission left her floating on air, fighting against a whirlwind of emotions washing over her. She'd known he loved her for a while, his every word and action had shown it, as had the glimmer in his eyes whenever he looked at her. It still rattled her to the core, fortifying her determination to get him out of the camp.

"Then you better think hard. Is there anyone who might help us?"

He kept silent for a long time, the tension growing unbearable. Just when she thought she couldn't take it any longer, he said, "Leutnant Hesse."

Roxi furrowed her brow. Sure, Frau Falkenstein's brother had organized a uniform for David, but it was a huge step from there to actively participating in a breakout. "Are you sure he'll help?"

David shook his head. "No. But we won't know if you don't ask him."

"He's never gonna trust me, he's never seen me before."

"Ask Amelie to contact him. There's a business card with his number in my drawer at home."

"I will." Suddenly, her skin tingled with fear. "Someone's coming. Stay put." She closed the window in the cell door and vanished behind a statue in the hallway moments before the door on the other side opened and two SS men stepped through. Chatting, they marched toward her. Roxi's blood froze in her veins, when they stopped directly in front of the statue, lighting cigarettes.

She stilled her heartbeat, slowing her breathing, as she imagined herself consisting of the same cold stone the statue was. Motionless she waited for the SS men to walk on. But those darned men leaned against the very statue she was hiding behind, taking their sweet time to smoke.

One of the guards spoke. "I hate these nightly patrols. What does Dobberke believe? Jews breaking out of their cells?"

"Come on. It could be worse. We could be at the Eastern Front."

Roxi sensed a shudder going through the other man, before

he drawled, "Right. But the way the war is going, it will soon catch up with us. Then only God can help us."

She suppressed the urge to give a snarky remark, focusing on keeping her breathing shallow, becoming an inanimate, invisible object. After what seemed like an endless time, the first man said, "Let's continue our patrol." He flicked off his cigarette butt and Roxi watched in horror as the glowing point sailed through the air to land on her naked foot. Gritting her teeth together she remained completely still, allowing the butt to burn a hole into her skin.

When the soldiers finally marched around a corner, she kicked off the defunct cigarette and got up to leave the building the same way she had entered it.

30

Thea returned late at night after celebrating an especially successful foray. She had not only caught a forger who'd slipped through her hands half a dozen times before, but also a former classmate. Nobody had seen or heard of Margarete Rosenbaum for years, assuming she'd either been deported or emigrated, until she suddenly stood in front of Thea, in the company of a rather ruggedly-handsome man.

"Dobberke wants to see you," the SS guard greeted her at the entrance.

"Thanks. Shall I go to his office right away?"

"Yes. It sounded urgent."

Thea climbed the stairs to Walter's office on the third floor and knocked on the open door.

"Thea, come in." Dobberke beamed from ear to ear. His mood was exceptionally upbeat, making her wonder what delighted him so much—until her gaze fell on the whip next to his desk. It usually hung in the closet, except if he'd used it and was waiting for Ingrid to wipe off the blood and shredded skin, before hanging it back in its proper place.

A shudder ran down her spine, as she remembered her own horrific experience with him yielding the whip.

"You wanted to see me, Herr Scharführer." While he requested her to use his first name in private, the same wasn't true for official occasions.

He beckoned her to sit on the chair in front of his desk. "Would you like a glass of wine?"

"I'd love one." Thea was tired to the bone after being out and about for close to sixteen hours. She settled in the chair, praying to God that Walter wasn't in the mood for intimacy tonight.

After making a show of pouring the expensive French wine, he raised his glass to toast: "The woman you caught, Margarete Rosenbaum, she's a truly fantastic catch."

"Thank you." She waited patiently for him to continue as she sipped her wine, leaning back in her seat with a soft groan.

"You must be tired, criss-crossing the city on foot all day." He looked at her, concern etched into his eyes.

"Indeed I am, but I'm happy to serve the Reich however I can."

"You truly are a special person, worthy of being a German citizen." He rounded his desk to come to stand behind her, putting his hands on her shoulders, his thumbs massaging the tense knots away.

Thea relaxed into his touch, the war, her daily worries and the exhaustion slowly vanishing together with her tightly wound neck muscles. After a while his hands wandered to her front, cupping her breasts, rubbing slow circles over her nipples. She groaned in dismay. Flogging a prisoner always invigorated his libido and she knew she was in for a long night.

Dobberke mistook her sigh for a sensual moan and wagged his finger at her. "Growing impatient, are you, my naughty little girl?"

"Yes, Walter." She cast him a seductive gaze. Indeed, she

was impatient to get it over with, so she could retire to her room and get some sleep.

"Your wish is my command." He gave an exaggerated bow and took three long strides toward the door, which he closed and bolted in one swift move. The first time he took her pressed against the wall. Then he bent her over his huge desk to enter her from behind.

Thea moaned and writhed at the appropriate times and finally sunk back into the chair, sore from his efforts, once he was satiated hours later.

"That was really good, wasn't it?" Dobberke lit a cigarette for himself and offered one to Thea. She took it eagerly.

Perusing her naked body, he rubbed his forehead. "You truly are the epitome of German beauty. I can't wait to make you an honorary Aryan."

Her heartbeat picked up. "Have you had any news about it?"

"We're almost there. The Führer is waiting for the right occasion. But rest assured, it won't be long." He patted her thigh.

She decided to take advantage of his good mood and asked, "Walter, would it be possible for me to see my parents again?"

A glint of something crossed his eyes, before he nodded. "I'll arrange for it, although it might take some days."

"Thank you." She wondered what exactly was so difficult to arrange since her parents were held captive in the same building, but she knew better than to voice her thoughts.

"You'd better get dressed. You'll need to get up early in the morning." He finally dismissed her.

As soon as she had put on her clothes, she left his office for her room. When she slipped into bed next to her husband, he woke and wrapped a possessive arm over her breast.

"Not now, I'm tired, Ralf." She pushed his hand away.

Sniffing into the air, he said, "You've slept with Dobberke, I can smell him all over you."

"Even if I did, it's none of your business." She turned her back toward him, ending the discussion. A second later, his hand grabbed her chin, turning her head to face him. To ease the strain on her neck, she shifted her body until she came to lie on her back, glaring at him.

"You're wrong. My wife sleeping around is absolutely my business." He shrugged. "I don't care how often you do it with whoever you want as long as I get sex with you whenever I'm in the mood."

Thea gave a sheepish nod and smiled at him. "Let's talk tomorrow, I'm exhausted. It was a long day."

"I'm not tired. I want you now." Without leaving her time to respond, he rolled on top of her, forcing her legs apart with his thighs.

It was pointless to fight him; he was her husband after all. She closed her eyes, cursing herself for her stupidity in marrying him. If she were single, she would be Walter's fiancée by now. Luckily Ralf didn't have Walter's stamina and finished within five minutes, letting her finally go to sleep.

If only Hitler would make her an honorary Aryan real quick, then she wouldn't hesitate for a second to divorce Ralf.

The next morning she woke up, tired and sore.

"Where should we start our hunt today?" Ralf asked her with a happy smirk.

She glared daggers at him. "Go to hell."

"What's wrong with you?" He looked at her confused, until it seemed to click in his brain. "Don't tell me you're cross about last night?"

A knock on the door relieved her from having to answer.

"Come in." It was Ingrid, neatly dressed in her nurse's

uniform. If the other woman loathed Thea for contending her position as first mistress to Dobberke, she didn't show it.

"You're needed upstairs, Thea."

"On my way."

"Morning, Thea," an SS guard greeted her. "Two kitchen workers didn't show up and they need someone to distribute breakfast to the prisoners."

"Why me?" She pouted.

"Because you're the only female currently available," he answered with a smug grin.

"Why don't they just skip breakfast for the prisoners, they'll soon be sent on a transport anyway."

He broke out into a chuckle. "I like your thinking. But you know, orders."

"Right, I'm on my way." Thea went to the kitchen and then delivered the trays of food with the full contempt she felt for Jews making her life so difficult. If it weren't for their damaging behavior, Hitler would never have had to resort to such drastic measures.

She opened the door to another cell and recoiled with shock. The tray would have plummeted to the floor, if the prisoner hadn't jumped up and caught it from her trembling hands.

"Thea? What are you doing here?" He seemed to be as shocked as she was.

"Me?" She swallowed hard, confusing emotions attacking her. Deep down she still harbored feelings for him, despite his refusal to let her move in with his family and the Falkensteins. None of this would have happened if he'd agreed to marry her, extending his status as a privileged Jew. "I'm just helping out in the kitchen."

He cocked his head, carefully perusing her appearance. "You wear quite nice clothes for a prisoner."

"Who says every prisoner must dress in rags?"

"The Nazis," he stated wryly, shaking his head. "So it is true? You work for the Gestapo?"

She felt herself flush, then pushed out her lower lip. "I had no choice."

"One always has a choice." David's eyes bore deep into hers, as if searching for something.

His haughty attitude pushed her shame away. "You can talk! You didn't have to live on the streets! You weren't arrested and hauled here! And you weren't flogged to shreds." Tears pricked at her eyes at the memory of Walter wielding the whip. He hadn't wanted to as he had explained later, when apologizing to her, but that didn't erase the horrific pain she'd experienced at his hands.

"Spare me the tears," David said, completely unmoved.

"You must believe me. I wanted none of this, they forced me. I had to comply in order to stay alive." More tears spilled down her cheeks. Why couldn't David understand that none of this was her fault? That she was the victim here? She wasn't one of the rascal Orthodox Jews invading Germany with their poverty, diseases and outdated ways of life. Everything was their fault. Without their existence, Hitler would never have pursued people like her.

David tilted his head. "There's a difference between complying and going out of your way to please them."

Fury snaked up her spine. How dare he ridicule her for giving her best? Did he know that catchers lived under the constant threat of joining the prisoners on their way to Auschwitz? Did he know that the only way to stay on good terms with Dobberke was to rise from the mediocre crowd and become indispensable? In more ways than one?

She glared at him, lacing her voice with ice as she answered, "You would have done the same, if you'd endured what I did."

"I absolutely understand that you caved in under torture, almost everyone does. But, Thea, did you really have to outdo yourself and become their star catcher? Not to mention Dobberke's little plaything?"

"It's not like that," she fumed. "He loves me. He even asked Hitler to make me an honorary Aryan."

David broke into a chuckle. "No shit! You're completely deluded. That man has lovers left and right. He's a one-hundred-and-fifty percent Nazi. What makes you think he's interested in more than cheap sex with you?"

"You're just jealous, because I chose him over you," she spat at him.

His expression grew serious. "You disgust me!"

"David, please." His rejection settled deep in her stomach, stabbing at her heart. If he hadn't set his mind on emigrating to Palestine, he'd never have abandoned her to live on that stupid Zionist training farm. Then, none of this would have happened and the two of them would have lived happily ever after.

Without another word, David turned around and settled on his cot, eating his breakfast, not deigning to look at her. Her shoulders slumped, she turned around, locking the door behind her, despairing at the world's injustice.

31

Helga had been a bundle of nerves ever since David hadn't returned home.

"What if he's dead?" she asked Heinrich.

"He probably got caught up somewhere."

"Or rather, he got caught by someone." Her voice was shrill.

"Mutti, please, calm down." Amelie had made careful inquiries through other members of the network the morning after David hadn't come home at night. She knew he'd been arrested, but she couldn't possibly tell this to her mother. Because then, Helga would start a full-on inquisition about the why and how. "I'm sure he's fine."

"How can you say that?" Her mother seemed near to tears. "For all we know he might be on the next transport to the East. Or worse..." Her shoulders heaving, she clung to the cupboard for balance.

"It won't do any good to fret until we know for sure what happened to him," Heinrich said.

"What if it's too late by then?" Helga looked as if she were going to have a nervous breakdown, but then recovered her aplomb and said, "I'll go to the police and ask for David's whereabouts."

"I'll come with you," Heinrich offered.

"No, you won't. I'm not risking your arrest, too." Helga shook her head, putting on her coat to leave the house.

Amelie fell in step with her. "Wait for me."

On their way to the bus station, she said, "Mutti. David has been arrested and is being held in the Jewish Hospital."

Helga turned, narrowing her eyes at her daughter. "How can you be so sure?"

Amelie twisted awkwardly. "Someone told me."

"Aha. Someone. May I ask who this someone is?"

"Not really."

Her mother exploded. "For God's sake, nobody in this house ever tells me anything! Even Julius with his broken thigh is secretive about whatever illegal things he does."

Despite knowing they were the only residents in the building, Amelie glanced over her shoulder. "You and Edith must be above suspicion. It is only because of you that the rest of us are still here. If they arrest you, we'll all be doomed."

"That doesn't mean you have to keep me in the dark about your activities." Helga's shoulders slumped.

Amelie chose to ignore her mother's gripe and explained, "David has been doing some stuff."

"Stuff?"

"Yes, you know—"

"No, I don't. As I already mentioned, nobody tells me anything."

"Because it's safer that way." Amelie shrugged. "If you wish, go and inquire at the Jewish Hospital, but it won't help. They won't let you go in there."

"How do you know?"

"Mutti..."

"You have tried that already, haven't you?"

"Not me."

Helga sighed. "And you're not going to tell me anything else, are you?"

"I can't." Amelie herself was out of her mind with worry for her brother, but she did her best not to show this to her mother, who had been on edge for weeks with all the burdens she already had to shoulder.

The bus arrived and Helga gave Amelie a quick embrace. "Take care, please. I can't lose you too."

"He's not dead yet, Mutti." It was poor consolation but it was all Amelie had to offer, as she watched her mother get on the bus before walking further down the street to the tram station.

She could have taken the bus, but preferred not to, so her mother didn't see her turning her jacket inside out before boarding. Just as she was about to do so, she sensed eyes boring into her back. Fear pooling deep in her gut, she turned around.

A black-haired woman dressed like a man approached her. "I need to talk to you, Amelie."

Narrowing her eyes at the peculiar stranger, she asked, "How do you know my name?"

The stranger glanced around to make sure nobody was within earshot, before she whispered, "I have news from David."

"Who are you?" Amelie's heart was beating wildly, yet she wasn't going to trust that easily.

"That's not important."

"It absolutely is, because I'm not trusting just anyone who walks up to me on the street, claiming she has news for me."

The stranger tilted her head, her electric-blue eyes perusing Amelie. "If you must know, I'm Roxi and I'm your brother's girlfriend."

What? Amelie almost toppled over. She knew David had gone out with a few girls after being cheated on by Thea, but it had never amounted to anything serious. Her jaw tensed. This must be a trap.

"I'd know you if you were." She turned on her heel and continued to walk down the street.

"Wait." Roxi hurried to fall into step with her. "I'm going to get him out of the transit camp, but I need your help."

Amelie froze in her tracks, turning to stare at the petite woman who'd made such a brazen remark. "And how exactly are you going to do that?"

"The same way David has retrieved others from police stations. Walk inside clad in uniform, demand they hand the person over and leave."

Amelie's eyes became wide. "How do you know about this?"

"I told you. I'm his girlfriend." Roxi glanced over her shoulder. "I'm also part of the network."

"With the pastor?" On purpose, she didn't mention his name, too deep ingrained was the necessity to be secretive.

A silent nod was the answer.

"Let's pretend I believe you." She wasn't fully convinced yet, but would give Roxi the benefit of the doubt. "How are you going to find him?"

"I already did. I visited him last night." Roxi cast her a smug grin.

"You're lying." The answer had convinced Amelie that Roxi wasn't honest.

"David knew you wouldn't believe me."

"If that is true, why did he send you? Doesn't make much sense, now does it?" Amelie inwardly shook her head. Whoever this woman was, she had to do better than that if she wanted to catch her unawares.

"Because you're the only person he trusts to help us."

"Us?" Amelie raised an eyebrow.

"David and me. Please, let me prove that I'm indeed who I say I am and want to break him out of prison."

"And how exactly are you planning to prove that?"

"Do you remember when his bicycle was stolen?"

Amelie involuntarily flinched at the memory. She quickly composed herself and said, "Maybe."

"He came home, beaten to a pulp. You found him on the staircase, helped him into your apartment and cleaned his wounds. You even gave him a towel to bite down on so as not to alert the Gerber children."

Amelie's eyes opened wider with every word. Back then, David had sworn her to secrecy, since he didn't want to worry their parents. Still, a doubt remained. One of his attackers might have spilled the beans, or the Gestapo had beaten the story out of David. But why would he divulge such a random detail?

She scrutinized Roxi's face, seeing only honesty and genuine caring there. "I'll have his head for keeping a girlfriend from me."

Roxi giggled. "He's all yours, but first, we need to get him out."

"How am I supposed to help?"

"Come with me for a walk?" Roxi answered with a question of her own.

"I need to get to work."

"It won't take long. We can't risk anyone overhearing us."

Fear flickered through Amelie's body, before she relaxed. The petite, lithe woman wasn't a threat to her. "Alright."

"Better reverse your jacket," Roxi said with a pointed gaze toward Amelie's chest.

Flushing, she replied, "He told you everything, didn't he?"

"Most of it. I have you covered while you make the star disappear." Roxi stepped in front of Amelie to shield her from the view of random passersby. When she was done, Roxi linked arms with her as if they were best friends. Seconds later she broke out into a girlish giggle.

Just as Amelie was about to roll her eyes at the stupid behavior, two SS men strode around the corner.

"...he's soooo incredibly handsome. I hope he asks me out soon," Roxi gushed with a dreamy expression on her face, before gazing at the SS men, as if she hadn't noticed them already.

The soldiers ignored them, and Amelie heard one of them say, "What a carefree life these girls have."

"Thanks," Amelie said, her heart racing at the thought of what might have happened if the SS men had asked for her papers.

"Don't mention it." Roxi unlinked her arm and walked toward a bombed-out house, clambering across a pile of rubble with surprising speed and agility, before she sat down in a spot shielded from view.

Amelie precariously slithered down the rubble and came to a halt next to Roxi. "So, what is your plan?"

"I need a uniform."

Amelie smirked. "I don't think they come in your size."

Roxi looked at her as if she'd gone nuts, before her mouth tipped upward. "You two have the same wry humor. It's not for me. If you haven't guessed already, I'm trying to keep away from the authorities."

Nodding, Amelie bit her tongue. This wasn't the time to ask questions about Roxi's background.

"David said to ask Leutnant Hesse to help us."

"Frau Falkenstein's brother? I don't even know how to reach him, and I wouldn't want to involve his sister."

"No need. In David's drawer in your shared bedroom is a business card with Hesse's office number."

Amelie's jaw dropped to the floor. "He really did tell you everything."

"Not everything, but a lot." Roxi cast her a pleading gaze.

"Will you contact him and arrange for a meeting with me? Please?"

Slowly, Amelie nodded.

"David told me he's earmarked for the next transport to Auschwitz." A visible shudder racked Roxi's frame and Amelie wondered how much she knew. Since no one had returned from that place to tell the tale, rumors were all they had. Regretfully, none of those rumors left space for hope.

"Don't worry, I want him back, too. If only to give him a good dressing-down for hiding you from me."

"Don't be too strict with him," Roxi chuckled. "It was my wish to stay hidden. I may not have to wear a star, nonetheless my mere existence apparently is a threat to the Reich."

Amelie could no longer keep her curiosity in check. "Are you a political or something?"

"Something. I'm Romani and the Nazis have all but expelled my people from Germany."

"Oh." Amelie had never talked to a Romani before. Roxi didn't at all fit the stereotype of a stealing, cheating, dirty, traveling person. Although on second glance, perhaps she did with her pitch-black hair, the darker complexion and the stealthy way she moved.

"Are you disappointed that I don't fit the Nazis' racial profile?" Despite trying to sound amused, sadness laced Roxi's voice.

Amelie shook her head. "I just never met a gypsy before."

"Romani."

"Isn't that the same?"

Roxi rolled her eyes. "Please. Don't make me explain to you how denigrating that name is."

"I'm sorry. I... I guess I was too caught up in our own misery to consider the other minorities suffering under that maniac."

"Back to our more immediate problem. When you call

Leutnant Hesse's office number, leave a message saying you have news from his sister." Roxi stood and made to leave.

"Wait. How do I let you know?"

"No need. He'll know where to meet me."

"You're not going to tell me, are you?"

"Nope. You know the drill." Without further explanation Roxi disappeared like a ghost.

Amelie stared at the place where she had been sitting seconds earlier, shaking her head at what she had learned over the last few minutes. Then she hastened toward the tram station, not wanting to arrive late for work. Several steps later she angrily shook her head and changed directions. The foreman could punish her all he wanted, but first she was going to fetch Leutnant Hesse's phone number and call him. If David truly was earmarked for transport to Auschwitz, time was of the essence.

32

"A moment please, Leutnant Hesse, there's a message for you," the receptionist said as Knut was about to leave for lunch. "The caller said she has news from your sister."

"Thank you." Knut frowned, wondering who that woman might be, since this was the code phrase he'd agreed on with David. "Did she say anything else?"

"No." She gave him an unsure look. "Should I have asked for more details? I didn't want to pry."

"Not at all. I was just wondering. I'll give my sister a call." As he walked toward the canteen he fought with himself to swing by Edith's place, instead of waiting to meet David—or whoever had called—at the zoo the next day. Then he dismissed the notion. After the failed Stauffenberg coup, he needed to avoid anything out of the ordinary. So far the Gestapo hadn't connected the dots. They'd let him go after a thorough interrogation, during which Knut had hopefully been able to show them his innocence.

In any case, he was most likely under surveillance. It wouldn't do any good to attract unwanted attention. If only he could talk to Bernd... out of the blue a wave of grief attacked him, pressing the air out of his lungs. For several long seconds he wasn't able to inhale, until black dots danced in front of his eyes and somehow his reflexes returned.

Welcoming the fresh oxygen streaming into his cells he willed himself to continue walking. For so many reasons, it was essential nobody knew about his crippling grief. At the canteen he greeted a few colleagues, made a friendly face when the traitor Fromm entered and engaged in idle talk, all while he fought the subdued atmosphere in the Bendlerblock.

Everywhere else men might celebrate the failed coup, but here, even those who stood firm on Hitler's side were afraid of being ensnared in the tightening net cast by the Gestapo, which no doubt would produce some incidental catches too. Left and right, colleagues were arrested and executed after a sham trial in the Volksgerichtshof, presided over by the vicious President of the People's Court, Roland Freisler. If there was ever a man unworthy of being called a *judge*, it was him. Theoretically bound to the law, his verdicts served exclusively the Nazi ideology. Furthermore, he enjoyed denigrating and humiliating the defendants during his trials.

A shudder raced down Knut's spine. Several hundred members of the resistance had been arrested so far and about one hundred executed. It was only a matter of time until he was going to be arrested as well. The thought surprised him. If he didn't have a chance to escape, should he even try to stay hidden?

He brushed his thoughts aside. Tomorrow he would meet David at the zoo and find out how he could help.

After not having been in the zoo for years, Knut entered for the second time in a few months. Even here, in the huge Tiergarten Park, Allied bombs had caused horrible damage. He passed by the lions' house, or rather the pile of rubble that used to be an enclosure, wondering what had happened to the lions. Hopefully they hadn't been able to escape, left to wander through Berlin's streets chasing the residents for their next meal.

As he reached the elephant enclosure, a woman with three small children stood there, the little ones gushing over the majestic animals. She surely hadn't come here to meet him, but there wasn't anyone else, either.

Knut decided to wait for a few minutes and settled on a nearby bench, pretending to admire the elephants. Suddenly, he sensed a person coming up from behind. Before he could crane his neck, a female voice said, "Don't look. Wait until the woman and her children are gone. Then walk toward the fence. I'll meet you there."

His mind going a mile a minute, he resisted the urge to risk a glance at her. She probably had a reason for being so secretive. The seconds ticked over painfully slowly, turning into minutes, when at long last the mother asked her children, "Who wants to see the monkeys?"

"Me! They're so cute!" The children fell into single file, following her to the next enclosure.

Knut had barely gotten up to leisurely stroll toward the fence, when he saw a black-haired woman with the most brilliant electric-blue eyes approach him with a wave of her hand.

"Knut, there you are." She linked arms with him, leading him away from the elephants and toward the hippo's pond, where a mother hippo and her cub were happily bathing in mud-crusted water.

"It's a lot quieter here," she said. Then she turned around to look at him, even as she frisked their surroundings. "I must apologize for the ambush. David has been arrested and taken to the transit camp at the Jewish Hospital. He's earmarked for transport to Auschwitz later this week."

Despite the shocking news, a heavy weight lifted from Knut's shoulders. Edith was alright. "And you are?"

"I'm... I help with his clandestine activities." She seemed to fight with herself, before she pushed out her lower lip. "And I'm David's girlfriend. I'm going to break him out of the camp, whether you agree to help me or not."

Knut bit back a chuckle at her fierce determination. "I haven't said anything yet. First I need to know your plan, Fräulein...?"

"Roxi. Just call me Roxi." Her shoulders relaxed. "So, we thought—"

He interrupted her. "Who's we?"

"David and I."

Immediately his brain raised an alarm. "I thought he was in the holding camp."

"He is. I broke in and talked to him two nights ago."

"You did what?" Appraising her sinewy stature and fierce expression, he almost believed she might be capable of pulling off such a feat.

"That's got nothing to do with it." Her expression became mulish.

"On the contrary. If you want me to risk my life breaking David out, we'll have to trust each other."

She seemed to mull over his words, because she averted her eyes. After observing the hippo cub for a full minute, she nodded. "Don't judge me. We all do things we're not proud of to survive."

At her pleading gaze, he bowed his head in agreement.

"I'm quite the proficient façade climber. It was almost too easy to get to an open window on the third floor, then find David in a cell on the first floor." She gave an apologetic shake of her head. "I would have freed him right away, but there was no way I could force the cell door open—and I wasn't sure how to get him out of the building."

Knut pursed his lips. The image of a catlike woman climbing up the walls suited her. "So you talked to him and came to the conclusion that I might somehow be able to help? I don't know anyone at the holding camp."

"I admit, the plan is a bit bare-bones, but it has worked before."

He raised his eyebrows, curious.

"You go to the holding center, wave your Wehrmacht ID card and demand you need to transfer the prisoner David Goldmann for questioning. Then you simply march out with him through the front door."

He broke into a chuckle. "Really? That's the plan?"

Roxi glared daggers at him. "Do you have anything better?"

"Calm down. A minute ago I didn't even know David had been arrested." He held up his hands in defense.

"I'm sorry."

"It's fine." Knut hesitated for a moment. "I believe I'm under surveillance."

Instantly the alarm went off in Roxi's head, as evidenced by her unsettled gaze. "You've been followed?"

"No." Knut shook his head. "I've been careful. You must have heard about the Stauffenberg coup?" After her nod, he continued. "Everyone in the Bendlerblock, including me, has been questioned. While the Gestapo let me go, I don't want to do anything to attract unwanted attention." *Like breaking out a Jewish prisoner from the holding camp.*

A flicker of admiration shone in her eyes, as she whispered, "You were involved."

It was made as a statement, not a question, therefore Knut didn't bother to acknowledge or deny her conclusion. He hadn't come here to be celebrated as a hero.

A long silence hung between them, only interrupted by birds tweeting in a nearby tree and the hippo calf's happy grunts. The little calf was perhaps a third of his mother's size, nonetheless it must weigh several hundred kilos.

Mulling over the implications, Knut finally decided that he had nothing to lose—and David had everything to gain.

"I'll do it."

"Really?" Roxi gazed at him, her eyes shining with gratitude.

"When?"

"The earlier the better—the transport is scheduled for Friday."

Thinking carefully about the usual procedure, he came to the conclusion it was best to request the transfer in the morning, since most interrogations were done during the day. "Alright. Tomorrow morning it is. I'll do it alone. If everything works according to plan, I'll drop him off at the fishing club *Gut Biss*, at Tegeler Lake. Do you know where that is?"

"I'll find out."

"At this time of year nobody will be there, so he can hide there during the day, but he must leave before curfew."

"I will—"

He raised his hand. "Don't tell me anything. And if David isn't there, you mustn't contact me, because that means something went wrong."

"Understood. Thank you again."

"Goodbye, Roxi."

As soon as she'd left, he sighed and in his mind he spoke to Bernd. *What have I gotten myself into?*

You're doing the right thing. You must continue our fight.

I miss you so much.

33

The door opened and an orderly entered David's cell.

"Get up, there's a visitor for you." The smirk on the man's face promised nothing good.

David suppressed a sigh, as he followed the order.

"Don't try anything stupid," the orderly warned him, pointedly gazing at the baton hanging from his hip.

After Roxi's visit, David had been mulling incessantly about her promise. Now he wondered whether this was part of her plan to break him out. If it was, he'd be alert and use whatever opportunity came along. In an attempt to get more information, he teased the orderly. "Why would I try to run? It's not like I can just walk out of here if I knock you down, can I?"

"You crazy or what? All doors are locked and we have guards." Another smirk followed his words. "Try if you want, you'll end up being flogged to shreds." A slight shudder racked his shoulders. "Or better don't. Not everyone survives the treatment."

David pretended to be cowed. "No, thanks. I'm not suicidal."

"Haha." The orderly prodded him forward with the baton. "Don't want to keep your visitor waiting, do you?"

In Dobberke's office, a tall blond man in Wehrmacht uniform stood with his back to David. Adrenaline shot through his veins. He almost didn't believe his own eyes, because he recognized Knut Hesse right away. David suppressed the happy smile wanting to spread on his face. Instead, he cast his eyes downward, pretending to be afraid.

"Is this the prisoner you want? David Goldmann?" one of the guards, an SS-Sturmmann asked, waving at the orderly to leave.

"Yes. He's one of our agents and you fools arrested him."

The Sturmmann flinched, but recovered quickly. "Your department staged a coup, not ours. So, who are the fools?"

Knut ferociously stared the other man down. "Is that the way to behave toward a superior officer?"

The Sturmmann seemed to deflate under the scathing gaze, yet didn't give up. "Excuse me, Herr Leutnant. Do you have a transfer slip?"

"Let me explain to you once more: this man is an *underground* agent on a *top-secret* mission. Naturally I do not have a transfer order. We don't usually broadcast the identity of our agents to the enemy."

"But... Herr Leutnant... I can't just give you a prisoner without a signed order."

Knut gazed at the young man. "Would it help if I sign a piece of paper for you?"

In awe, David gaped from one man to the other, feeling strangely detached from the discussion, despite being the reason for their argument.

"I would rather wait until Scharführer Dobberke returns, he's in charge of the camp," the Sturmmann said, visibly unsure.

"When will that be?"

"He's expected back tonight."

"You don't really want me to wait around here all day?" Knut's voice was surprisingly calm, belying the pulsating vein in his temple.

"Perhaps if Scharführer Dobberke gives you a call at your office when he's back?"

Knut's fist slammed on the desk. David hadn't seen it coming and jumped backward against the wall, seeing the Sturmmann flinch in his seat. "This agent has to continue his work immediately, or your unwillingness to cooperate will destroy the entire mission. Do you want to be responsible for that?"

David watched in awe how the haughty SS man shriveled to a piece of nothing in his seat and mumbled, "But... but... I thought the Abwehr operates only abroad?"

Knut fixed him with an ice-cold stare, one corner of his mouth tipping up. "And how do you think the agent will get there, if you hold him captive?" Seeing how the Sturmmann was at the point of breaking down, Knut issued another threat. "If this mission goes belly up, I'll make sure to let Brigadeführer Schellenberg know who is responsible for it." Knut pulled out a notepad and pen from his breast pocket. "Name, rank and department, please."

"Wait." The Sturmmann blanched. "I don't think that will be necessary. If you just sign a paper, stating that I handed the prisoner—"

"Agent," Knut corrected, in a clipped tone.

"That I handed the agent over to you, it should suffice." His eyes were filled with anxiety.

Knut gave an exaggerated sigh and returned his notepad and pen to his pocket. "Alright, where do I sign?"

"Here, please." His hands trembled as he pointed at the line with David's name on a list of inmates.

David craned his head. He didn't dare to move for fear the Sturmmann was tempted to ask questions about his supposed role with the Abwehr. Narrowing his eyes, he believed to make out the word "Auschwitz" next to his name. Whatever it was, Knut scratched it out and wrote "Transfer to Wehrmacht" next to it, then scribbled an illegible signature next to it.

"Thank you. Don't mention the incident to anyone." Knut turned around, nodded at David and said, "Let's go. We've lost enough time as it is."

"Yes, Herr Leutnant," David said loudly, hoping this was the expected form of behavior for an agent. While he followed Knut to the exit, he barely dared to breathe as he hoped he wouldn't meet anyone—least of all Thea.

At the exit Knut showed the transfer slip to the guard and they stepped into freedom.

"Thank you," David whispered, unsure what to do next.

"Follow me." Knut led him to a parked Wehrmacht vehicle and motioned for him to get into the passenger seat, while positioning himself behind the steering wheel. His anxiety was evident in the white knuckles as he drove them through the morning traffic.

After a full minute, Knut let out a sigh. "That went surprisingly well."

"Thank you so much. You saved my life."

"Don't celebrate just yet. You need to disappear. Completely."

David raised an eyebrow. So far, he hadn't given it much thought, but Knut was correct; David couldn't return home and pretend nothing had happened.

"I can't help you with that and I don't want to know where you are, either. For the sake of both of us, make sure nobody finds you before this damned war is over."

"I will." David had no idea, how, or where he was going to hide. "Rest assured I will never mention your name."

Knut snorted. "If you're found that won't be necessary, surely the Sturmmann at the camp will gladly testify as to who got you out."

A worrying thought shot through David's mind. "What if Dobberke phones Schellenberg?"

"He won't." Knut narrowed his eyes. "I wish Admiral Canaris was still in charge, he was on our side."

"Unbelievable." David's eyes threatened to fall out of his head at the revelation. He'd never once considered the possibility that the Wehrmacht leadership might be against Hitler, not even after the failed Stauffenberg coup.

"I'll drop you off at a fishing club." Knut turned his head, a small smile lighting up his features. "Hide there until your girlfriend picks you up. Just make sure you're gone before curfew."

"You met her?" Suddenly David was giddy to give Roxi a passionate kiss.

"Yes. Quite the impressive young woman. Take care of her."

"She doesn't need taking care of." David slightly relaxed, leaning back into the passenger seat, watching the landscape pass by. It had been ages since his last ride in a car, with the exception of the police car after his arrest.

"Everyone needs someone." Knut's expression saddened, and David wanted to put a hand on his arm in consolation. Since that was completely inappropriate, he simply offered, "Your sister speaks very highly of you."

"I failed her. I'm a lousy brother." The grief in Knut's voice was overwhelming.

"You certainly aren't. I don't know you all that well, but I can assure you, you're a very fine man." Gazing at Knut's brooding look, he added, "My mother told me that you protested at the Rosenstrasse alongside the women. That was very brave of you."

"Too little, too late. I should have plotted against Hitler much earlier, perhaps then..." His face became a mask of guilt and exhaustion.

"Should've, would've, could've. It's no use regretting anything. Nobody could have known how this would unfold.

The important thing is that you changed your course and are fighting back now." David genuinely meant it. His communist ex-colleagues at the workshop had hated Hitler and his politics from the first day, yet even they had never taken up arms to fight him. What Knut had done was a lot more than ninety-nine percent of German citizens could say for themselves.

A small smile crept onto Knut's face, but he kept silent, steering them through backstreets until they arrived at a lake. "I'm going to drop you off over there. Seek shelter in the open shed next to the boathouse. Hide for the day, but be gone before curfew, there's a guard patrolling at night due to the vicinity of the Bergmann-Borsig Factory."

"Alright." David knew about the munitions factory and the frequent Allied air raids on it, which increased the fire risk in the adjacent areas, and apparently in the fishing club, too.

"Just in case someone is watching us, I'll walk to the boathouse and get my fishing gear, presumably for repair. While I'm gone, you sneak out of the vehicle," Knut said as he parked next to a hedge.

"Thank you again for your help," David croaked out past the lump forming in his throat. "I hope we will meet again after the war."

Knut looked at him with terrible sadness in his eyes. "I don't believe I will survive that long. If you see my sister, tell her I love her very much and I'm sorry to have been so blind for so many years. I should have acted much earlier."

"I will." David tilted his head, perturbed that Knut seemed so certain not to survive the war. "You're a good man."

"Good luck to you." Knut stopped the motor and got out to walk toward the boathouse in long, confident strides.

David slipped out of the driver's door, which Knut had left open and disappeared around the bushes, into the open shelter.

. . .

When Knut arrived at his apartment, the Gestapo was waiting for him.

"Leutnant Knut Hesse, you are arrested for high treason and participating in a conspiracy against our Führer."

"Excuse me? That is an absolutely ridiculous accusation! I'm a loyal member of the Abwehr."

"Save your breath for the interrogation."

Knut inhaled. He intended not to confess anything. It wouldn't make a difference to himself, but he hoped to spare those who were still free. If he was tortured, he'd put the blame on those already dead or sentenced to death by Roland Freisler's notorious sham of a People's Court.

But there was nothing to deny, because the Gestapo had his crimes in black and white, obtained through confessions of others who either hadn't withstood torture or had tried to save their own necks, ratting out their colleagues. It didn't matter how they'd obtained it.

After two days, Knut literally threw up his hands and admitted his involvement in planning the Stauffenberg coup, not caring what would happen to him next. He half-expected a bullet to his head right then and there, but that wasn't to be. Instead he was returned to a cell in the Gestapo prison at Prinz-Albrecht-Strasse. The next day, he was transferred to Plötzensee Prison, without being told a word about his fate. He spent several days agonizing about what would become of him, when the guard announced, "You have a visitor."

34

Edith was worried. Knut hadn't shown up to their bi-weekly meeting in a café, so she decided to pass by his apartment. As soon as she entered the building, an elderly lady shot out of the ground floor apartment, wearing the party sign on her collar.

"Where are you going?"

It was none of her business, but Edith wasn't interested in causing trouble with the person who appeared to be the Block-wart, therefore she answered, "I'm visiting Leutnant Hesse."

The woman's face turned into a stony grimace. "He was arrested about a week ago."

Edith's knees threatened to give out under her. "But... why?"

"I've seen you visiting before, who are you?"

Again, none of her business, yet Edith indulged her. "I'm his sister. Edith..." She hesitated for just a beat, before using her maiden name. "Hesse. Very pleased to finally meet you, my brother has praised you most highly."

The woman's eyes went wide, showing surprise and plea-sure, before they dimmed with suspicion. "Lisa Stenzel, I'm the Blockwart. So, you don't know?"

"I'm afraid not." Edith had lived under the Nazi yoke for such a long time, deceit had become second nature. Without batting an eyelid, she gracefully lied. "I was out of town for several weeks, attending to my ailing parents."

"I shouldn't be telling you anything," Frau Stenzel said, clearly itching to tattle everything she knew.

Edith had met the type: gossipy people, filled with their own little importance, never able to shut up about anything, however secret, unsavory or untrue it was. She simply had to give Frau Stenzel a tiny nudge for her to spill the beans.

"I hope he wasn't doing anything detrimental to the war effort, it would bring such a shame over our family."

It was the cue the Blockwart had been waiting for. She puffed herself up. "It's a rather delicate issue."

Now Edith was intrigued. What on earth could she mean? Knut had never introduced a girlfriend to her and she couldn't imagine him engaging in anything improper, or whatever this woman was suggesting. She pursed her lips to show disapproval. "Do tell me."

Lowering her voice to an important whisper, Frau Stenzel bent forward. "He's been having male visitors."

Confused, Edith answered, "He was arrested for inviting friends over?"

"*Gnädige Frau.* He was inviting *that* kind of friend, if you know what I mean."

Slowly it dawned on her. If what the woman said was true and Knut truly loved a man, he was in serious trouble. The Nazis disliked homosexuals almost as much as Jews. Even his rank of Leutnant wouldn't prevent him from being sent to a concentration camp. She felt her heart crack open, but she had to keep up appearances.

"How horrific!" Edith threw her hands up in the air.

"Isn't it? Just thinking such an abomination lived under the same roof as me," Frau Stenzel grimaced with disgust. "I'm glad the Gestapo arrested him. We surely don't need perverts in this building."

Edith nodded in agreement. "It looks like I won't visit him after all." Then she tilted her head. "Thank you for warning me."

"No problem at all, I'm here to serve."

"And it seems you're doing an outstanding job." Edith gave her a measured smile, about to bid her goodbyes, when the Blockwart suddenly offered, "If you'd like to retrieve any family memories before everything goes up for auction?"

"Such a generous offer, you can't imagine how grateful I am."

"Here's the key, go ahead and leave it in the mailbox for me."

Edith climbed the stairs, unlocked the door and entered Knut's place. She settled on the same sofa where he'd witnessed her devastation after being turned away at the Swiss border. As she relived the scene, she remembered the handsome man sitting at the dinner table with him, who'd quickly taken his leave when she'd shown up.

"Oh, Knut, why didn't you tell me?" She stared at the wall, tears pricking at her eyes as she considered how lonely he must have been, always hiding who he truly was, unable to share his burden with anyone.

After sitting in silence for several minutes, she grabbed the few things of value—both material and sentimental—to safe-keep them for him, hoping that one day soon, when the Nazis were defeated, he'd return from prison.

On her way home she took a detour to the Gestapo head-quarters, chilling fear all but petrifying her, as she asked after her brother's whereabouts, until she was finally told that he'd been transferred to Plötzensee Prison a few days prior.

. . .

The next morning she skipped work to pay Knut a visit, equipped with a chunk of bread and spare clothes she'd taken from his apartment. After a lengthy discussion with the receptionist, a sympathetic guard showed up and she was granted permission to see Knut for twenty minutes.

Unlike the Gestapo headquarters, which exuded danger and fear, the air in Plötzensee reeked of suffering and despair. As she was being led through the maze of cold and empty corridors, she thought she saw a puddle of blood on the floor. Blinking twice, it vanished. Her heart drummed faster against her ribs and she hastened her steps, while at the same time leaden dread seized her mind, slowing her way forward until she was about to turn on her heels and bolt.

Digging her fingernails deep into the flesh of her palms, she forced herself to follow the guard, who'd been kind enough to facilitate the unannounced visit.

Finally, he came to a stand before a steel door and said in a loud voice, "Twenty minutes. No touching. I'll be watching you." Then he winked at Edith and whispered, "What your brother did is admirable."

Confused by his admission, she was lost for words and merely nodded her agreement.

In the visitors' room, a disheveled figure slumped in a chair at the only table. He looked up when he heard the door opening, delight bursting over his features as he exclaimed, "Edith! What are you doing here?"

"Visiting you, of course."

"How did you pull this off? I was told traitors to the Reich aren't allowed visitors." He looked frightfully thin and battered.

Edith thought being homosexual was hardly treason. Yet, with the Nazis everything was possible. "Why didn't you tell me?"

"It wouldn't have been safe for you. The less you knew, the

better." His expression hardened, as he pressed his jaws tight, scrutinizing her face. "Did the authorities harass you?"

"No." She shook her head, confused by his apparent worry that he had somehow implicated her with his personal affairs. Kin liability was often used against political dissidents or resisters, but she'd never heard about someone punished for the sexual preferences of their family members. "I went to your apartment because you didn't show up to our meeting at the café—"

He sighed. "You shouldn't have. I should have told you not to come looking for me, if something happened."

"Oh, Knut." The urge to get up and wrap her arms around the picture of misery sitting on the other side of the table became overwhelming. Mindful of the guard's warning, she folded her hands in her lap and became businesslike. "We won't have long. I brought you a bit of food and some spare clothes."

"Where did you get them?" he asked, looking at the bundle she pushed over the table.

"At your place. Your Blockwart let me inside. She was also the one to tell me you had been arrested for your relationship with another man."

His jaw fell open, as he looked at her with utter shock. "That's what the old hag told you?"

"So, it isn't true?" Embarrassment flooded her system, even as she wished to hide in a mousehole.

"Yes, and no." He ran a hand through his greasy hair. "I do love another man—did love, because he's dead."

Edith couldn't stop her hand from reaching over the table to put over his, the immeasurable pain in his eyes hitting her very soul. "I'm so sorry."

The silence hung heavy in the room for a minute, before he spoke again. "That wasn't the reason for my arrest though. As far as I know, the authorities never found out," he scoffed. "At least unless the nosy Blockwart has told them. I was arrested for high treason, accused of participating in the planning of the Stauffenberg coup."

"Oh dear heavens!" She'd known for a long time that Knut disagreed with many issues of the Nazi ideology, yet she'd never once considered him actively partaking in a coup.

"That's why I never told you a word. I wanted to protect you in case they captured me."

"That's laudable. You still should have told me about your partner though." For the last day, she'd been warring with her conflicting emotions. The shock of Knut being one of *those* men still sat deep, as did the feeling of betrayal that he hadn't believed he could confide in her. She hadn't told anyone else, not even Julius. Hours of mulling over the issue all night and she finally concluded that it wasn't important. Knut was her brother and she'd continue to love him with every fiber of her soul.

If he survived the war, which she hoped with all her heart, they could talk about his reasons to keep the secret from her and start over fresh. For now, she simply wanted to give him all the support he needed.

"I would have wanted to meet him." Sadness choked Edith to a point that she needed to clear her throat several times. "After the others disowned me, you are the only family I have left."

Knut's eyes shone with affection. "You actually met him once. Do you remember your first visit at my place after being denied entry to Switzerland?"

She nodded, remembering all too well her very inappropriate breakdown, when she'd been lying on Knut's couch, bawling like a hysterical baby. "A handsome guy."

The smile on her brother's face lit up the entire room. Just then, a commotion outside caught their attention.

"Wait, you can't just go in there!"

"I can and I will!"

The next moment the door was flung open and a man in black SS uniform strode inside. The anger emanating from him all but pressed the air out of Edith lungs, making her gasp. "Joseph!"

Joseph tore his gaze from Knut, perusing Edith with so much cold hatred that she shuddered. "What are *you* doing here? I hope you don't feel sympathy with this traitor?"

Aware that any criticism of Führer or Fatherland would land her in a cell adjacent to Knut's within the blink of an eye, she chose her words carefully. "I wasn't told the reason for his arrest, so I came here to offer comfort to my brother."

"Now that you know, you should spit at him and leave."

"How can you say such a thing?" Edith was appalled.

Joseph ignored her and approached Knut with a menacing expression. Edith shot desperate pleas for help at the guard, who'd followed Joseph into the room. But he seemed too intimidated by the Standartenführer's insignia to utter a word, much less intervene.

"You disgust me! Scum like you don't deserve to wear this uniform!" Joseph made to rip the tunic from Knut's body. Just in time, Edith stepped between the two brothers.

"No touching," the guard ordered.

From somewhere she found the strength to straighten her shoulders and peer into Joseph's eyes. What she saw in there sent ripples of horror mixed with grief into her heart and body. This wasn't her brother, he was not even a feeling human being any longer. Nothing but glaring hatred resided in him. A monster disguised as a person.

"Step out of my way!" Joseph growled through tightened jaws, seemingly ready to pounce at her if she didn't follow his order.

Just as Edith feared he'd shove her aside, the guard, who must have raced away to call for help, returned with reinforcements.

"Standartenführer Hesse, while I completely understand your anger, I must ask you to step away from the prisoner." A man in his sixties with completely white hair stood in the room, exuding natural authority.

Joseph snapped out of his fury, turning his head toward the man. "Herr Director."

"The traitor will receive his due punishment, but I hope you'll understand that I can't allow you to take the law into your own hands."

"Certainly." Joseph visibly fought for calm, before he added, his voice dripping with contempt, "I shall personally see to it that this son of a bitch will be sentenced to death. Consider that a promise." Then he clicked his heels, shot his arm forward and shouted, "Heil Hitler! Down with the traitors!"

Too stupefied to utter a word, the director and the guard followed suit, shouting the *Hitlergruss* back at him.

Edith stepped into Joseph's path. "You can't do that. Knut's still your brother."

"I don't have a brother." His eyes fixed her with such coldness, her entire being chilled. "Step out of my way, or I'll get another death sentence for you."

Deep in her soul she realized that this wasn't an empty threat. This person standing in front of her was consumed by idolized love for his Führer and hatred for everyone who opposed him.

"I'm sorry," she said, stepping aside. "I'm so sorry for what has become of you."

Joseph didn't acknowledge her words and strode out of the room, the director and the guard on his heels.

Edith turned around and locked eyes with Knut, who'd risen from his chair. A feeling of desolation shattered her heart. It wasn't only his imminent fate that terrorized her—because she didn't doubt for a second that Joseph would follow through with his promise—but also the consequences for the rest of the country. As long as dehumanized men like Joseph occupied the positions of power, there was no hope to end the senseless blood shedding.

Using the unobserved moment, she fell into Knut's arms, whispering into his ear, "I love you and I'm incredibly proud of what you did."

"God bless you, Edith. I love you too. Promise me to stay safe and do everything to survive this war. It won't be long now."

Then the guard returned. "I'm sorry, Frau Falkenstein, but you need to leave."

"Thank you for allowing me to visit my brother," she told the guard, fighting against the tears wanting to drop.

A week later she received a package with Knut's wristwatch and a half-smoked packet of cigarettes, along with a note to inform her that he'd been executed for high treason.

35

JANUARY 1945

It was the third time her monthlies had not arrived and after a visit with the doctor, there was no doubt that Thea was with child. She had no time for a pregnancy. The incessant Allied air raids bombing Berlin to shreds combined with her personal precarious situation made it a folly to want to birth a child into this world.

She settled into a café, drinking a glass of cheap wine and smoking a cigarette to cope with the shock, as she entertained the idea of abortion. Despite it being strictly forbidden for Aryans, the procedure was welcomed and sometimes even enforced for Jews.

A thought struck terror through her as she realized that in order to get off scot-free she had to own up to being a Jewess, which was the last thing she wanted. Just a week ago Dobberke had told her that, finally, her Honorary Aryan certification had been signed by Hitler and merely had to go through some formalities before it could be officially announced.

Thea smiled. With that certificate, her future was looking a lot brighter. It wasn't worth risking her future status by asking the doctor for an abortion. She certainly wasn't going to use some back-alley midwife to get rid of the baby, because she intended to stay alive until the war ended.

Leaning back in her chair, observing the other patrons, she had an epiphany. While she couldn't pinpoint who had fathered the baby, Walter Dobberke was the most probable candidate.

Perhaps it was time to think strategically and use the pregnancy for her own benefit. Her husband Ralf was a loser, whom she'd completely lost interest in. Walter, on the other hand, held her life in the palm of his hands. Tying herself to him via his offspring would strengthen her position. He might even marry her, elevating her above anyone else in the camp, removing the stigma of being a Jew once and for all.

Yes, that was the solution! She paid for her drink and hastened back home, where she knocked on Dobberke's office door.

"Thea? You're back early, has something happened?"

"Can I talk to you for a minute, Herr Scharführer?" On his nod, she closed the door, mulling over how best to broach the topic. A shudder raced down her spine as she wondered whether she should have waited until he called her to his bed.

"If this isn't a good time, it can wait," she hedged.

His features softened as he stood up and walked around his desk to put his hands on her shoulders. "If it has to do with your Aryan certification, I have it from a trusted source that it's about to be delivered within the next days."

"That's fantastic news." She beamed at him. Seeing how he involuntarily licked his lips she decided there was no time like the present. "I do have good news myself."

"Do you now?" His hands moved downward to pinch her nipples. "Let me guess. Another successful catch? How many did you arrest this time?"

Her smile broadened and she tilted her neck to gaze into his eyes. "I'm pregnant."

His hands fell away and he stepped backward, as he said in a clipped tone, "Congratulations to you and your husband."

She shook her head, the lie leaving her lips without remorse. "Ralf and I haven't... in a long time. The child is yours."

His features derailed, as he took another step backward staring at her as if she were a monster. "You're lying!"

"But, Walter—" she tried to appease him, shocked at his appalled expression.

"Don't you dare call me by my first name! You lying Jewish whore!"

"But... but... I thought you loved me?" The betrayal sent hot tears into her eyes.

His sneer cut deep into her flesh. "Love you? A dirty Jewish bitch? Did you really believe I would fall for a subhuman lout?"

Biting her lip, she nodded with big eyes as the realization dawned on her that he'd been using her all this time. The sweet words, the soft caresses, nothing had been genuine—it had been a calculated move to make her pliant to his every desire. Another, even graver discovery sent icy chills into her limbs.

"My certification as an Honorary Aryan?"

"You really believed that shit?" He guffawed, slapping his knees. "You're even more stupid than I thought. Hitler despises your kind, he would never."

Shaken to the core, she sensed tears rolling down her cheeks, unable to keep them at bay any longer.

Dobberke stared at her pensively, before he stepped nearer, took her chin into his hand and forced her to lock eyes with him. "If you as much as insinuate to anyone that I ever touched you, I'll personally flog you to death."

Fighting not to break down, she rasped, "I won't."

"Good girl. Now leave and forget everything that happened between us."

Sniffing, she stood up, a leaden exhaustion pressing down

on her. With the doorknob in her hand, she turned around and asked with a small voice, "May I still see my parents?"

His eyes became wide with disbelief, before he snorted. "Never seen anyone as gullible as you. They went on a transport weeks ago."

It took a few seconds before Thea understood the meaning behind his words, then an agonizing burn made its way through her body, spreading all the way into her fingers and toes, rendering her brain useless as the only thing she felt was hot, searing pain.

"You... you vile liar!" she spat out.

Dobberke's answer was a bored shrug. "If that is all, I'd like to get back to my work."

She couldn't resist the small flame of rebellion lighting up in her soul. The safety of her parents had been her initial reason to work for the Gestapo—before she'd become addicted to success, praise and esteem, before she'd become Dobberke's mistress, enjoying the benefits he bestowed on her.

Deprived of his benevolent hand held up over her, what did she have to lose?

"You broke our deal."

"I didn't realize we had a deal." His voice was calm as a pond in still air.

"We had. You promised to keep my parents here if I worked for you."

"Did I?" He raised an eyebrow.

Fuming with scorn, she straightened her shoulders. "I'm not going to catch anymore Jews for you."

"Is that so?" Finally, something akin to a smile showed up on his lips.

"Yes." Thea was filled with jubilation. He was lost without his star Jew catcher. He needed her as much a she needed him. She was the reason his superiors held him in high esteem. She was the reason he never lacked for newcomers to fill his quota.

Recovering her sangfroid she gazed at him daring him to contradict her.

"That's very unfortunate."

Dread crept over her skin as he took up a notebook and opened it. Hot and cold shivers raced down her spine when she recognized the transport list. She inched toward him, hissing, "What are you doing?"

"Putting your name on the list. Wasn't that what you wanted?" He looked up at her, his eyes completely devoid of emotion.

The consequences of her rebellion seeped into her brain, a paralyzing fear taking over her heart, soul and body. All she could do was shake her head.

Dobberke cast her a questioning gaze, raising one eyebrow. The hand holding the pen hovered motionlessly an inch above the paper, ready to plunge down and write her name on the list, condemning her to unspeakable horrors before her inevitable death.

In that moment she realized that he had craved to possess not only her body, but also her mind. He relished the absolute power he held over her, making her do whatever his heart desired, for the simple reason that he could end her life with a stroke of his pen. It was the most embarrassing situation: having to admit that she, Thea Dalke, neé Blume, master manipulator, had been played. To add insult to injury, Dobberke apparently expected her to beg.

Shaken by the injustice, she seethed with anger at his twist. How dare he play such a dirty trick on her? Hadn't she always obeyed his every whim? Why did he now turn against her? Hadn't she proven her worth over and over again? Wasn't a promise worth anything these days?

"Please, don't send me on a transport." Since she knew from SS men on home leave that all the rumors were true, she was prepared to throw herself to her knees and lick Dobberke's boots to make him change his mind.

"I might not, if..." He fixed his gaze on her, remaining silent for an excruciating long amount of time, while Thea lowered her eyes, her heart beating rapidly in her chest. After a while she sank down to her knees, willing to submit the essence of her being to him. "I beg you. Please allow me to stay in the camp."

Even a flogging, which he seemed to enjoy so much, held its appeal over being sent to Auschwitz and just as she considered offering herself up for his cruel penchant, he finally raised his voice again. "Go back to work. Step up your game—catch a dozen Jews by the end of the week and you're off the hook."

A dozen? She shut her mouth before she could utter the words. Dobberke knew as well as she did that this was virtually impossible, as nearly all Jews had been swiped from Berlin's streets. Those remaining were the most savvy, cunning ones who knew how to evade SS, catchers and everyone else after them.

"Thank you, Herr Scharführer," she croaked and left his office on wobbly knees. Back in her room, she cried at how unfairly she'd been treated and how miserable her life was.

36

At first, David had wanted to seek shelter in the Swedish church, but Roxi convinced him that it wasn't a good choice, since Pastor Perwe had explicitly forbidden to stage a rescue operation, out of fear of exposing the network and risking many more lives in the process.

Sadly, the pastor had died shortly after David's breakout in a plane crash on his way home to Malmö. David believed the rumor that the Nazis had caused the plane crash to get rid of the man whom they had suspected to work against them. From the first day he'd taken up his post as Birger Forell's successor—who had returned to Sweden at the Gestapo's instigation—he'd been a thorn in the Nazis' side.

Perwe's successor, Erik Myrgren, a former seamen's pastor, had yet to get his bearings in his new parish and harboring David would cause undue friction.

"I can't stay out here all winter," he complained to Roxi, who only laughed.

"Spoilt much? What do you think I've been doing all these years?"

"I swear, this is the coldest winter in my life, and it'll only get worse. Also, with the incessant bombing there really aren't any safe places in the city." He'd been mulling over the issue for several days and had come to the conclusion that the risk of getting re-captured was increasing with every day he stayed in Berlin.

"Where else would you go?" Roxi asked.

"I've told you about my Aunt Feli, haven't I? She's living in Oranienburg in a huge house."

"She is also a Nazi of the first order." A shudder racked Roxi's frame.

David put his arm around her shoulders. "That has never hindered her from helping my family. I'm sure she'll take us in. She might not be delighted about it, but she'll do it nonetheless."

"Perhaps she'll take you, not so sure about me."

He'd naturally assumed Aunt Feli would welcome Roxi for the sole reason that she was David's girlfriend, so he hurried to assure her. "Don't you worry about that. She'll love you the same way I do."

Finally, Roxi grinned. "I hope, not *exactly* the same way."

"Yes, that image is rather yucky." He got up from the frozen ground in the bombed-out ruin they'd spent the night in. "Come on, we have a train to catch."

"Are you sure?" she drawled.

"Absolutely." He stretched out his hand to help her up, surprised when she took it. A little devil whispered into his ear, so he pulled her hand a little harder than necessary. Unprepared, she lost her balance and fell square into his arms, giving him the opportunity to steal a quick kiss.

"Hey, that's not fair," she protested laughing and wagged her finger at him. "When you expect it least, I'll get my revenge."

"Can't wait," David sniggered.

· · ·

Two hours later, they arrived at Aunt Feli's. The smoking chimney promised a warm house, despite the thick layer of snow in the garden and on the roof.

Just as David was about to ring the bell, Roxi tugged at his sleeve. "I should probably leave."

"Don't, please."

With discomfort written on her face, she said, "But if she doesn't want me, you must promise to stay with her without me."

David agreed, although he had no intention of obeying her request. He'd never leave Roxi to fend for herself.

The maid answered the door, her eyes opening wide as she recognized David, whom she had known since he was a little boy. "David! What a surprise!"

"Hello, Laura, can we come in?"

Only now did Laura seem to notice Roxi, who'd been hiding behind David's back. A flicker of uncertainty crossed her eyes. "I don't know. Frau Ritter is out visiting with a friend." Then, she pulled herself together and stepped aside. "Of course you can wait for her inside, it's awfully cold."

David entered the hallway, dragging Roxi behind. "Thank you, Laura. This is my girlfriend, Roxi."

"Why don't you wait in the salon, while I make coffee? You must be chilled to the bone."

"That would be nice." David helped Roxi out of her coat and led her to the salon. There, they settled in front of the fireplace, soaking up the warmth they'd missed for such a long time. They'd barely finished their coffee, when the door opened and Aunt Feli rushed in.

"David, darling!" She pulled him into a hug. "Your mother told me you'd been arrested. When did they let you go?"

"They didn't."

She stiffened and took a step backward. "Then, how come you're here? And who's this young lady?"

"She's my girlfriend. Roxi."

"Please excuse my manners, Roxi. I should have greeted you first." Aunt Feli was back to her usual behavior toward strangers.

"Frau Ritter." Roxi attempted something like a curtsey, clearly inhibited by his aunt's presence, which was very unusual for her.

"Now back to you, David. Would you care to explain how you got out of the prison, if you weren't released?"

"Someone helped me to break out."

Feli shook her head in disapproval. "Don't you think you should have waited for justice to do its work? Now you're a fugitive of the law and will be mercilessly chased."

"Aunt Feli. The Nazis have been hunting Jews for years."

She pressed her lips into a thin line. "I admit, they've gone too far. Locking our families up in the Rosenstrasse camp was wrong on so many levels. At least they let you go in the end."

"Because women like my mother stood up for us."

"I was there, protesting, too. I won't let anyone harm my family." Red dots appeared on Felicitas' cheeks.

"You just don't mind them hurting people who're not your family?" Roxi asked in a soft tone.

Aunt Feli looked flustered. "As I said they've gone too far. Many of the things the Nazis did might have been well intended, but have now got out of hand. I certainly don't condone injustice, regardless who is affected. There are laws—"

David cut her short. "Unfair laws, issued for the sole reason to make life for Jews"—he looked at Roxi—"and other minorities unbearable. Do you even know what happens in these camps? Do you have any idea how awful conditions are?"

Visibly shaken, as if she had indeed a good idea, but tried her best not to confront the truth, she said, "You can't expect the government to provide luxuries for criminals, we're a country at war."

"Criminals! Am I a criminal?" David was close to losing control. He loved his aunt to bits and desperately wanted her to take off the blinkers. Why couldn't she see the Nazis for what they really were?

"Your arrest must have been a misunderstanding and you should have waited for the authorities to sort it all out and release you. The same way it happened last year when everyone at the Rosenstrasse camp was let go."

"Do you know why we were released?" David studied Aunt Feli's face, getting the impression that she knew very well. "Not because of law and order, but because Hitler was afraid the housewives might rouse other parts of the population to rise up against him and topple his tyrannical regime."

"It's only tyrannical during a transition time, until the war is won."

"You know that's not true."

Aunt Feli's shoulders crumpled. A wave of sympathy hit David at the epiphany that she had been clinging to her deluded opinion in order not to lose hope and sanity. Unfortunately for her, he wasn't going to allow it. He'd tear down her dream castle and make her cope with reality. Roxi must have sensed his intentions, because she sidled up to him, laying a hand on his back.

"Frau Ritter, do you know what happens with the people who are deported?"

"Well, not really. There are rumors..." Felicitas shook her head. "They can't be true. They're too atrocious to even contemplate."

"Whatever you have heard, the reality is probably worse," David said in a sad tone.

"It can't be," her voice was but a whisper.

David decided to seize the opportunity and ruthlessly confront her with the truth. If she was going to hide them, she needed to know. "Let me tell you what really happens there.

People are taken to camps that have the most appalling living conditions than you can imagine. They have to do hard physical work for twelve and more hours a day, while fed even less rations than Jews receive here. They don't get proper clothing to keep them warm in winter, and certainly no medical treatment if they are sick. Hundreds perish every day from starvation, exposure and sickness. A hundred more are beaten to death or otherwise tortured by the SS guards. But the vast majority are killed minutes after stepping off the trains."

"That's not true!" Aunt Feli cried out. "Those are nothing but lies. Vile rumors spread to agitate the population against law and order." Then she sunk into the armchair next to the cozy flames lapping in the fireplace, burying her face in her hands.

When David went to walk toward her, Roxi stopped him with a silent shake of her head.

After a minute of silent sobbing, Aunt Feli raised her eyes to David with a pleading look. "Please, tell me this is not true."

"I only wish I could. Ever single word is true."

"How do you know all of this?" Her voice was coarse, the horror etched deep into her face.

"Smuggled messages, the odd person who has escaped, SS guards on home leave bragging about their gory deeds, photographs of skeletal inmates. There's enough evidence if you want to see it." David almost felt sorry for her, because her entire world was crumbling right in front of him.

Everything she'd believed about Hitler's world, deluded by official propaganda, shattered into a million pieces like a building razed to the ground under the onslaught of bombs.

"I... I... I don't know what to say," she stammered.

Again, Roxi put a hand on his arm to keep him from walking over to his aunt, whispering into his ear, "Let her be. It's a lot to take in."

Tugging at his sleeve, she led him into the adjacent dining room. David repeatedly glanced with worry at the picture of misery slumped in the armchair. "Are you sure I shouldn't console her?"

"I am. It's a harsh awakening when you finally realize you've gullibly soaked up the lies told to you for years."

Something in her voice made his ears prick up. "Do you speak from experience?"

She nodded sadly. "Perhaps one day, when all of this is over, I'll tell you."

Despite sensing that it would help her to talk about her past, he resisted the urge to ask. By now he knew her well enough to understand that it would have the opposite effect: even the gentlest pressure caused her to freeze up and block. She might even run away, if he pushed her too much.

Sometimes he wished for a girlfriend that was easier to handle. The next moment he dispelled the thought. He loved Roxi with all her shortcomings, quirks and infuriating habits.

"I love you and I can't wait to get to know more about you," he said, rubbing his thumb over the back of her hand.

She sighed. "I just hope you won't run away scared once you learn about my past."

"I won't. We have all done awful things to stay alive."

"You haven't."

Perhaps that was true. He hadn't killed anyone or betrayed people to the Gestapo. "That doesn't make me any better. I could have done so much more to fight the Nazis."

Soft steps made him turn his head.

"I'm so sorry," Aunt Feli said. "I've had my doubts for a long time, but it was more comfortable to keep believing the lies. I'm so ashamed." She looked down at her feet. "Thinking of all the suffering I condoned. It's hard to accept."

"You're a good person," David assured her.

"I don't think so. I've been a part of this system for much too long to be innocent." She took a deep breath. "The two of you are welcome to stay as long as you want. Laura will prepare the guest room for you. I assume you don't want separate rooms?"

"One will be enough." David felt a wave of euphoria warming his insides.

"You'll have to excuse me, it's not every day your entire world gets turned upside down. I'll see you at dinner tonight." With these words, she walked out into the hallway, instructing the maid to prepare a room for her nephew and his fiancée, while she took her fur coat from the hook and disappeared into the snow.

"Do you know what happened to Frau Ritter?" Laura asked.

"It seems she finally accepted the reality about the Nazis."

"Oh," Laura gasped. "She's such a kind-hearted woman, I never understood why she defended them so much." Then she seemed to realize that she probably shouldn't gossip about her mistress and added, "Would you be so kind as to get me a basketful of firewood from the shed, while I prepare your room?"

"Sure." Usually a male servant would carry the heavy load, but since all of them, including the old gardener, had been drafted, it was all on Laura.

"Come, I'll show you the gardens," he told Roxi, taking her hand and guiding her outside onto the snow-covered grass. As they approached the wood shelter, he heard a squeak. Walking around it, his eyes became big, as he observed two happy rabbits chasing each other through the cage. A third one peeked out from the little house in a corner.

"If those aren't Cuddly, Fluffy and Gizmo!" he exclaimed.

"How beautiful they are." Roxi walked to the enclosure, making guttural sounds. Much to David's surprise, Cuddly stopped chasing her playmate and carefully approached to snuffle Roxi's outstretched hand.

"She likes you."

"She's beautiful. An angora rabbit."

"I had no idea they were here," David mumbled.

"Aren't they your aunt's?"

"No. You remember the three Gerber children who used to live in our house?" At Roxi's nod he continued. "One day they brought the rabbits home, supposedly from a classmate who emigrated. We kept them in the backyard until the Nazis issued a decree saying that Jews had to put down their pets."

"I remember." She scrunched up her nose. "Heartbreaking scenes were playing out in the queues in front of the veterinarians. How vile can one man be?"

"Very vile unfortunately." David collected the firewood in the basket, whereas Roxi cuddled the animals.

When she noticed he was ready to leave, she got up, saying, "Such a cute little fur ball. I could cuddle her all day long."

"You may cuddle me instead," David responded with a smug grin.

"Your fur isn't half as soft as Cuddly's," Roxi teased him.

On their way back to the house, David planned to give his sister—because no other person could have brought the rabbits here—a good dressing-down for never telling him. The thought was immediately followed by a sharp pang to his heart. He wasn't going to see her again until Hitler was finally defeated, maybe not ever.

"Come on. I'm getting cold," Roxi urged him.

"All of a sudden?" He raised his eyebrow. "Weren't you the one to tell me I'm a sissy for not wanting to spend the rest of the winter sleeping rough?"

She laughed. "See what a bit of luxury can do to a girl? Better get used to me wanting a roof over my head."

In the guest room, they found a set of clothes for each of them.

"Gee whiz." Roxi whistled. "Have you seen this fine woolen dress?"

THE BERLIN WIFE'S VOW

"Hmm. Why don't you try it on right away?"

"While you are sitting here, watching me peel off my old clothing?"

"If you insist."

She swatted him. "No way, mister. I'll take a hot bath, behind locked doors."

His disappointed pout made her laugh. "Don't you have some talking to do with your aunt?"

"I guess I do, even though I'd rather stay here with you, doing other things than talking." He watched her back as she disappeared into the connected bathroom, before he changed into the clothes, probably from his late uncle Ernst, the maid had left on the bed. Then he walked downstairs into the living room, where he found Aunt Feli.

She got up as soon as she saw him. "I must apologize, David. All these years I've done my best to reason away my doubts. I didn't want to acknowledge what I knew to be the truth."

He wanted to say something, but she held up her hand.

"Don't. Ernst was so convinced Hitler would lead Germany out of the crisis into a better future. He, and I, we didn't realize the prosperity was never meant to include everyone." She gave a deep sigh. "It's hard to admit you've been fooled. I have found excuses for everything they did, because I couldn't stand to have been so gullible. Instead of eagerly soaking up Goebbels' words, meant to lull citizens like me into complacency, I should have critically challenged the things I saw and heard. I should have believed your mother, instead of chalking all the bad things up to inevitable false positives." Aunt Feli seemed about to start crying, so desperate was her face. She took a few choppy breaths, before she continued, "What the Nazis have done, and are still doing, is appalling. How can I ever atone for being a part of the machine that caused so much suffering?"

David didn't know what to say. "It's never too late."

"I'm afraid it is. We can only hope the war will end soon.

Until then, you and your girlfriend may stay with me. But you must be careful and avoid being seen. Even my house is not above suspicion and if the Gestapo finds out you're here, nobody can prevent them from bursting in and dragging you out."

"We'll be careful. Thank you for letting us stay."

"It's the least I can do." She took his hand and led him to the fireplace, beckoning him to sit down. "Now tell me everything about your family. Are they alright?"

37

In the basement shelter Helga leaned against Heinrich. Plaster fluttered from the ceiling, covering the floor in a thick layer looking like snow.

"Do you remember how we used to go sledding with the children?" she asked into the darkness, lit up only by a small flashlight in the corner.

"I do." His voice was thick with emotion. "They've grown up."

"I always thought we would have grandchildren by now." Helga had looked forward to welcoming a cute little bundle into her family, but then Hitler had come and then the war... right now she would be content if everyone in her family survived.

"Not much chance to meet anyone these days." Half-Jews weren't allowed to marry an Aryan, and getting married to a full Jew—if they even found a special someone—would deprive them of their protected status, resulting in immediate deportation.

A powerful detonation shook the walls.

"Ouch." Edith's voice rung out.

"What happened, Frau Falkenstein?" It was Amelie who asked.

"Just a piece of plaster. Nothing serious."

From the corner of the room, next to the curtain, behind which they'd installed a makeshift toilet, came heavy puffing.

Julius' femoral fracture hadn't healed properly. The poor man was writhing in agony most of the time. He'd decayed to a point that it was painful to look at him. Since he wasn't able to climb the stairs, David and Heinrich used to carry him into the shelter as soon as the air raid siren came.

But David wasn't with them anymore, so Herr Falkenstein lived more or less permanently in the basement.

Helga was out of her mind with worry and grief for her son, fearing he might be long dead. Several days after his arrest she'd found a note pushed through under the door, saying he'd escaped from prison and was on the run. Looking at her daughter, she knew for sure that she had somehow participated in the breakout, although Amelie refused to talk about it, only giving a supposedly innocent pout.

While Helga understood that it was too dangerous for her son to return home—the Gestapo had showed up three times to search for him—she still wished he would let her know where he was, or at least drop a note every now and then. Since he didn't, every day she lived with the terror that he'd been caught, killed or deported.

She made out Amelie's pale face on the other side of the shelter. At least her daughter was safe, as safe as one could be while bombs were being dropped on one's head.

Weeks ago, the Red Army had reached the Oder River about eighty kilometers east of Berlin. It was only a matter of time until they arrived in the capital. Nobody in their right mind still entertained the idea that Germany could win this war.

"We should leave the city," she whispered after another particularly vehement detonation nearby.

"Where to?" Heinrich grabbed her hand, rubbing his thumb over the back of it. "We're not exactly welcome anywhere."

"Felicitas." Due to the deteriorating infrastructure she'd lost contact with her sister months ago.

"Your sister, who joined us during the demonstrations?" Edith asked.

"Yes. She lives in Oranienburg." Despite receiving its share of bombings, due to the presence of munitions and chemical factories, the town was still better off than the center of Berlin, especially because Felicitas lived on the outskirts in a huge mansion surrounded by gardens.

"It's a good idea," Amelie joined the discussion.

"Would she take us in? You know she doesn't want to do anything illegal," Heinrich asked.

Helga thought about Feli's reaction after they'd been expelled from their previous apartment, before the Falkensteins had offered to sublet a room to them.

"Oh come on. By now even Aunt Feli must have realized how horrific the Nazis are," Amelie objected.

Heinrich, who always weighed his words carefully, raised his voice. "I think—" He was cut short by a bone-jarring screeching. Something heavy smashed against the walls above their heads. "I'll go and have a look."

Everyone's biggest fear was to be trapped in the shelter while a firestorm rampaged the streets, effectively sucking all oxygen from the air.

"I'll come with you," Helga said.

"Let me." Amelie pushed her mother back to her seat, whispering into her ear, "I'm afraid Herr Falkenstein won't make it much longer if we don't get him out of here."

Inhaling deeply, Helga closed her eyes, fighting against a wave of nausea rushing over her. As soon as Amelie and Heinrich had left the shelter, she sidled up to Edith. "You are naturally coming with us to seek refuge with my sister."

"We can't possibly impose on Frau Ritter in such a way."

Helga was glad for the almost complete darkness, so Edith wouldn't be able to decipher her features as she bit her lip in worry.

"Of course you can, you've become like family. We won't abandon you here, it'll only become worse and your husband needs to see a doctor."

"No doctor will treat him." Edith sounded tired.

"There must be a sympathizer somewhere." Helga used an upbeat voice, hoping to instill hope in her friend.

The steel door opened to let daylight inside, as Amelie and Heinrich returned with soot-covered faces.

"We got the fire under control, but the entire building is on its last legs, I'm afraid it might crumble under its own weight," Heinrich announced.

"It should be safe in the basement," Julius said from his bed in the corner. "It was reinforced with steel before the war and should withstand even if the building above topples over."

"We can't stay here," Heinrich said in an authoritative tone. "Our best bet is to leave for Oranienburg as soon as the all-clear siren sounds."

"I'll race to the station and check whether there are trains going, while you stay here and pack," Amelie suggested.

"We can't possibly join you," Edith protested.

"But whyever not? I'm sure my sister will welcome you in her home." Helga counted on Feli's kind heart, regardless of her support for the Nazi party.

"Because I won't make the trip. I can't even climb the stairs." Julius' voice was devoid of emotion as he stated the obvious.

"I'll stay with you." Edith walked over to the cot, where he was fighting to sit up.

"No, my love. I'm old and tired. I'll await my destiny, but you're still young. You must go and save yourself."

"I'm certainly not going to leave you alone. Who'll bring you food and drink? Help you to the toilet? Change your clothes? I'm not signing your death warrant by abandoning you." Edith's voice was firm, despite the slight tremble of fear beneath the determined words.

"What about the handcart in the backyard?" Amelie asked.

"It should still be there, why?" Edith sounded confused.

"If we carry Herr Falkenstein upstairs, we can put him in there and pull him to the train station."

"That's a fantastic idea." Helga smiled at her daughter's ingenuity. "We'll stuff the handcart with our blankets, cushions and spare clothing. Julius will be comfortable and we don't have to carry our luggage."

"Then it's a deal." Amelie beamed with delight. "I'll rush to the train station, while you prepare everything." Without waiting for an answer, she dashed off, leaving the older generation in a pensive mode.

"I do think it's possible," Heinrich finally said.

"My presence will only inconvenience you," Julius croaked from his corner.

Heinrich though, would have nothing of it. "You've helped our family many times over the years, how can you expect us to leave you to your sure death? If you refuse to leave, we're all going to stay here with you."

Helga held her breath, hoping it wouldn't come to that. Surely, Julius must understand that it was the best solution for all of them.

"If you insist. But the moment I become too much of a burden, you must leave me behind."

Heinrich agreed, although Helga sensed that her husband had no intention of keeping this promise. They wouldn't leave an old and helpless man to die a wretched death. She quickly squeezed his hand, silently telling him that she was of the same opinion.

They went upstairs to pack their few belongings into suitcases. Just as they had placed Julius into the handcart, Amelie hastened around the corner, her face a mask of misery. "There aren't any trains. The bombing last night destroyed the tracks."

Despair sucked the energy out of Helga's limbs. They'd never survive if they stayed smack dab in the center of Berlin.

"We'll walk," Heinrich decided, naturally assuming the role of household head.

Her eyes bulging, Edith gazed at him. "All the way to Oranienburg? That's how far, forty-something kilometers?"

"A bit less."

"We'll never manage it in one day." Nobody mentioned that the handcart would further slow them down.

"Luckily we have a handcart full of blankets with us, so it shouldn't be a problem sleeping en route." Helga tried to cheer up the mood, even as she dreaded the march and the night out in the cold, exposed to the bombs that would invariably rain down come evening.

"If we can make it past Heiligensee before nightfall, we have a good chance of avoiding the bombs," Heinrich said, since the forested area between the cities of Berlin and Oranienburg was rarely the target of air raids.

"Dear God, please help us," Edith murmured, straightening her spine. "I'll pull the cart first."

Helga looked at her friend, rail-thin after years of insufficient rations, yet so determined never to give up. Fighting against her own fear, she said cheerily, "Off we go."

It was a sad procession as they made their way through a city reduced to rubble with very few buildings standing unscathed.

After an hour, Helga offered to pull the handcart, which Edith gladly accepted. Julius hadn't uttered a single word since their departure, lying pale between the blankets, his forehead covered in sweat despite the icy temperature.

The thin rope cutting deep into the flesh of her palms, Helga trudged forward until her arms and legs were numb from cold and exertion. Still, she forged on, driven by the prospect of a warm fireplace at the end of their journey.

At one point in time, Heinrich sidled up to her, taking the rope from her hands. "Let me."

"I'm so tired. Can we rest for a while?"

He shook his head. "No. It'll only get harder if we don't keep moving."

Edith came up next to her, offering a Thermos with a hot infusion she'd prepared before their departure. "Here drink this, it'll revive you."

"Thanks." Falling in step with her friend, Helga drank a few sips, before she handed the Thermos back.

Amelie, who seemed to never tire, returned from scouting ahead for the best route to take. "The railway tracks are over there, if we follow them, they should take us directly to Oranienburg."

Helga nodded wordlessly. Her only hope was to arrive at her sister's mansion in one piece. Whatever happened then, she didn't care, since her capacity for worry was all but used up.

Long after darkness had fallen around them, Heinrich finally pointed at a forlorn three-sided shack with a dilapidated half-rotten roof and announced, "This will be our shelter for the night."

"I guess this is better than nothing," Helga mumbled under her breath. Not daring to make fire for fear of enemies both in the air and on the ground, they ate the last slices of bread and then huddled together, hoping a few hours' sleep would replenish their strength.

38

MARCH 1945

Everyone but the most deluded knew the war was coming to an end. The Red Army had Berlin in a pinch grip, simultaneously fighting at the Lausitzer Neisse in the south and the Seelower Höhen in the north. It was just a matter of days, or perhaps weeks, before they broke through the German defensive and attacked the capital.

Thea didn't plan on being present when they arrived. She threw her belongings into a bag and walked out of her room, not caring where her husband was or what would become of him. For all she cared, he could rot in hell. Alone, and heavily pregnant, she had a better chance of finding a sympathizer to shelter her.

As she crossed the entrance hall, which had been severely damaged during a recent air raid, Dobberke called after her, "Where are you going?"

She pursed her lips, his betrayal throbbing like a thorn in her flesh. "To work."

"There are no Jews left in Berlin. And I may say, no more transports either."

Nobody knew what had become of Auschwitz after the Red

Army had conquered Polish territory in January and February, but it certainly wasn't functioning anymore.

Thea looked at the man she'd feared for such a long time. Deprived of his power he looked weak. "I'm not going to wait for the Russians to arrive."

"Exactly my thoughts." Dobberke smiled at her. "Come with me, together our chances are better. I'll protect you from bandits."

She snorted. It was rather the opposite. An SS officer had little chance of survival, mercilessly hunted by his peers loyal to Hitler if he deserted, as well as a prime target of the enemy.

"Thank you, but I'd rather try my luck on my own." She turned on her heel.

He caught up with her in three long strides, grabbing her upper arm. "Don't be silly, Thea. In your condition, there's no way you can manage without help."

Glaring daggers at him, she replied, "With you by my side, it's guaranteed nobody will help me." Seeing his fearful face, a little devil whispered in her ear and she spat out, "And God help you when the Russians arrive. I certainly don't want to be anywhere nearby to watch how they make mincemeat of you."

Using his shock to free her arm, she hastened her steps and escaped from the camp that had been her home for more than a year. But that lay in the past. It was time to shed the identity of Thea, the star catcher of Jews, and become a persecuted Jewish woman with child.

On her walk toward the suburbs she was held up by road-blocks, pot holes bigger than meteorite craters and heaps of rubble. Seeing the devastation around her, she finally came to the worrisome conclusion that she'd made her bed—quite literally—with the wrong side.

Germany was going to lose the war. Hitler would not turn the tide, however many miraculous wonder weapons he promised, and soon the Russian soldiers would swarm the capital like locusts. Then, nobody could help those who'd supported the Nazi government.

Thea had no intention of sharing the punishment for the atrocities the Gestapo and SS had committed. She fumbled in her pocket for her papers, stamped with a red "J". Having fought for years not to be recognized as one, she realized that the loathed heritage might be her only ticket to survival.

Once the decision was taken, her steps became lighter. Now she must only get away from Berlin not to be recognized by her former prey. Thinking on her feet, she chose Potsdam, near enough to walk there in one day, yet far enough away to minimize the risk of meeting someone she knew.

Late at night, she reached the neighboring city, unsure what to do next. For lack of a better idea, she entered the train station, where no trains passed since the complete infrastructure had all but broken down. At least, here she had a roof over her head, which sheltered her from exposure.

Wrapping the shawl around her shoulders and bulging belly, she settled in a corner and immediately fell into an exhausted sleep. A touch to her shoulder startled her awake.

"There aren't any trains going," a white-haired woman with kind eyes told her.

"I know." Still not fully awake, Thea said, "I've come here on foot all the way from the center of Berlin, just to find out that my friends' house was bombed and they are gone."

"You can't stay here, not in your condition." The woman cast a pointed gaze at Thea's belly.

"My husband was killed in action a few weeks ago." She pressed out a tear.

"Come with me, there's a shelter for orphaned children. The nuns will take care of you."

"Thank you so much." Thea laboriously got to her feet. The long march had depleted her strength, therefore she gratefully took the woman's outstretched hand.

At the orphanage, a young nun greeted them. Thea told her the sad story of her husband's demise valiantly fighting for the Fatherland and her being all on her own in this world, afraid she wouldn't be able to properly raise the child she was bearing.

"The Reverend Mother has the last word, but I'm sure she won't send you away," the young nun assured her.

"I'm so grateful."

The next morning, after a meager breakfast, she was led to the Reverend Mother's office. It took only a few critical questions under the elderly woman's stern gaze until Thea broke down in tears, confessing her lies.

"Please, Reverend Mother, don't send me away. My entire story is a lie. My husband wasn't killed in action, he was sent to Auschwitz months ago."

The old nun raised an eyebrow. "What did he do?"

"He is... I am..." A heart-rending sob rose from her chest. "We're both Jews. We've been hiding in the underground, always on the run, until he was caught, trying to buy food on the black market for me and our unborn child." Thea raised her eyes at the Reverend Mother, giving her a pleading look. "Please forgive me, for I have sinned. I should not have lied last night, but I was so afraid I'd be sent away if I told the truth."

Just as she had hoped, the Reverend Mother pursed her lips, but nodded, kindness emanating from her.

"I forgive you, my child. Lying is an understandable sin to save your life and that of your unborn. You can stay with us for as long as is needed, but I'm afraid you'll have to do your share of the housework."

"I'll gladly do everything you ask of me. How can I ever thank you for such generous help?" For a fleeting moment, the thought of falling to her knees at Reverend Mother's feet crossed her mind, before she decided that would be a bit too theatrical.

"Pay it forward to those who need your help." Mother

Reverend got up. "Welcome to our orphanage. Sister Caro will show you around."

It was everything Thea could have hoped for and more. Here she'd hunker down until her baby came; the war surely would be over by then.

39

Before being forced to live in hiding, David had never considered how luxurious it was to live in a real house with running water and electricity. At the breakfast table laid with home-baked bread, butter, plum jam, cheese and watered-down cherry juice, he said, "We should put your garden to good use."

"What do you mean?" Aunt Feli looked at him.

"Growing eatables."

"Oh, we've done that for years. There's the orchard and a patch with salad and kitchen herbs in the back."

"Most of the garden is just grass." He gazed at her intently. "The war will be over soon, and things won't miraculously return to normal."

Her eyes twitched.

"I'm afraid we'll have to rely on our own produce for quite a while."

"What do you mean? There are shops, ration cards, and..." Her voice teetered off, an expression of shocked disbelief settling on her face.

David gave her a minute to cope with the revelation. "We should take a portion of the potatoes in the cellar and plant them alongside other vegetables, basically anything we can get hold of. We might even consider buying chickens to give us eggs, and a pair of goats."

"Goats? Chickens?" Aunt Feli slunk against the backrest of her chair. "This is not a farm, you know?"

"I agree," Roxi said in her soft voice. "Chickens are a good idea, whereas for goats we first need to build a sturdy fence, or they'll eat anything and everything in the garden."

David turned his head to look at her. "I had no idea you knew so much about keeping animals."

The sad expression in her eyes reminded him there were many things he didn't know about her. "It will be next to impossible to organize the building material for a fence, so perhaps we should stick with chickens for now? And the potato patch."

Aunt Feli seemed to have recovered from her shock, because she clapped her hands. "Then it's decided, I'll have Laura retrieve a sack of potatoes from the cellar and tell the gardener..." Her eyebrow twitched as she remembered the elderly gardener had been drafted to the Volkssturm and wasn't likely to return soon, or ever.

"I'll do it," David offered, fully aware that breaking up the grassland to prepare it for planting potatoes was back-breaking work.

"Not under my watch," Aunt Feli hissed at him. "If someone sees you, they might turn you over to the police."

"I doubt the police is still working, since they are busy shooting deserters," David said.

Aunt Feli's glare all but pierced through him. "Or they might mistake you for a Wehrmacht deserter and shoot you on the spot. Being a young able-bodied man and all that."

A chill raced down David's spine, since that was the one threat he'd not considered. After a while, he shrugged. "Are you going to dig the soil yourself?"

His aunt gave an embarrassed smile. "You'd have to show me first."

"I'll do it," Roxi offered.

David, though, wasn't going to allow his girlfriend to bear the brunt of the burden. "Actually, I thought you might visit a few farmers and buy or exchange chickens and seeds, anything useful you can get."

"I'll pay some farmers I know a visit." Aunt Feli looked as if she was about to storm out at that very moment.

Roxi glanced at David, apparently unsure whether his aunt was savvy enough not to be shortchanged.

"Aunt Feli, do you know how to judge the quality of the things we need?" David asked, understanding Roxi's concerns without a word. It was one of the issues that continued to amaze him: they both seemed to be able to read each other's mind, much like his parents did. A warmth spread from his heart to his limbs, making it difficult to restrain himself from wrapping Roxi in his arms right then and there.

"We should go together. Frau Ritter will use her negotiating skills and I will examine the wares they offer us."

Meanwhile I'll break up the soil. He didn't voice his thoughts, hoping Aunt Feli had forgotten that he wasn't supposed to be seen outside. Regretfully that wasn't the case.

"You're not allowed into the orchard." She fixed him with a stern gaze. "Your mother would never let me see the light of day if something happened to you under my watch."

"I'm old enough to take care of myself," he protested. After all, he was about to turn twenty-six soon.

Her stern gaze rested on him, shifting him into the schoolboy of years ago. He recovered quickly, grinning at her. "Aunt Feli. Your glare isn't half as frightening as it used to be. Don't worry, I'll be extra careful not to be seen."

"You could wear a dress and a headscarf." Roxi giggled.

"Very funny. I don't think the women in this household own dresses in my size."

"A headscarf and a coat might do." Aunt Feli apparently was serious about the ridiculous suggestion, ringing the bell for her maid.

"Over my dead body," he growled.

"It will be dead if someone sees you, and I'd rather not have to explain that to your mother."

"Alright." His intention was to shed the stupid disguise the moment she and Roxi left the house to pursue their black-market activities.

Laura had to turn her face away with laughter, when Aunt Feli explained the plan to her.

Glaring daggers at Roxi, who seemed to be equally amused, David stood from the table to look out the window, just as a group of bedraggled people trudged toward the mansion, pulling a seriously overloaded handcart behind them.

"There's a bunch of refugees coming," he said, his eyes not leaving the peculiar bunch.

"Do you think they want to rob us?" Aunt Feli's voice betrayed her fear.

"These sorry figures? I doubt it." He squinted his eyes to see better.

Roxi stepped next to him, her nearness sending a happy feeling into his bones. "Goodness! The woman pulling the handcart, isn't she your landlady?"

"Frau Falkenstein?" David sincerely doubted it, despite knowing that Roxi had eagle eyes. "Are you sure?"

"In fact, I am." A big grin spread across her face as she elbowed him. "And the rest of that sorry crowd, that's your family."

Tears sprung to his eyes, completely flustering him. He put a hand on Roxi's shoulder to steady himself. Aunt Feli was the first one to recover her composure—or rather recover her ability to move—and she raced out the front door, heading for the visitors with outstretched arms. A petite, scrawny figure separated from the group dashing straight into her embrace.

"Amelie," David murmured, frozen in place.

"Don't you want to go and greet them?" Roxi asked.

He nodded, yet his feet seemed to have developed roots, keeping him firmly in place, watching how two more people broke away from the handcart to greet Aunt Feli.

Finally, he saw their faces. "Mutti and Vati."

"Go out and say hello." Roxi's nudge dissolved his rigidity and he dashed off.

"David!" his mother cried out as she spotted him, throwing herself into his arms. "I feared you were dead."

"I'm sorry, Mutti, there was no way to communicate." He didn't mention that he wouldn't have told her his whereabouts, even if it had been possible, for fear the Gestapo might beat it out of her.

"My sweet little boy," she sobbed, pressing herself against his chest.

Normally he would bristle at being called a little boy, today he was just deliriously happy to see his family again. As his mother's small frame was racked by vicious sobs, he gazed at his father pleading for help.

"Good to see you, son." Heinrich slapped him on the back, then took charge of Helga, who clung to her husband for support.

Amelie and Aunt Feli strolled toward him, hand in hand, his sister visibly fighting to control her emotions.

"Can't get rid of you, can I?" he said to lighten the moment.

"Better get used to it," she snapped back, a small smile dispelling the treacherous pools in her eyes.

"We need to ask you something," Helga told her sister.

"That can wait. You must be exhausted and hungry." Aunt Feli was taking charge, calling for Laura to prepare a meal and rooms for the visitors. "You're going to stay here until..." She broke off, giving a tired wave, followed by a shrug.

"And our friends?" Helga asked.

Apparently until now, Felicitas hadn't noticed Edith, who was standing several steps away next to the handcart. "Isn't that Frau Falkenstein? Naturally she's welcome to stay as well."

"Her husband is very sick, he urgently needs to be seen by a doctor."

David's eyes roamed the area, since Julius was nowhere to be seen. "Where is he?"

Amelie poked him in the biceps. "You sure you don't need glasses, *Blindschleiche*? He's in the handcart."

On second glance, it was obvious. To make up for his shortcoming, David offered to carry him inside. As he sidled up to the handcart, shock rippled through his bones. Julius had shriveled since he last saw him. He was but a skeletal figure, his face white against the blankets. Despite the cold wind, sweat drops adorned his forehead. David bent down to pick him up and carried the old man—who weighed next to nothing—into the guest room, as Laura hastily prepared the bed.

THERESIENSTADT, APRIL 24, 1945

It was disappointing, to say the least. After long negotiations, the Swedish Red Cross had been allowed to evacuate 1200 Danish Jews in a long convoy of autobuses. Just a week later, Joseph accompanied his family to the train station.

"Will you join us at Carsta's house?" Liesl asked, as she put little Maria on her hip, holding their first-born, three-year-old Adolf, by her other hand.

"On the contrary, my darling. The Wehrmacht will soon push the Red Army back and you can return to my side."

Her trembling lips betrayed her fear. "Are you sure, Joseph?"

"I am. Don't you worry, nothing will happen to you or the children. My sister is happy to take you in for a while and our children will be happy to play with their cousins." He softly kissed her cheek, patting her swelling belly. "I would keep you here if it weren't for the unborn. This is just a precautionary measure, it's really nothing to be worried about."

Liesl was the perfect wife in every aspect, just sometimes the age difference of twenty-five years showed and he wished for a more life-experienced companion. He put the thought aside. A woman his age wouldn't be capable to birth future soldiers for the Führer.

"I love you," Liesl whispered, visibly fighting for composure.

"Say hello to Carsta for me, will you?" He bent down to Adolf. "While I'm gone, you must take good care of your mother and sister."

Joseph's heart swelled with pride, as the little boy answered, "Yes, sir," followed by the perfect *Hitlergruss* with a shouted, "*Sieg Heil!*"

"It won't be for long." He stroked Maria's hair, then he gave Liesl a last kiss and nudged them into the waiting train that would take them into the Old Reich. Carsta would take good care of them. It was a temporary setback to be rectified as soon as the promised wonder weapons were ready to be deployed on a large scale.

He waved at the leaving train, his heart squeezing. He'd miss his family. Unfortunately, he had work to do and duty always came first. Another precautionary measure waited for his attention: headquarters had given orders to burn any and all paper evidence.

During the next days Joseph supervised the remaining inmates as they committed cartload after cartload of precious lists and documents to the flames. His heart wept as he observed how everything he'd worked so hard for turned into ashes. The burnt remnants of documents scattered all over Theresienstadt, blemishing the camp that had been meticulously embellished just weeks prior to welcome a second Red Cross commission. Under the supervision of SS men, the paper scraps were constantly collected by a Sonderkommando, a special unit of inmates, to avoid any of them falling into the wrong hands.

If, God forbid, the Russians arrived at the camp, they mustn't discover a trace of the true happenings. Slavic subhumans themselves, they would be led by misguided empathy and take their revenge on the German master race.

Joseph shook his head. It was a horrible shame. Twelve years of busting his ass for a future paradise was coming to an end— he caught himself and pushed the defeatist thought away. The war wasn't lost yet, the wonder weapons were waiting to be deployed and turn the tide. Then, Germany would be victorious.

Even as the burning and cleaning continued, dozens of evacuation transports from camps further east arrived on a daily basis.

"I wish they would have properly dealt with this half-dead riff-raff in the other camps, instead of sending them to us," he commented to his adjutant Mayer.

"They probably had neither time nor capacity," Mayer lamely excused their colleagues.

"I'm sick and tired of having to pick up the slack for others! Why can't people do what's expected of them?" Joseph burst out, the vein on his temple pulsating dangerously. Without Liesl's soothing presence, he found it difficult to keep his volatile temper at bay.

"*Jawohl*, Herr Standartenführer," Mayer shouted quickly, even as he ducked his head as if expecting a knock on the ear.

"Where are we supposed to put the new arrivals? And how are we to process them if we aren't allowed to produce a paper trail?" Red haze was clouding Joseph's vision as his shouts increased in volume. "Tell me how!"

"Perhaps, if we just herded them into the barracks, without counting—"

"We can't do that! We abide to laws and order! Every sack of potatoes and every piece of meat is counted, written down, and put onto a list. In this camp order prevails! Every nail, every piece of cloth is accounted for! Nothing gets lost or stolen." The bottled-up disappointment over the Reich's possible defeat erupted in a powerful explosion.

Mayer took a few measured steps backward, before he proposed, "Jews are trash anyway. We don't keep books about the trash in the camp."

Joseph froze mid-movement, glaring at his aide in disbelief, until the revelation hit him. It took several long breaths to calm down enough to speak in a normal voice. "You might have a point there. Who cares about names and dates of death, as long as we're sure all of them perish. Go ahead and pen them up." Finally, calmness settled in his soul. "Make sure the crematorium is working at full capacity."

"*Jawohl*, Herr Standartenführer!"

Joseph had never seen his aide dash away at such fantastic speed. He retired to his apartment, fiercely missing Liesl. By now she should have arrived safely at Carsta's place. Liesl was in the best hands with his sister until the baby arrived. By then, he'd either join them or order his family back to Theresienstadt to pick up their normal life.

He settled into his favorite armchair, a bottle of the Czech national liquor Slivovitz by his side and a cigarette in his hand. As he did every night, he switched on the radio to listen to the news. It was already late, when suddenly sounds of Richard Wagner and Arnold Bruckner rang out through the ether.

Joseph's ears pricked up, a horrible feeling of foreboding making him sick to his stomach. Taking up a glass of Slivovitz, he peered at the radio, waiting for what he realized must be an ominous announcement. After a long pause, during which his own heartbeat was the only sound, the speaker announced, in a carrying voice, at exactly 10.26 p.m.: "The Führer's headquarters have reported that our beloved Führer, Adolf Hitler, has died fighting Bolshevism to the last breath."

Joseph threw the glass against the wall, watching as it shat-

tered into a thousand pieces, Slivovitz running down the wall-
paper, leaving an ugly spot.

"Traitor!" he screamed. "You promised to be immortal! You
promised Germany would win! You lied!" Then he collapsed to
the floor, weeping with grief. Much later he crawled toward the
table, taking the bottle to his lips.

He was still lying on the floor in a crumpled heap, when the
cleaning lady arrived in the morning.

"Herr Standartenführer, what has happened? Are you
hurt?" She fussed over him.

"Our Führer is dead," he mumbled through the headache,
the pain and the grief.

"It's a tragedy. What will we do without him?"

"We're doomed. Without him, our dream of a better world
will never come to fruition." Looking at the woman, he
suddenly became aware of his sorry state and barked at her,
"Get out. I don't want to see anyone."

She was quick to obey his orders, afraid of his volatile
temper.

The sun stood high on the horizon when Joseph finally
picked himself up from the floor and dressed in a freshly-ironed
uniform. Adolf Hitler might be dead, but Joseph wasn't going to
neglect his duties. There was still hope for Germany. He knew
a mountain of work waited for him as he arrived at the office,
only to find a stranger in his chair.

"Good afternoon," the civilian greeted him, unimpressed by
Joseph's uniform. Next to him, Mayer stood, guiltily hunching
his shoulders.

"This is my office, if you haven't noticed." Joseph tried to be
polite, although he seethed inside, wanting to drag the intruder's ass across the floor.

"I believe we haven't met." The man had the brazenness to
extend his hand. "I'm Paul Dunant, delegate of the

International Red Cross. I have taken Theresienstadt under my protection."

Joseph was so completely nonplussed, he accidentally shook the offered hand. As soon as he regained his sangfroid, he clarified who was in command. "I'm Theresienstadt's commandant, SS-Standartenführer Joseph Hesse and I forbid you to assume control over my camp."

Dunant's lips pursed. "I'm afraid it's much too late for that. If I were you, I'd go into hiding before the people you tormented seek their revenge and lynch you."

"I have nothing to fear, and much less to repent." He glared at the insolent man.

"That is to be seen. If you'll allow, I need to organize medical support." Dunant took up the telephone receiver and dialed a number, completely ignoring Joseph's furious grimace.

There was nothing for him to do, but to leave his own office with his tail between his legs. It was beyond humiliating. Since he apparently had become superfluous in his own camp, he decided to travel to Stralsund to join a fighting unit there and later to reunite with Liesl.

As he marched toward the train station, where so many subjects had arrived throughout the years, a young man dressed in rags stepped into his path.

"Get out of my way, scum!" Joseph ordered, but the man didn't obey. For the second time that day, his opposite didn't cower in fear to do his bidding.

The brazen man glared at him with bloodshot eyes, spitting at him. "I've come to kill you."

Joseph sighed. "I'll have you torn to pieces if you don't step out of my way."

"You have no authority anymore." Then, the man plunged forward.

Something glittered in the sunlight, but before Joseph conceived what it was, a sharp pain stabbed deep into his gut.

The revelation dawned on him as he noticed the satisfied expression on the other's face. Joseph's hand shot to his stomach, sensing a warm liquid spilling out, pulsating with the rhythm of his heartbeat. He didn't have to take a look to know it was his very lifeblood seeping out of him.

"Rot in hell, bastard." The former inmate turned the knife before he retrieved it and walked away, leaving Joseph to die, in pain and alone.

41

The Red Army stood in front of Oranienburg. They couldn't be seen yet, although the incessant shelling sounded day and night. Even after Hitler's death—suicide it was rumored—the Wehrmacht continued to fight literally to the last man.

Heinrich and David were confined to the upper floor, the women watching their every move with eagle eyes. They weren't even allowed downstairs for fear a passerby might spot them. Even if David wasn't shot for being a deserter, the Wehrmacht might just decide that even a half-blood was man enough to die for the Fatherland in a last foolish attempt to ward off the Russian victory.

Amelie entered with two bowls of hearty soup, quickly closing the door with her foot, her eyes darting to David.

He growled, "Sis, I'm not suicidal, even I know better than to run outside."

"Good to know." She put the bowls on the small table, then removed cutlery from her apron's pocket.

"Thank you, Amelie," Heinrich said. "Do you want to keep us company for a while?"

She hesitated, before she nodded and sat on the bed, watching David and her father eat.

"How are you holding up?" Heinrich asked.

David noticed how much pain it caused him not be in charge of his family. Indignation snaked up his spine, because neither he nor his father were capable of protecting the women against the Russian soldiers—if what the grapevine shouted from the rooftops was true. A lump formed in his throat and he quickly shoved the horrifying images away. He'd talk to his father once Amelie was gone, no need to worry her even more than she already was.

"We are running out of produce," Amelie said, chewing her lip. For more than a week no one had ventured out of Aunt Feli's property and they lived exclusively from the dwindling supplies in the basement—sufficient for four people, certainly not enough for nine, especially after having paid the doctor who came to see Julius in kind.

"I meant how are *you* doing." Heinrich gazed at his daughter.

She fidgeted under his scrutiny. "Holding up alright, I guess..."

Heinrich put his knife and fork aside and walked over to sit next to his daughter, wrapping an arm around her shoulders. "We'll get through this together. We've made it this far already."

Amelie leaned against him, the worry lines on her forehead easing up. A low rumble shook the ground, followed by the sound of mortars. The front must be nearer than they'd realized, since the rumble could only come from tanks rolling down a street somewhere in the vicinity.

"I should go. Herr Falkenstein's leg isn't healing. Someone has to go into town and get medicine."

Once she had closed the door, David asked his father, "Why didn't you order her to stay in the house?"

A pained groan was the answer. "It's not my place to tell her what to do."

David jumped up, concern mixing with fury. "Mother and Aunt Feli are forcing us to stay up here so we won't get killed, but Amelie is thrown to the wolves?"

"Ach, David. You and I, it doesn't hurt anyone if we stay hidden, but if she doesn't buy the medicine for Julius, he'll die."

"I'll go." David was at the door in two big strides.

"Stop."

Reluctantly he turned around to face his father.

"You won't even make it down the main street before you're either drafted or shot. Then you and Julius will die. How is that any better?"

David hated to admit that his father was right. He stayed next to the door, his shoulders slumped, racking his brain as to whether there was another solution. A scream from downstairs cut his mulling short.

"The Russians. They're here!" Laura screeched in a bone-piercing tone.

Before David's brain had processed the meaning of her words, his feet were already set into motion, racing down the stairs. He wouldn't idly stand by when his family was in danger.

In the hallway Aunt Feli distributed white pillow cases to hold as a sign of peaceful capitulation. David doubted it would make much of a difference. The Soviet soldiers hadn't come to shoot unarmed women—according to popular knowledge they usually had different plans.

"We should wait for them to knock," David said.

"No. Better to meet them halfway, perhaps we can persuade them not to raid the house," Aunt Feli said. During the past week they had buried everything of value in the garden. Yet, there was enough left for the Russians to pilfer, including food supplies.

"I'll come with you," David added after a look at her tight face. "They certainly aren't going to draft me."

He felt Roxi approach from behind, handing him his reversible jacket with the star-side out. "Put this on."

Aghast, he stared at her. "You want me to..." Then it occurred to him. "Oh, wait. I think it's a fantastic idea."

Slipping into the jacket, he sensed how she slipped away, clearly going into hiding somewhere. His tension slightly dissipated. Roxi was a master at concealment, the Russians would never find her.

He looked at Amelie and his father, both shaking their heads. "We left the stars in Berlin, not wanting to risk being caught at the last minute."

Helga took a step forward. "Let's go and deal with the Russians."

The family barely stepped out of the door, when they came face to face with a group of four Soviet soldiers. The Russians seemed surprised, jerking their guns upward and aiming them at their heads.

One of them stepped forward, ordering in broken German. "Out of the way."

David raised his hand, palm out, willing the man to look at the yellow star on his chest, as he said, "We are Jews."

The soldier smirked and shook his head, apparently not believing him. "You, German."

"Please, we really are Jews, we've been in hiding with our aunt. She is the only reason we're still alive," David pleaded with him.

Continuing to point his weapon at him, the Russian's face turned into a leer as he gave Amelie the once over.

David's blood was close to boiling with indignation on his sister's behalf, when a dark-haired soldier with heavy bones stepped forward and asked him something, he didn't understand. The language wasn't Russian. Despite not understanding the words, it sounded somehow familiar.

The dark-haired man shook his head and talked to his leader—this time it was unmistakably Russian. In the next moment, the leader grabbed Amelie by her hair and planted a kiss on her mouth. The smacking sound kicked David's brain into overdrive and suddenly it clicked. The familiar sounds had been Yiddish—a language he neither spoke nor understood, despite having heard it often during his *hachschara*.

"Wait!" he cried out, drawing all eyes to himself. Even the leader released Amelie, who immediately wiped her mouth with the back of her hand, her face a grimace of revulsion and fear.

With four guns trained at David's head he scrambled to form a coherent sentence, before he said in—admittedly poor— Hebrew, "Please. I tell truth. We are Jews."

The dark-haired man's eyes lit up, as he raised a hand and approached David. "How come you speak Hebrew but not Yiddish?"

David wished he'd listened better to the teacher at the Zionist training camp, because it took all his effort to understand the question and form an answer. "I learn going Palestine. But..." He shrugged to express the futility of his efforts to emigrate. Then he crossed his palms over his chest and bowed his head. "You liberate us. We welcome you."

After a short discussion in Russian, the leader broke into a huge grin and said in German. "Now we drink, friends."

Helga was quick to react. She ushered them into the house, making sure she positioned herself between the soldiers and Amelie, while she whispered to Felicitas, "Go and get the liqueur from the basement to make our new friends happy."

The Russian soldiers stayed for five hours, drinking to their newfound friendship, talking in a mish-mash of Russian,

German and Hebrew, until they finally left, promising to return the next day with medicine for Julius.

"Oh my God," Amelie groaned. "I thought I was going to die for sure. Thanks for rescuing me, David."

He hugged her. "It's over, sis."

"The war is over and we survived." Helga leaned against Heinrich, tears shimmering in her eyes.

"Yes, we finally made it," Edith mused.

"None of us could have done it alone." Helga gazed at Edith. "Without you, I'd have given up so many times. It was amazing how you organized everything during the Rosenstrasse protests. And when you warned everyone about the upcoming raid your brother had told you about."

"I miss him." Edith pressed her lips into a thin line.

"Knut is a hero, without him I wouldn't be here." David fondly remembered the man who'd most likely saved his life.

"He never told me."

David tilted his head. "It's a long story. I'll tell you everything later. Do you know what happened to him?"

"In fact, I do." Edith paused, seemingly having to gather courage. "He was executed. On Joseph's personal request."

"Your other brother, who's in the SS?" Helga's mouth hung agape.

"Yes. I really don't know how I can ever look him into the eye again." Edith shook her head.

"Humans are capable of the most atrocious things and still feel like they're doing the right thing," Heinrich said.

"Just because he's family doesn't mean you must like him. Sometimes water is thicker than blood. And friendship is more valuable than family ties." It was Roxi who offered the sage words.

Helga was quick to console Edith. "That's true. Where I'm concerned, you and Julius have become part of our family."

"Thank you." Edith stopped looking as if she was going to

break out in tears. "I'm grateful for all of you. I doubt I'll ever completely forgive my parents and Carsta for how they treated Julius."

The only person still looking miserable was Felicitas.

"What is wrong, Aunt Feli?" Amelie asked her.

"It's just... I feel so guilty." Feli stared intently at the floor.

"You never turned against us." Helga hugged her sister.

"I should have seen through the Nazis much earlier and—"

"Stop!" Heinrich put a hand on her shoulder. "You came through when we needed you most. Without you none of us would have survived the war."

Felicitas sighed. "I guess."

"It's time to look forward. We have our lives and a country to rebuild." Again it was Roxi, offering the words everyone needed to hear.

42

SIX MONTHS LATER

Soon after the Russians, the Americans, the British and the French arrived and divided Berlin amongst them into four sectors.

Thanks to his good connections to the occupiers and his status as a Nazi victim it didn't take long for the ownership of both the mansion in Schwanenwerder and the Falkenstein Bank to be returned to Julius.

Naturally he'd offered the Goldmann family to move in with them until they had found another place to stay. Especially because the city apartment lay in ruins—and in the Soviet sector. Despite the Russians' friendliness after David had talked to them in Hebrew, Julius never fully trusted them.

His broken thigh finally healed after a lengthy convalescence, but his health never fully recovered. Thus, he'd offered Heinrich Goldmann the position as Managing Director of the Falkenstein Bank. His former deputy, Herr Dreyer, would stay on for several months to ensure a smooth handover before he retired.

Amelie found a job as a secretary for the British, thanks to the English lessons at the Lemberg School. Julius received sad news. Inquiries with the Red Cross had confirmed that his sister, Silvana, and her husband, Markus, had been sent to Auschwitz after the *Fabrikaktion* in February 1943 and both had died there. He missed his youngest sister more than he was willing to admit.

David and Roxi initially moved into the Schwanenwerder mansion, too. Recently David had been offered a job in the Ruhr area where skilled mechanics where highly sought after. Julius still hadn't found out what profession Roxi had learned, if any, or how she earned her living. In any case, she'd agreed to move with David to pursue their luck away from Berlin.

Julius' own life had returned to almost as it had been before the war, with one exception: Edith. Much to his chagrin, she'd decided caring for him and the house wasn't enough and had taken up a position with the Americans, organizing anything from accommodation, food, party supplies and official events. Perhaps he was a little bit proud too, that her talents were so much in demand, even if he seethed inside at this new world.

One day on his return after his weekly visit to the bank headquarters, he found a letter from the Soviet Administration on his desk. Wondering, what they might want, he slit it open with a paperknife. Once he'd read the contents, he settled onto a chair in shock. There, Edith found him shortly after.

"Julius, what has happened?" Due to his frail health, she worried way too much about him.

"It's nothing. It's just..." He handed her the letter.

"A summons to court? As a witness?" Her eyes darted down the paper. "Who is this woman and why does she think you can help her?"

He rubbed his nose. "It took me a while, because she used a different last name when I met her. You remember the girl who saved me?" He flinched, unwilling to speak out loud that he'd attempted to take his own life. "When the van almost ran me over."

She furrowed her brows for a moment. "Oh, yes. She came to visit us at the city apartment after your liberation from the Rosenstrasse. What was her name again?"

"Thea Dalke. She calls herself Thea Blume these days."

"What do you think she wants?"

"Apparently, she's been accused of working for the Gestapo." Julius tried to merge the image of the sweet, adorable young woman with a ruthless collaborator.

Edith's eyes became big. "Oh dear."

"It seems she was a catcher, finding Jews and handing them over to the authorities."

"Wasn't she Jewish herself?"

"Yes." Julius wasn't very proud of the way he'd behaved during the first years of the Nazi reign. Back then, he'd eagerly complied with every rule, believing that being a law-abiding citizen was the correct thing to do. Yet, his gut twisted as he contemplated Fräulein Stunning's, as he'd called her before knowing her name, betrayal of her own kind.

"What are you going to do?" Edith broke into his musings.

"I'll have to attend the court hearing, don't I?"

Later over dinner, Edith casually mentioned, "Julius has been summoned as a character witness by a Soviet court."

"Not another Nazi who secretly helped a Jew and now wants a denazification certificate." Amelie rolled her eyes. Every one of them had vouched for people who'd actively helped, like Aunt Feli or Herr Dreyer. They despised the frightened ex-Nazis popping up and begging the very people they had persecuted to put in a good word for them.

"She's Jewish herself," Julius said.

"What is she accused of?" Helga asked.

"Apparently for working as a catcher for the Gestapo."

David went pale, dropping his fork onto the plate. "Don't tell me you're talking about Thea."

"How do you know?" Julius rubbed his nose, not quite

understanding what was going on. "The summons mentions Thea Blume, although I know her under the name of Thea Dalke. She saved my life, pushing me out of the way of an oncoming vehicle."

"I forbid you to vouch for her!" David jumped up, his chair toppling to the ground.

"David!" his mother scolded him.

Since Julius had such a high opinion of the young man, he decided to overlook the lack of manners and indulge him. "Would you care to elaborate?"

"I'm sorry." David at least had the grace to look contrite. "I met her when I was imprisoned at the Jewish Hospital. She was quite the celebrity. Not just any catcher, she was the Gestapo's acclaimed star catcher. She has at least two hundred Jews on her conscience."

Roxi tugged on David's sleeve to coax him into his chair again. He growled, but obeyed the unspoken plea.

"Perhaps that's an exaggeration? I'm sure she wasn't there of her own free will," Julius defended Thea.

"She probably wasn't, yet she still had a choice," Amelie said.

"What do they want you to testify?" Heinrich, as always, was the voice of reason.

"A character witness, that's all I know."

"I heard about her case," Roxi interjected. She always knew more than others. It was a mystery to Julius how a woman without formal education was so intelligent, and where she got her information from. "The prosecution is asking for the death sentence, her court-appointed lawyer is running from pillar to post to find extenuating circumstances. So far, nobody has been willing to speak in her favor, whereas about a dozen survivors from the camps have denounced her." Roxi cocked her head. "You might be her last recourse, Herr Falkenstein."

Inwardly shivering, Julius sensed the weight of responsibility on his shoulders. Whatever Fräulein Stunning had done, he didn't want to be the one to condemn her to death by not speaking out. "She saved me once. And offered help a second time, that must account for something."

David shook his head. "Thea is utterly selfish. Everything she does is done for her own benefit. She deserves to rot in hell."

"She has a child." All eyes were on Roxi, as she divulged this bit of information.

"Well, that settles it, then. I will speak on her behalf." Julius wasn't going to let yet another child become a war orphan.

David gazed at him with contempt without saying a word.

Once they retired into their personal quarters, Edith said, "You don't have to do that, you know?"

"I want to. She won't get off scot-free. Hopefully several years in prison will give her the chance to reflect on what she did and repent."

"You're a good man, Julius."

"And you're a good woman." He reached for her, planting a kiss on her lips. "I never believed we would survive. Not after they turned us away at the Swiss border. Perhaps you and I could have a fresh start?"

"There's nothing I would like more in this world, my darling."

A LETTER FROM MARION

Dear Reader,

I want to say a huge thank you for choosing to read *The Berlin Wife's Vow*. If you did enjoy it, and want to keep up to date with all my latest releases, just sign up at the following link. Your email address will never be shared and you can unsubscribe at any time.

www.bookouture.com/marion-kummerow

It's always sad to end a series, because I've come to like the characters so much. After the Rosenstrasse Protest in Book 3, *The Berlin Wife's Resistance*, Edith and Helga hand over to the younger generation and I was curious to explore the relationship between Roxi and David, as well as their participation in resistance activities.

The same applied to Knut, since I'd hinted at his relationship with Bernd in the last book. It was only logical that he would share his disdain for Hitler and both of them would engage in subversive activities.

If you've read other books of mine, you know that I always get new ideas while writing. This time was no exception. There's a spinoff to the series forming in my head and I've put a few clues in this book to keep you guessing.

As for the historical facts, the briefly mentioned Operation Valkyrie indeed existed. Initially it was a contingency plan to regain control over the nation in case of an uprising. The resisters in the Abwehr under the lead of Admiral Canaris took this plan and transformed it into a playbook to usurp the power after a coup. For that to happen, Hitler had to be dead, though. Throughout the years, many assassination plans were made. Most had to be abandoned due to one problem or other; those that were set into motion all failed.

Knut's planned suicide attack was one of them. In reality, Axel Freiherr von dem Bussche was the officer who agreed to sacrifice himself. He waited two days at the Führer's headquarters Wolfssschanze for the presentation of Wehrmacht uniforms, during which he planned to detonate a bomb. The opportunity never materialized and he returned to his unit at the Eastern Front, where he was severely wounded—luckily as it later turned out.

His leg had to be amputated and he spent several months in an SS-hospital, unable to participate in the preparations for the Stauffenberg coup. Thus he survived the war as one of the few resistance members and died in 1993 of old age.

The Stauffenberg coup was the last attempt to put Operation Valkyrie into motion. After its failure, the resistance was shattered and hundreds of men were arrested and executed.

Thea has had smaller appearances in previous books including *Daughter of the Dawn*, the final book in the Margarete's Journey series. She is a complex and conflicted character, inspired by a real person, Stella Goldschlag. Stella was caught by the Gestapo after living in hiding for several months and tortured until she agreed to work for them. She wasn't the only one who turned; many victims succumbed to the pressure and did shameful things for their own survival.

But I believe she was the only one who completely embraced her new work. Furthermore, she never showed a trace of remorse. After the war Stella was denounced by survivors and sentenced by the Soviets to ten years in prison. Upon her release, she returned to Berlin to be near her daughter, to whom she'd given birth shortly after the war.

In 1957 she was tried again—this time by a German court—and sentenced to another ten years in prison, which she didn't have to serve because she had already completed the time in a Soviet prison.

Throughout the two trials and her prison time, she never reflected upon her actions. On the contrary, until her death in 1994 she was convinced that she had only done what was necessary to survive and believed herself to be a victim of the Nazis, even trying to be awarded compensation from the government. Shortly before her death, her former classmate, Peter Wyden, who'd emigrated to the United States before the war, interviewed her several times for his biography about her, which I used as a reference book for the different periods in her life.

Walter Dobberke is a real person. He was a member of the Gestapo's *Judenreferat*, the department responsible for the deportations. He worked as director of the transit camp from 1942 to 1945. Most deported Jews in Berlin passed by his desk, even if only as a name on a list and not physically.

Many survivors returning from the camps attested to his penchant for cruel punishments. He especially enjoyed lashing prisoners with his whip. There were rumors that despite being an anti-Semite, he had several lovers among the female prisoners. His relations with Ingrid and Thea are completely fictional.

Toward the end of the war, he fled from Berlin. His luck didn't last long, because a few weeks later a survivor recognized him and denounced him to the Soviets. He was sent to a prisoner of war camp, where he died in July 1945.

The Swedish Pastor Erik Perwe took over the parish and the underground network from his predecessor, Birger Forell, who'd been declared a persona non grata by the Nazis and had been forced to leave the country, despite his diplomatic status. Erik

Perwe tirelessly worked to help Jews and other illegals. He died in November 1944 when his plane crashed into the Baltic Sea on a trip home to Malmö in Sweden. Rumors have it that his death wasn't an accident. That theory, though, has never been proven.

The chapters in Theresienstadt, especially about the "city embellishment" closely follow eyewitness reports. The visit of the International Red Cross was the culmination of successful Nazi propaganda. Instigated by critics of the Third Reich to shed light on the horrific treatment of Jews, the visit turned into the complete opposite. The delegates let the Nazis pull the wool over their eyes during the inspection and wrote positive reports about the camp, perpetuating the Nazi propaganda. This considerably damaged not only the Jewish inmates, for whom the Red Cross had been their last hope, but also the credibility of eyewitnesses who reported on the inhumane treatment.

After the war the two Danes, Eigil Juel Henningsen and Frants Hvass, as well as the Swiss delegate, Maurice Rossel, were confronted with their reports. While Rossel apparently never expressed regret over his report, the two Danes defended themselves, claiming they had to write a positive report in order not to endanger the Danish Jews in Theresienstadt who might have been punished for any negative words.

Perhaps greater politics were at stake here, putting other interests over those of the inmates, or perhaps the delegates truly didn't see through the sham. In any case it was a lost opportunity to help the Jews.

Thanks again so much for reading *The Berlin Wife's Vow*.

Marion Kummerow

KEEP IN TOUCH WITH MARION

www.kummerow.info

facebook.com/AutorinKummerow

x.com/MarionKummerow

instagram.com/MarionKummerow

goodreads.com/MarionKummerow